Crown
Prince

The Brookmeade
Young Riders Series

Crown
Prince

Linda Snow McLoon

TRAFALGAR SQUARE
North Pomfret, Vermont

First published in 2012 by
Trafalgar Square Books
North Pomfret, Vermont 05053

Printed in the United States of America

Library of Congress Cataloging-in-Publication Data

McLoon, Linda Snow.
   Crown Prince / Linda Snow McLoon.
      p. cm. -- (Brookmeade young riders series)
Summary: Sara Wagner's dream of having her own horse comes true when,
after she keeps a runaway school horse from hurting himself and others, the
owners of Brookmeade Farm give her the racetrack rogue, Crown Prince, for
her own.
   ISBN 978-1-57076-546-9 (pbk.)
[1. Horsemanship--Fiction. 2. Race horses--Fiction. 3. Horses--Training--Fiction.
4. Interpersonal relations--Fiction.] I. Title.
   PZ7.M478725Cro 2012
   [Fic]--dc23

2012024425

Book design by Lauryl Eddlemon
Front cover design by Jennifer Brandon
Cover artwork and points-of-the-horse illustration by Jennifer Brandon
(www.jachestudio.com). Copyright and all reproductive rights to the artwork,
inclusive of complete ownership of the physical artworks themselves, are the
property of and reserved to the artist.
Typeface: Palatino

10 9 8 7 6 5 4 3 2 1

Dedication

To Jeanne Moriarty and Arla Cohen,
who read every word and
cheered me along the way.

Contents

CHAPTER 1

The Farm

THE SILVER SUV SLOWED ABRUPTLY, its tires crunching on the gravel roadway as it turned off the highway at the sign for Brookmeade Farm. Sarah Wagner hurriedly twisted her dark hair into a ponytail before reaching into her tote bag and feeling for her black riding helmet, riding gloves, and spurs. Along with the carrots she'd grabbed at the last minute, everything was there. She checked her watch. It was going to be tight, getting her horse groomed and tacked up before the lesson started. Even if she got to the class before her instructor did, there wouldn't be much time to warm up.

"Can we go faster, Mom? I'll never be ready in time!"

"Not on this bumpy road. With all the money Chandler DeWitt has, I don't understand why he doesn't get it fixed," her mother complained, slowing to steer around the ruts. "This road is like a washboard, and I'll bet it's almost a mile long."

Sarah said nothing, but silently willed the SUV to go faster. They topped a rise where a panorama of gently rolling pastures divided by split rail fencing unfolded. Mares and foals grazed in the fields, some in the shade of the giant oak trees that lined the road, their long limbs reaching into the pastures. As the car approached, a leggy bay colt exploring near the fence bolted back to his mother's side, his short black tail streaming behind. The mare continued to graze on the lush grass, seeming not to notice the car as it passed.

Sarah's gaze shifted to an unfenced field on their right, which on their last visit had been tall with timothy and orchard grass. Now it was an emerald carpet of closely mowed grass, the June afternoon sun casting far-reaching shadows on the smooth surface.

Just then a horse and rider burst out of the woods and splashed through the broad brook at the far edge of the field. Sarah recognized her riding instructor's wife, Kathleen O'Brien, riding Wichita. The splotches of black on the Pinto's mostly white body glistened like polished ebony as he sailed over a chicken coop jump near the brook. Kathleen, trim and athletic, reached down to pat Wichita's neck for his good effort. She rode easily in the saddle as they cantered across the field.

A larger horse ridden by Jack O'Brien, Sarah's instructor, followed behind them. The horse was Hedgerow, one of the two Thoroughbreds that had come to Brookmeade Farm directly from the racetrack a few months ago to be retrained as sport horses. If all went well, they'd eventually be put on the market as potential show hunters or event horses, each with a hefty price tag. Sarah would give anything to have one of them.

Slowing as he approached the brook, the bright bay with a wide blaze pricked his ears as he lowered his head to focus on the moving water. This was something new, and he wasn't sure he wanted any part of it, even after seeing Wichita bound through the brook. Sensing his hesitation, Jack reached back with his crop and smacked the horse's side. Startled, Hedgerow sprang into the brook, dashed through the water, and easily jumped the coop on the other side. Jack only laughed when the horse tried to put his head down to throw in a buck as they cantered across the field after Wichita. Hedgerow's coat gleamed in the afternoon sun, showing off the powerful muscles that rippled beneath.

Sarah watched as both riders came down to trot, smiling as they turned their horses back in the direction of the brook to repeat the exercise. Jack and Kathleen were having a good time, doing what they loved most. The horses carried them briskly across the field, their heads high and their ears pricked forward. They liked the mowed surface and arched their necks like circus horses, pulling against the reins to go faster.

"Kathleen's horse is pretty, both black and white," Sarah's mother said, as she steered sharply around another pothole. "I don't think I've seen that one before."

"That's Wichita. Jack picked him up last winter to use as a school horse. They're using him to show Hedgerow it's okay to go through water."

"You know a lot about this horse training business these days," her mother said. "Is that from reading horse books and your *Practical Horseman* magazines? Or have you learned more from your lessons with Jack?"

"I've learned tons from Jack," Sarah replied without hesitation, "and not just about riding. He's always telling us how to take care of horses, what the different breeds are, stuff like that."

"You're pretty lucky, you know. How many stables have an instructor from Ireland who once rode in the Olympics?"

Mrs. Wagner's eyes left the road for a moment to glance at her daughter. With Sarah's high forehead, dark eyes, and olive complexion, she looked so much like her father. She also had his slender build and serious manner. If only she wouldn't worry so much about every little thing. She'd always been a hard worker in school and brought home excellent grades to show for it, but Sarah's mom thought it would be nice if her daughter would relax and laugh more.

Looking at her watch again, Sarah frowned. She remembered the day both Paige Vargas and she had been late to their class. Jack wasn't pleased. "'Tis not fair to riders who are on time when someone else holds us up," he'd said. She felt a knot tightening in her stomach.

"I'm going to be late again. The other kids are probably warming up right now. Even Kayla and Rita, and they had to truck their horses here." Sarah paused. "Like everyone else in the class except me, they have their own horses." Her voice trailed off. As soon as she spoke she regretted it. Complaining wouldn't change anything.

Sarah knew her mother's afternoon physical therapy sessions sometimes ran late, and they were important. Therapy had played a big role in her recovery after the accident. It seemed longer than just a year ago that Alison Wagner had nearly died—she'd been driving alone when she swerved to avoid hitting a cat. Her car sheared off three guard rails when it went off the road and crashed into a tree, leaving her with internal injuries, a badly shattered left leg, and several broken ribs.

The night of the accident, Sarah and her sister Abby had huddled on the hospital waiting room sofa with their dad, Martin Wagner, while their mother underwent surgery. Few words were spoken, but the girls had known their mother was in bad shape. It was a miracle she had survived the accident that left her car a mangled piece of metal and broken glass. Finally a doctor in blue-green scrubs came to tell them the operation was over.

"It was close," the doctor had admitted, "but I'm pretty sure she's going to make it. It's a good thing the car's airbags inflated and she was wearing a seatbelt." Sarah remembered how she, Abby, and their dad hugged each other, tears streamed down the girls' faces.

The road to recovery had not been easy for Alison Wagner, with more than one surgery needed to set all her broken bones in place. But a year later she was capable of driving Sarah to her weekly riding lessons. Mrs. Wagner could get around using a cane, although slowly and with care. She hadn't yet been able to return to her fourth-grade classroom, but the part-time job she had keeping the books for a gift shop at the beach in Yardley helped pay some of the medical expenses insurance didn't cover.

Sarah had realized for some time that having her own horse was not in the cards. With high medical bills to pay, her parents weren't in any position to buy her one, not now and probably not ever. They did their best to help with her riding lessons, which she mostly paid for with money she earned at the ice cream shop her father managed in the summer when he wasn't teaching.

"Do you expect everyone will be here today for the lesson?" Sarah's mother asked, changing the subject.

"I'm not sure about Paige. Quarry was a little lame last week, and Paige had to ride a school horse. Tim would never miss a jumping school for Rhodes if he could possibly help it. I know Kayla will be here with Fanny, and of course Rita will show up with her big-bucks horse in her fancy van driven by her *groom*." Sarah emphasized the last word. "Maybe today they'll bring the maid to serve her lemonade when we have a break."

Sarah's mother looked at her sharply. "That wasn't very kind, Sarah. Rita's father does give her a whole lot of support, but in many ways she doesn't have the greatest life. Richard Snyder is all the family she has, and I hear he's away on business a lot. I don't like it when you knock someone just because she has more than you do. So you don't have your own horse. But you do have a lesson with your friends every week, and some kids who love horses don't get to ride at all."

Sarah stiffened. Why did her mother make her feel guilty? Rita was doing well enough without having Sarah's mother on her side. *It doesn't seem fair,* Sarah thought. *Rita's father will buy her anything in the world she wants, but I'll never have my own horse, the one thing I want most.*

They rode in silence as the car dipped into a hollow before rumbling over the wooden bridge that crossed the brook at its narrowest point. Water, which a few months before in early spring had roared under the bridge, now moved serenely along the banks. A slight hill brought them to the quaint bungalow where Jack and Kathleen O'Brien lived, the only house on the entry road.

"I'm afraid I won't see you ride today," Sarah's mother said. "I'm going to watch Abby's softball game, so I'm not sure what time we'll be back to pick you up. It's the last game of the season."

"No problem. I don't mind hanging out at the barn. Maybe Jack will let us take the horses for a walk on the woods trails after the lesson to cool them out. Sometimes we go up to the old orchard on the ridge."

At the crest in the road by the bungalow and its attached carriage shed, a large double-aisled gray barn came into view. An indoor riding arena was attached to the westerly side of the barn, and just beyond it horses grazed in a series of white-fenced paddocks. Even from this distance they could see a bulging hay wagon hitched to the farm's John Deere tractor parked close to the barn. A crew was at work grabbing bales of hay from the wagon and tossing them onto a moving conveyer belt that whisked them up to the loft.

The SUV coasted down the hill toward the barn office, approaching the area where Rita Snyder's late model horse van with the green Pyramid Farm lettering on its side was parked. The Snyder's ruddy faced and balding hired man, Judson, was sweeping the van's ramp, but there was no sign of Rita. *She must already be warming up Chancellor in the indoor arena,* Sarah thought.

A pickup truck attached to a silver horse trailer was parked near the van. Sarah's best friend, Kayla Romano, had tied her Quarter Horse to the trailer and was tacking up for the lesson. She lifted her saddle onto her mare's back as they passed. Kayla's curly, auburn hair so closely matched her horse's coat color that Paige got a lot of laughs when she referred to them as "the twins." The mare's registered name was Fanfare, but the red chestnut with a white diamond on her forehead was better known as Fanny. Her high white markings on all four legs made her a flashy head-turner. "Lots of chrome," Kayla liked to say.

Sarah waved as they passed. She and Kayla had known each other as long as Sarah could remember. They were finishing up their freshman year at Yardley High where they were in the same Spanish and math classes. Since they lived only a few miles apart on Ridge Road, they also rode on the same bus. It was their love of horses that had first brought them together, but now they could talk to each other about anything.

When the SUV came to a stop by the main entrance, Sarah grabbed her tote bag and sprinted for the stable's office to check the ride board. She bounded up the cement steps, pushed through the entry door, and turned from the foyer into the office. Lindsay, one of the farm's assistant instructors, was seated at a large oak desk doing paperwork while she waited for her class of beginners to arrive. Before Sarah could check the board, Lindsay greeted her.

"Hi, Sarah. You'll be riding Gray Fox today. Don't forget he goes in a standing martingale. Not everyone can do as nice a job with him as you do."

Sarah's heart sank. The wily old school horse that had been at Brookmeade Farm from the beginning was the last horse she would have chosen. Everyone said Gray Fox could size up riders the minute he felt their weight in the saddle. He was easygoing with small children and beginners, traveling slowly and taking his cues from the instructor's verbal commands, but with experienced riders he had a whole bag of tricks. You had to be on your guard with him. If he wasn't guided straight to a fence, at the last minute he might run out to the side. Sometimes he would "quit dirty," putting on the brakes right in front of a jump, a move that had pitched more than one unlucky rider over his head. He also tended to be slow and lazy, which was fine for beginners, but not for the more demanding work Jack O'Brien expected of the students in his classes.

Sarah had felt badly for Paige in their class the week before. With Quarry a little off, Paige was forced to ride Gray Fox, and he'd been especially difficult, repeatedly breaking from canter back to trot. This was a switch for Paige, because her own horse, Quarry, was a Thoroughbred, sensitive and quick. The farm owners, Mr. and Mrs. DeWitt, had been watching the lesson that day, too. Paige had been embarrassed when Jack had to repeatedly remind her to insist Gray Fox be more forward.

"Thanks, Lindsay," Sarah replied, trying to sound enthusiastic. "I only hope he won't be as stubborn as he was last week. He was a real jerk for Paige."

"Paige is riding Quarry today. But you'd better scurry along. I expect Jack will be back from his schooling session soon."

Sarah rushed to the tack room to pick up a saddle and the bridle with the martingale strap Gray Fox always wore to keep him from throwing his head in the air. Stepping inside, she was immediately aware of the strong aroma of saddle soap and leather as she scanned the bridles hanging on the pine paneled wall. On the bottom row she spotted Gray Fox's bridle with the fat snaffle bit and the martingale attached to the noseband. Grabbing it off the hook, she turned to the racks on the opposite wall and picked up the all-purpose saddle and pad she'd used on Gray Fox before. It was good for both flatwork and jumping, and fit him well.

Sarah started for the door with the tack over her arm, but hesitated by the wall cabinet. Jack's words came back to her: *Better to have a crop and not need it, than to need it and not have it.* She pulled a sturdy black crop off the rack, stuck it in her tote bag, and hurried out the door. Sarah was glad she had brought her spurs—with Gray Fox, they'd probably be needed. She quickened her pace down the aisle. After riding at Brookmeade almost two years, she knew where every horse's stall was located in the big barn, and she headed for the back side where most of the school horses were stabled. She noticed the barn was unusually quiet, which meant Tim and Paige were already warming up in the ring. She hurried even faster.

The place seemed deserted except for the DeWitts' two Jack Russell terriers, Taco and Spin, who came running to meet her. There was no sign of Mrs. DeWitt near her mare's stall, but if the terriers were around, she couldn't be far away. The brown-and-white dogs were excited to see Sarah and wanted to play, their short tails whipping furiously.

When Sarah stopped by Gray Fox's stall and placed the saddle on a collapsible saddle rack pulled out from the wall, Spin jumped up on her leg, asking to be petted. She nudged him aside. "No time right now, Spin." Not giving up easily, both dogs persisted in jumping up, fully expecting their usual playtime with Sarah. "No!" She spoke sharply, and then was sorry to see the terriers turn and start back down the aisle, Taco with his head low, dejected, and Spin almost slinking away. But it couldn't be helped. She'd make it up to them later.

Sarah rummaged through the wooden box of grooming tools by the door to pick out a hoof pick, curry comb, mane comb, and a stiff brush before sliding the stall door partly open and easing inside. Gray Fox was standing on the far side of his stall near the window with his eyes half closed, his tail lazily swishing off the occasional fly. He turned his almost white head to gaze at her nonchalantly.

"Come on, boy. No more dreaming. Time to go to work." She offered the horse a carrot before attaching a stall tie to his halter. She quickly picked the packed bedding and manure out of his hooves before currying and brushing his flea-bitten gray coat. Not much dust and dirt appeared as she brushed him—thank goodness he hadn't rolled in his paddock that morning! She hastily ran a comb through his mane and went over his face with a soft brush.

Gray Fox stood quietly for grooming, seeming to enjoy it. When Sarah had finished, she lifted the saddle and pad onto his back, and ran the girth through the martingale loop before tightening it. He obligingly opened his mouth to accept the bit when Sarah put on his bridle. So far the old gelding was being cooperative; a good sign.

Sarah put on her helmet, picked up the crop, and was about to lead Gray Fox out of his stall when she remembered her spurs. She quickly strapped them to her boots, but on this warm afternoon, she left her riding gloves in the tote bag. Gray Fox's hoofs rang on the cement floor as she led him down the aisle toward the side exit. Cutting across the courtyard would be the quickest route to the indoor arena.

Once outside, Sarah began jogging, not easy in her tall boots, and she was relieved when Gray Fox willingly trotted beside her. The arena's large entrance door was open, with only the wooden swing gate closing off the opening. She looked in to see if the coast was clear. Taking a deep breath, she called out, "Gate!" to the riders inside and led her horse into the arena.

CHAPTER 2
The Lesson

THE AIRY INDOOR RIDING ARENA was brightly lit from the afternoon sun filtering in through the skylights when Sarah led Gray Fox inside. She was relieved there was no sign yet of Jack O'Brien. The other four riders in her class were mounted and warming up their horses, all wearing helmets, riding breeches, and tall black boots.

These four teens were experienced riders, the best of the young equestrians at Brookmeade, and they took their riding seriously. They hoped to do well in competition and knew Jack O'Brien would help them achieve that goal. Sarah had felt honored when she was invited to join the class, even though she had to ride a school horse while they all owned their own mounts. Jack said she deserved to be challenged along with his top riders and shouldn't be held back. "To be sure, there's much good that comes from riding many different horses," he'd added.

Paige Vargas was riding Quarry near the ingate and came closer when Sarah entered. Quarry, an eye-catching dappled gray Thoroughbred, turned his head to Gray Fox, who pinned his ears. Fox wasn't friendly with most horses; the barn crew was careful to turn him out with only the few he tolerated.

"You're late," Paige said. "What's up?" A few strands of blonde hair escaped from under her riding helmet as the girl with the perfect complexion and violet eyes halted her horse.

"My mother's appointment ran late, that's all," Sarah said. "I'm glad Quarry is okay now."

"We think he was just footsore after being shod last week. You know how brittle his feet are. He had a few days off and now he's fine."

Paige glanced at Sarah's mount as she asked Quarry to move off. "I'm glad it's your turn to ride Gray Fox," she called over her shoulder as Quarry broke into trot. "Be prepared to work hard!"

As Sarah walked Gray Fox to the center of the arena to mount, she saw Kayla trotting Fanny in a circle at the far end. She caught Kayla's eye and gave her a thumbs up—Kayla and Fanny looked great. Sarah knew Kayla was a little nervous about jumping Fanny today, as things hadn't gone well in their last lesson. Fanny had stopped in front of a triple bar jump, something she'd never done before.

"It was my fault, not Fanny's," Kayla admitted later. "Jack said Fanny needed more impulsion. If I'd ridden her stronger to the jump, she wouldn't have refused."

On the far side, Paige's boyfriend, Tim Dixon, was doing walk-canter-walk transitions. His horse, Rhodes Scholar, was mostly Thoroughbred except for a Cleveland Bay grandfather, which accounted for his large frame and generous bone. A rich blood bay, his only marking was a white stocking on his left hind leg. Tim sat tall in the saddle, a good-looking guy on a striking horse. When Rhodes took a few trotting steps before cantering, Tim brought him back to walk and asked again. After a few tries, Rhodes seemed better in tune with what Tim wanted, and finally went directly into canter.

As Sarah prepared to mount Gray Fox, Rita Snyder trotted briskly by on her elegant Dutch Warmblood, Chancellor. She was spotlessly neat, wearing full seat breeches, a polo shirt monogrammed with her Pyramid Farm logo, and highly polished custom boots. "You're late!" Rita called out as she passed, without slowing to hear a response.

Chancellor was a splendid horse, standing well over sixteen hands with a gleaming jet-black coat. His head was large, like the rest of him, as were his long somewhat heavy ears. A white ring in his left eye contrasted sharply with his dark coat, and an irregular star on his forehead trailed down to a snip on his muzzle. For a big horse, he was light on his feet, and with each stride he pushed off with elegance and power, his luxurious black tail swinging from side to side. Although Chancellor could be irritable at times, Rita never complained. Instead she took every opportunity to brag about her horse.

Gray Fox raised his head to look at the spectators on the bleachers near the door. In winter the heated observation room was usually the preferred place to watch lessons, but it put viewers behind a plexiglass window. This time of year they liked the bleachers, where they could get a closer look and hear Jack's comments. After halting Gray Fox in the middle of the arena, Sarah quickly tightened the girth and adjusted the length of the stirrups before easily mounting the medium-sized gelding. Unlike some of the taller horses at Brookmeade, mounting Gray Fox didn't require a mounting block, but his stocky frame enabled him to carry riders of all sizes. Sarah took up the reins, switched her crop to her right hand, and turned the gray gelding to join the others.

Just then, Jack O'Brien, wearing a tweed cap and buff riding breeches with his black boots, strode into the arena. A clean-shaven man in his forties with legs somewhat bowed from years in the saddle, Jack's square jaw and snapping dark eyes set him apart even before he spoke. His black hair was liberally sprinkled with gray, and he admitted being a little long in the tooth. His competition days were over, and now he was content to teach riders and train young horses. Occasionally a problem horse was brought to Brookmeade for retraining, and Jack was also in demand to instruct at clinics organized by other stables. But he seldom took time to travel. "I'll not be doing justice to the horses and riders at Brookmeade Farm if I'm running all around the countryside helping other folks," he'd once said.

Most of Jack's students had heard the story of how he and Kathleen came to Brookmeade Farm. Chandler DeWitt was determined to have a high-caliber director head up his riding program, and he found the man he was looking for in Ireland. DeWitt had heard about a talented Irish horseman who was looking for a position, and he made a special trip to meet Jack and Kathleen O'Brien. DeWitt proposed they move to the States to take over the Brookmeade Farm riding and training program.

At one time, Jack was a member of the Irish eventing team, riding his horse, Donegal Lad. Lad had been somewhat high-strung, so dressage was not his strong suit, but he compensated by being an incredibly athletic and bold jumper. In his prime he had never been known to stop at a cross-country obstacle, and in stadium jumping he tucked his knees high into his chest to clear huge fences. The big liver chestnut could be counted on to go fast and clear, but an unlucky fall at a water complex while competing in the Olympic Games cost them a competitive placing. Jack dislocated his shoulder in the accident, but he insisted on remounting his horse and finishing the course.

As a condition to accepting the job at Brookmeade, Jack asked to bring Donegal Lad to America to retire on the farm. DeWitt agreed to pay for the horse's transportation, and he had a stall built for him in the corner of the former carriage shed next to the O'Briens' bungalow. Lad quickly settled into his new home with his own pasture, where he was close to Jack and the broodmares. Although the horse was getting along in years, sometimes Jack could still be seen riding Lad through the old orchard high on the ridge in the early morning mist.

Lindsay and Kathleen taught the less experienced riders, but most of the students hoped their riding would improve so they could eventually ride with Jack. He could be tough, expecting riders to work hard and take their riding seriously. "This is not a class for fair-weather pleasure riders," he frequently announced. "I'm here to teach serious riders who are determined to ride as well as they can and have their horses perform as well as they can." Some who preferred an easier approach didn't like his challenging lessons. A few who bristled at his demands had gone elsewhere, but those who stayed were quick to admit that Jack's instruction made them better riders.

"And 'tis hello to everyone," Jack began in his usual booming voice with more than a trace of Irish brogue. On this day he needed to speak loudly to be heard over the drone of the nearby conveyer belt taking hay to the loft. "You'll be forming a line behind Quarry one horse's length distance apart. Then knot your reins in preparation for doing your stretching exercises."

As usual when a class was starting, Jack carefully eyed the horses for any signs of lameness. He had worked with most of the riders in this group since he had taken the job at Brookmeade eighteen months earlier. He expected them to understand the importance of a slow warm-up and make time for it prior to starting a lesson or schooling session. Sarah was relieved when Jack didn't find Gray Fox a bit stiff. The horses continued walking as the riders bent down to touch their toes on alternate sides.

After finishing the regular exercise routine, Jack asked the class to take up their reins once again and prepare to trot. Sarah applied enough leg to let Gray Fox know what was coming, and when asked, he reluctantly moved forward into the faster gait. The spurs definitely helped. Not many months before, Jack had said Sarah was riding with a steady lower leg and should learn to use a small blunt spur as the other riders did—with the exception of Paige. Quarry didn't need to be more forward! Sarah mentioned it to her mother, and a pair of Prince of Wales spurs made a perfect birthday gift a few weeks later.

Sarah checked to be sure she was posting on the correct diagonal, and as they trotted down the long side of the arena, she looked at Gray Fox's reflection in the mirror that ran the length of the wall. His gray coat made him stand out, although with Quarry back in action, there were two grays in today's class. She concentrated on her riding—heels down, hands steady, head up with her eyes looking ahead—as she put Gray Fox on the bit and asked him to move forward energetically.

The riders followed Jack's directives, sometimes circling and sometimes changing direction across the diagonal of the arena. Frequently he spoke to individuals. "Paige, sit taller in the saddle without leaning to the inside. Breathe deeply and open your shoulders." Paige's forehead furrowed in concentration as Quarry circled at one end of the arena, trotting with a steady rhythm. The girl who loved to joke and goof around with her friends was dead serious and determined when it came to riding. "Make sure you support your horse with your inside leg pushing him forward into a steady outside rein," Jack continued.

"Tim, Rhodes is traveling too fast and too strong," Jack called. "Try circling at the other end of the arena and use half-halts to slow the pace. Slow your posting to encourage him to slow his trot, and try to relax."

Several times he addressed Sarah, telling her Gray Fox needed more impulsion. When it was time for individual work at the canter, Sarah was reminded how much effort riding Gray Fox required. She held the reins taut while communicating with her legs and seat to prepare for the faster gait. But when she gave the signal to canter with her outside leg, Gray Fox only trotted forward. "Bring him back to walk, and don't be afraid to use your spurs and your crop behind your leg if it's needed. You *must* get his attention. Now insist he goes forward," Jack said.

On the next try, Sarah asked for canter with a strong and deliberate motion. Grey Fox must have felt the spur, because he responded by jerking his head down and trying to buck. Sarah instinctively sat back so she wouldn't be thrown out of the saddle, and used the reins to bring his head back up.

"I guess old Fox isn't used to being ridden with spurs," Jack called. "Try that again, and remember to use just enough spur so he understands what you're asking, but not so much he overreacts." On the next attempt, Gray Fox seemed to have learned his lesson. With a swish of his silver tail to show his irritation, he responded to a more subtle leg action by smoothly springing forward into the three-beat gait. Sarah was happy when Jack commented, "Excellent! Much better."

As usual, Chancellor needed little correction from Rita, who got only praise from Jack when her horse immediately broke into a well-balanced canter. It was obvious the horse had received years of excellent training long before Rita's father purchased him. "Brilliant!" Jack called out as Chancellor cantered past.

When their flatwork was finished, and they were allowed to let their horses walk on a long rein, Gray Fox gratefully stretched his head and neck down. It had been a long canter session for him, and Sarah leaned down to stroke his neck as a reward for his hard work. But her throat tightened when Jack announced, "'Tis a grand afternoon. We'll use the outside hunt course for our work over fences." Sarah was afraid Gray Fox might be emboldened to try more of his usual tricks out in the open.

One by one the riders followed Jack from the arena into the bright sunlight, heading to the grassy, unfenced hunt course dotted with a number of brightly painted jumps. Near the entrance to the indoor arena a crew continued to toss hay bales onto the loudly whirring conveyor belt. Quarry and Fanny sidestepped nervously past the machine, not liking the noisy contraption, but

Chancellor and Rhodes were more interested in the hunt course beyond. Gray Fox snorted as he passed, looking warily at the moving belt.

Before Jack let the class focus on the hunt course, he led them to a cross-rail followed two strides later by a low post-and-rail vertical fence. "We'll do a short warm-up over these fences," he said. "Beginning with Rita, spread out at least four horse's lengths between you to form a large circle. When I signal to pick up trot, you'll follow Rita through the low combination. Continue cantering on the circle until you've all jumped it three times." The simple exercise provided a good warm-up before jumping higher fences, posing little challenge to the horses and riders in the group, and soon they were back at walk, gathering in a spot near Jack just off the hunt course.

Many of the striped poles, standards, and the gray roll top on the hunt course had recently been painted. The brush box had also gotten a coat of white paint and was filled with fresh evergreen boughs. The course looked tidy and inviting, the grass a bright green from the rain of the day before. After Jack had adjusted the height of the poles on some of the jumps, he explained the short course they'd be jumping.

"You'll first balance your horse by cantering a circle at this end. Since we've been working on it, let's make the transition to canter from walk. Start with the brush box. Then it's five strides to the in-and-out, six to the roll-top, and finally four strides to the red striped oxer." Jack turned to study the combination. When his gaze shifted back to them, he said, "The in-and-out is a long one stride, so it's good impulsion your horses will be needing on the approach. And remember that the striding will work only if you ride a straight line with a steady pace into each fence." He paused to survey the riders. "You're up first, Tim."

Tim was rewarded for his earlier work practicing canter transitions, as after walking Rhodes Scholar away from the class, the horse neatly sprang into the gait directly from walk. Circling once, Tim guided the bay to a straight path to the brush box. Rhodes got into it perfectly, soared over, and continued to jump well until he approached the final fence. Tim overshot the direct line to the oxer, and when he attempted to straighten Rhodes, he pulled too hard on the reins. Now his horse had to jump the oxer at an angle, and Rhodes seemed unsure how to compensate.

The other riders gasped when at the last second Rhodes left out a stride and launched into a giant leap over the jump. Out of sync with his horse, Tim was thrown back and yanked the reins sharply in the air. The pain Rhodes felt when the bit pulled hard against his mouth caused him to throw his head high in the air upon landing and bolt forward. It took Tim several strides to bring his horse back under control.

"You can all see how important 'tis to ride a straight line to the fence," Jack said. "The last thing we want to do when jumping is to get left behind and grab our horses in the mouth. But except for the last fence, your ride was nicely done, to be sure. You didn't turn quickly enough after the roll top, so you didn't have enough room for a good approach to the oxer. I'd like you to do the course again."

Tim once more started his course with a circle before the first jump. Rhodes seemed unsure and cautious at first, but Tim rode him straight into all the fences, helping restore his horse's con-

22

fidence. Rhodes finished with a beautiful jump over the oxer. "Well done, Tim," Jack said.

Paige was next, and as usual Quarry was a little quick to his fences. He was excited at the prospect of jumping, and that excitement translated into speed. He wanted to get the jump behind him, the sooner the better. "Sit quietly," Jack called. "Keep your eyes up and look beyond the fence. He just needs more assurance that he can do it, and it will help him a great deal if he senses you're quiet and confident. If he persists in rushing the fence, then circle once in front of it." Paige continued on and was very pleased with her horse and herself when on the last two jumps Quarry settled down.

Kayla was next, and she looked worried as she asked Fanny for canter to begin the course. Sarah knew Kayla desperately wanted to avoid the problems she'd had with her horse the week before. As Kayla circled Fanny in front of the first fence, Jack called out, "Kayla, you appear tense. That won't help your mare. She's going well. She can do this course with ease, to be sure. Try to relax and let her know you're confident."

Kayla made a point to turn her head to look at each fence well in advance, and she pressed her legs on Fanny's sides as they approached. Fanny moved forward at a steady pace and pushed off easily to jump each obstacle, all taken from a straight and accurate line. When the oxer loomed ominously ahead, Kayla sat deep in the saddle while squeezing her legs harder to make sure Fanny knew they were committed. Fanny rewarded her with a beautiful round jump from just the right spot. Kayla was happy and relieved when Jack clapped his hands. "Brilliant, Kayla!"

When it was Rita's turn, she oozed her usual confidence as she turned Chancellor toward the hunt course. "Let's show them how it's done, Chance," she said loud enough for the others to hear as her horse moved off in long rhythmic trot strides. Rita brought him back to walk for the canter transition, and after he obediently picked up canter on the correct lead, she rode a perfectly straight line into each jump with all the right striding. Jack complimented Rita for a first-rate ride when she had finished. "Nicely done, Rita. I expect you'll be doing well when you compete him this year."

Rita trotted back to the group, a look of supreme satisfaction on her face. Sarah watched, her resentment feeding a slow burn. She couldn't help being irritated by Rita's cocky attitude. *Just because she has a to-die-for horse, does she have to look so totally smug?*

Sarah was the last to go. She walked Gray Fox onto the hunt course and was relieved when he smoothly picked up canter when asked, willingly moving forward. "A bit more impulsion, Sarah," Jack called out. "Gray Fox will have trouble jumping the fences unless he's moving with more energy." Sarah closed her calves, being careful not to press hard with her spurs, and Gray Fox responded by increasing the pace. Coming out of the circle, she turned her head to look at the first jump. The gray gelding's ears pricked forward as he also focused on the jump ahead, but as it loomed closer, Sarah felt him hesitate slightly. Again she squeezed her legs to urge him on, and Gray Fox responded with renewed energy. As the horse rose into the air to clear the jump, Sarah's body went forward in unison with him.

On landing, they made a right-hand turn to the in-and-out.

Gray Fox wasn't blessed with a long stride, but he managed to jump the combination in good form. Sarah again felt him lose energy as they approached the roll top, and she closed her legs firmly, moving him forward. He finished with a straight line and a good jumping effort over the oxer. "Very good, Sarah," Jack said. "You kept your lower leg steady over the fences, something that's surely important when you're wearing spurs. Your lines were accurate, and you moved Gray Fox forward when you needed to."

As Gray Fox trotted along the driveway back to the other horses, Sarah noticed Chandler and Dorothy DeWitt standing by the stable entrance. Mr. DeWitt, a tall man with a thick head of white hair and a neatly trimmed mustache, was intently observing the lesson through steel-framed glasses over his steel-gray eyes. Mrs. DeWitt was leading their five-year-old granddaughter, Grace, on the chestnut pony Pretty Penny. Grace's face looked tiny in her riding helmet, with her straw colored braids hanging to her shoulders. Even on the small pony saddle, her short legs barely extended below the saddle flaps. Sarah wasn't sure how long the DeWitts had been watching, but she was glad Gray Fox had performed well. That would account for the Jack Russells being at the barn. Mrs. DeWitt waved and cheered her with "Good job, Sarah!" as she rode by.

It was time for the hay crew to return to the north field for another load of hay, and at that moment Gus Kelso, the barn manager, tried to start up the tractor. "Dang," he muttered when it sputtered and died. On the second try the engine caught, and the aging tractor began moving along the roadway. Gray Fox stopped and planted his feet as the tractor neared, raising his head to get a better look at the scary green machine chugging toward him. Sarah stroked his neck to reassure him while she asked him to move forward.

Suddenly, just as the tractor was passing by, its engine backfired with a thunderous crack, belching a giant plume of black smoke. Throwing his head skyward, Gray Fox reared high, the force of his movement snapping his leather martingale. Rising far above the ground on his hind legs, he seemed to linger in the air as if waiting for Sarah to slip from his back. Her crop fell from her hand as she frantically grabbed his mane to stay in the saddle, praying he wouldn't go over backward.

After what seemed like an eternity, the horse began his descent. When he hit the ground, he spun on his hind legs and bolted in the opposite direction. He accelerated to a full gallop, with Sarah clinging to his mane, trying desperately to stay on. Heading for the entry road, Gray Fox ran like a racehorse out of the starting gate, his long tail streaming straight out behind. Sarah heard shouts, but they were muffled by the roar of the wind in her ears.

Down the road they plunged, with Gray Fox seeming to gallop faster with every stride. Sarah let go of his mane to pull back on the reins as hard as she could, but there was no change in his breakneck pace. If only she'd worn her riding gloves, she'd have a better grip! She remembered the ruts in the road and a terrible thought came to her. What if the horse stepped in one of the holes? Going this fast, he would certainly injure himself. Perhaps he would fall, and even break a leg. She had to stop him! Sarah felt her heart pounding as she started to panic. Again she pulled back hard on the reins, but with only the mild snaffle bit in his mouth and his martingale broken, Gray Fox lifted his head to defy the rein action.

They flashed past the O'Briens' bungalow with no slackening in the horse's speed. Sarah was bent low in the saddle, Gray Fox's mane whipping in her face. The broodmares were startled by the thundering hooves and took flight to the far end of the field, with their tails up and their foals running fast by their sides. As the bridge came into view, Gray Fox continued to run at full tilt. He might lose his footing on the wooden planks! Sarah pulled hard on the reins again, but to no avail. She grasped his mane tightly as the horse flew across the bridge with no slackening of his pace. At this speed, they would soon reach Ridge Road. If she couldn't stop Gray Fox by then, he would run blindly out onto the road and maybe be hit by a car. Perhaps one was approaching, coming up over the hill right now!

Sarah tried desperately to remember anything she might have read or heard over the years about how to stop a runaway horse. And then it came to her. When Paige was having a problem with Quarry going too fast on a cross-country school, Jack had taught them a way to slow down an out-of-control horse: the pulley rein. She'd never had an occasion to use it, but she remembered what Jack had told them.

While tightening her grip on the left rein, she draw her right rein back and slightly over the horse's neck toward the other rein. Once in place, she mustered all her strength to pull the reins as hard as she could. Gray Fox tried to resist, but even with his head in the air, there was no way he could avoid the effective technique. Sarah pulled hard again, and this time she felt his speed lessen slightly. She pulled even harder with her right rein, and at last the gray gelding resignedly slowed his pace. He seemed to surrender. In a few more strides, just as the farm sign and Ridge Road came into view, Gray Fox was under her control.

As Gray Fox came grudgingly back to trot and then to walk, Sarah suddenly felt utterly exhausted. She steered the horse to the side of the road where he came to a stop. He stood with his head lowered, his coat drenched with sweat. His flanks heaved in rhythm with his rapid breathing as he gasped for air. Sarah fell forward with her arms around Gray Fox's lathered neck. She closed her eyes, her breaths coming as fast as his. Time stood still for horse and rider.

CHAPTER 3

The Friends

SARAH REMAINED MOTIONLESS on Gray Fox as she waited for her strength to return. The horse was equally exhausted. He stood quietly, his sides rising and falling in quick succession. At some point Sarah heard the low drone of a car approaching from the rear. She sat up slowly and twisted in the saddle. It was Mr. DeWitt driving his red Blazer with Jack on the passenger side. When the vehicle came to a stop, Jack jumped out and hurried to her, his face grave.

"Sarah, are you all right?" Chandler DeWitt was right behind, looking equally worried. They saw she was pale and shaken, slumping limply in the saddle.

"I guess so," Sarah said. She had finally caught her breath, but felt drained. She looked down at the horse. "But I don't know about Gray Fox. Is he okay?"

Jack's eyes quickly scanned Gray Fox's legs for any obvious sign of injury. He bent to run a hand down the horse's forelegs, pausing to feel the tendons and ankles.

"His legs seem fine," he said, straightening, "but time will tell. Any swelling will come later."

"I couldn't slow him down by circling—there wasn't room. I was afraid he would step in one of the potholes, and a few times I felt a jerky stride."

"It's not an easy task to pull up a horse running at a flat out gallop," Jack said. "'Twas a fine bit of riding."

Gray Fox continued to stand quietly, still gasping for breath.

"I was pulling as hard as I could, but it didn't seem to make any difference," Sarah said. "Then I remembered the pulley rein you taught us when Quarry was taking off with Paige on the cross-country course. It really worked."

"Ah, the old pulley rein," Mr. DeWitt said, reaching up to stroke Gray Fox's neck. "It's stopped many a fast running horse."

"'Tis lucky you remembered it," Jack said.

Their gazes shifted to a blue sedan turning into the farm road. As the car approached them, Sarah recognized the passenger, a girl who came regularly for riding lessons. The driver slowed as they got closer, and eying the lathered horse, she ran down her window.

"Is everything okay?" she asked.

"Yes," Mr. DeWitt said. "Gray Fox will be fine. But thanks for asking." He smiled broadly. "Perhaps we'll see you back at the barn."

After the car had driven away, Mr. DeWitt turned back to Sarah. "You are a fortunate young lady. It's a stroke of luck that car didn't start up the farm road ten minutes ago." He was scowling as he turned to Jack. "Has Gray Fox ever pulled this stunt before?"

"Not that I know of," Jack replied. "Oh, he has a few evasions if he's not ridden well, like running out of fences or even quitting right in front of a jump. But if he's ridden properly, like he was today by Sarah, Gray Fox is a good jumper. He goes in a fat snaffle bit, which works well as long as he wears a martingale. 'Tis too bad it snapped when he reared, so he could do as he pleased."

Jack reached for the dangling martingale and felt where it had broken. "No wonder. The leather in this martingale is bone dry." He looked at the horse, who was still breathing fast, and then back at Mr. DeWitt.

"This is a spooky side of Gray Fox I've not seen before. He's usually quiet and a bit on the plodding side. Though not a push-button ride, Fox is a grand mount for beginners who aren't ready to jump. But he's a challenge to handy riders who are accustomed to riding horses that are more forward."

"Gray Fox has been with us from the beginning," Mr. DeWitt said. "This may be the first time he's ever run away with anyone, but I can tell you this—it will be his last. From now on, Jack, please see that this horse is used for lessons only in the indoor riding arena or the outside ring. Today he's shown us he can't be trusted outside an enclosed area. He'll continue to do what he has done so well up to now, but with a few constraints."

Jack nodded as he took hold of the reins. "Sarah, I picked up the crop you were using. Now 'tis best if you hop down and go back to the stable with Mr. DeWitt. You've had a pretty stressful ride. We should get Gray Fox moving, so I'll ride him back to the barn. 'Twill give me a chance to feel if he's off. This has been quite a workout for the old soldier, and for you, to be sure."

Soon, with Jack in the saddle, a weary Gray Fox retraced his steps along the farm road, but slowly this time. For once, Sarah was glad not to be riding. She was still shaken, and it felt good to be sitting on the comfortable seat of Mr. DeWitt's Blazer, even though she didn't know the farm's owner very well. She rested her head back and sank deeper into the seat.

"I had a horse run away with me once," DeWitt said, "so I know how terrifying it can be. I was living in Virginia at the time. A horse right off the racetrack came to foxhunting too soon. A mild bit was in his mouth, and I guess he thought he was back at the track. When the hounds started baying, that horse took off just like Gray Fox did today, except he was leaping stone walls and ditches along the way. We must have gone over a mile before I could pull him up."

"Did you ever ride him again?"

"Many times. The horse's name was Happenstance, and once he had more training, he became a first-rate field hunter. But after that I always rode him in a Kimberwicke bit."

They drove in silence for a while, lost in their own thoughts, as the Blazer moved steadily along the rutted road. Mr. DeWitt glanced over at Sarah.

"I understand you're quite a dedicated rider," he said. "Dorothy gives me good reports on how hard you work in your lessons. She tells me you also take good care of the horse you ride."

"I really like riding here, especially since Jack took over," Sarah said, pleased with the compliment. "It's great to be in Kayla's class. She and I have been friends forever."

"I see your mother comes to watch your lessons sometimes. I hope she's made a good recovery after her accident."

"Mom's doing great. Her doctor was surprised how quickly she walked again. But she still goes to therapy and uses a cane. I think she made up her mind that the accident wouldn't get the best of her." Sarah's usual shyness had vanished, and she found herself enjoying the conversation with Mr. DeWitt. She often talked with Mrs. DeWitt, but had never had a conversation with her husband.

"Your father teaches at the community college, doesn't he?" Mr. DeWitt asked as they passed the O'Briens' bungalow and the carriage shed.

"Yes, Dad's taught at Bromont for as long as I can remember. He's in the history department. He has tons of books on the presidents, more than he could get in his office at the college. He built some bookcases for them at home."

Mr. DeWitt mulled this response before asking another question. "Do you have any plans for this summer, Sarah?"

"I'll be working for Dad at Seaside Creamery, like I did last summer. It helps pay for my lessons. Dad manages the one at the beach when he's not teaching. I've been working there on weekends since it opened on Memorial Day."

"It sounds like you have a little pull down there," Mr. DeWitt teased. "Are there any other family members who work for your father?"

"I know my sister, Abby, would be totally into it. Dad says maybe next year."

Mr. DeWitt steered the Blazer around a large pothole. "Well, today's events have pointed out one thing. The farm road is scheduled to be graded next week, and it's not a minute too soon. The spring rains took a heavy toll, washing it out in many places."

Sarah couldn't help but smile. "My mother will be glad to hear that."

Mr. DeWitt chuckled. "And so will Dorothy and probably most of the people who ride here."

Back at the stable, Sarah thanked Mr. DeWitt for the ride and headed across the parking area toward Kayla and Rita's horse trailers. Chancellor and Fanny wore shipping boots, and Rita was holding Chancellor while Judson wrapped a bandage around the horse's tail.

"Sarah!" Kayla called out when she saw her. She hurried to meet her friend, pulling Fanny, who broke into a trot. "Are you okay? Is Gray Fox okay? How did you stop him?"

"Do you remember when Jack told us how to use a pulley rein? Well, I can tell you—it really works. I didn't think of it until we were almost to Ridge Road." Sarah paused for breath. "We're both okay, I think," she added.

"Yeah, I remember the pulley rein," Kayla said. "It was when Quarry was taking off with Paige down in the lower field."

Rita handed Chancellor's lead shank to Judson and came over to join them. "I've been riding here for ages, and it's the first time I've ever seen Gray Fox run like that," she said. "He was going like a cruise missile! Funny, since he's usually pretty lazy. Chancellor would never take off like that. He's too well trained."

Kayla gave Sarah a knowing look. Sarah reached up to give Fanny a pat, trying to ignore Rita's bragging. It was nothing new.

Kayla's mother had finished filling the hay net in the trailer. She poked her head out the side door and beckoned to Kayla. "Bring her on."

Kayla turned Fanny and started back toward the trailer. In the past, the mare had put up a fight when loading, but now that she'd gotten on and off the trailer many times, and she no longer had any fear of it. Fanny walked confidently up the ramp, and once inside, immediately grabbed hay from the net. Sarah helped Mrs. Romano lift the ramp to close the trailer.

"Fanny is much improved about loading, isn't she?" Kayla's mom said to Sarah.

"Yeah, it's hard to believe she's the same horse."

"Taking her places is so much easier, now that getting on the trailer isn't a battle," Mrs. Romano said, as she opened the pickup's door and climbed in.

Kayla closed the trailer's side door and called to Sarah, "See you in school tomorrow. I can't believe it's the last day!"

As the Romanos' pickup and trailer moved slowly out of the parking area, Sarah walked over to Rita's van. Rita was putting her saddle into the van's dressing room as Sarah approached. "Do you need help loading Chancellor?" Sarah asked.

"Oh, Judson can do it. Or maybe I should say Chance can load himself." Rita laughed. "He knows the drill." She became serious. "You know, it's a wonder Gray Fox didn't break a leg running on that road, with all those ruts. It's a real bumpy van ride for Chance, even with Judson creeping along. My father is thinking about writing a letter to Mr. DeWitt demanding the road be fixed. He says coming here is like driving through a minefield."

"I was worried Gray Fox would stumble," Sarah admitted. "But the road didn't seem to slow him down any, and somehow he managed to miss the potholes. Would you like to hear some really good news?" Sarah paused a moment, enjoying the drama as Rita waited expectantly. "Are you ready for this? Mr. DeWitt said a construction company is coming next week to fix the road. They're going to fill all the potholes and smooth it out."

"That's awesome!" Rita said. "My dad will sure be happy. But there's no excuse for letting it go so long." She placed her riding helmet in its box and hung up her protective riding vest. She leaned down to brush some dirt off her navy full-seat breeches before stepping outside the dressing room. Judson was bringing Chancellor around the side of the van, and the horse obediently followed him up the ramp to his roomy stall on board. After Judson closed the door and slid the ramp under the body of the van, he climbed into the cab. As the diesel engine came to life, Rita got in on the passenger side. Through the open window she waved to Sarah. "See you next week."

Sarah watched as the van slowly pulled out of the parking area and inched along the farm's roadway. *How lucky can one girl be*, she thought. *Besides Chancellor, Rita still has her old pony, her first horse, two extra horses for house guests, and of course the horse that's supposed to be her father's. It doesn't seem fair!*

Looking at her watch, Sarah saw she'd have time to see Paige and Tim before her mother came to pick her up. She went to the barn and started down the aisle where the school horses and the two Thoroughbreds in training were stabled. All the horses had been brought in from the paddocks, and Gus was tossing down their evening hay from the loft. As expected, Gray Fox's stall was empty.

Sarah came to the extra roomy end stall belonged to Mrs. DeWitt's gray Arabian mare, Medina, who was nickering for the hay she knew was coming. Sarah whistled for Taco and Spin, and was disappointed when there was no sign of the terriers. After riding Medina, Mrs. DeWitt often stayed to chat with riders, but today she and her dogs must have already made their way up the hill to the farmhouse.

To the Brookmeade riders, Mrs. DeWitt seemed like a grand-mother from central casting—a friendly woman with plump cheeks, twinkling blue eyes, and silver hair neatly done up in a bun. Her kind face and quick smile immediately warmed every-one she met, and she was well liked by everyone at the barn.

Passing by the lesson program's tackroom, Sarah looked in on Wichita, who jumped back to avoid flakes of hay falling from above. Next to him the former polo pony, Max, circled his stall, and directly across the aisle a stall housed the bay Morgan gelding, McDuff, who was trained to both ride and drive. Last winter, when a storm dropped over a foot of snow on the farm, the DeWitts offered students and boarders rides in their antique sleigh, with McDuff between the shafts.

She stopped at Lady Tate's stall. The mare left her hay when Sarah slid the door open enough to slip through. Lady Tate had come to expect a carrot or peppermint from Sarah, but Gray Fox had gotten all of them today. "Sorry, Lady." She stroked the friendly mare while Lady Tate nuzzled her shirt and jeans' pock-ets. "Next time, I promise."

Outside the stall, Sarah looked for Paige and Quarry. There was no sign of the gray Thoroughbred, but Rhodes was cross-tied in the aisle. He rested one hind leg in an easy relaxed posi-tion while Tim went over him with a dandy brush. Tim's tanned face spoke to the amount of time he spent outside, much of it in the saddle. Standing a little over six feet tall, with intelligent brown eyes, dark hair, and a cool personality, it was easy to understand why Paige liked him so much. Sarah walked up to Tim, and while he continued to groom Rhodes, she told him the story of the runaway.

"Wow!" he said when she finished. "So you stopped him with a pulley rein. Awesome. I remember Jack talking about it. I think I might try it some time when Rhodes is moving out, especially in the big field where I let him gallop. He never wants to slow down."

Sarah reached up to stroke the bay gelding as Tim ran the brush over his rump. "He's really nice, Tim. You're lucky to have such a super horse. Where did you get him?"

"In Canada." Sarah waited for Tim to continue his story. "Last year, when my parents could see their way clear to buy me a horse, Rhodes was advertised on Dreamhorse.com. A man who liked to foxhunt decided he was too busy to ride much. We requested a sales video, and my dad thought it would be worth a trip to Toronto." Tim grinned. "With a name like Rhodes Scholar, we knew he must be smart. Anyway, the next weekend we piled in the van and headed for Canada. He was supposed to be a large framed horse with good bone, and he was. And just like he was advertised, he's quiet under saddle with three good gaits, although he's stronger on his right lead canter." He paused. "I should say quiet under saddle *most* of the time!"

Tim began to brush the tangles out of Rhodes's tail with a wide comb. "I thought he was just what I wanted, and my parents were also impressed. We had a vet do the pre-purchase exam while we were in Toronto. The only concern was a slightly capped hock, but the vet didn't think it would ever bother him. Dad wrote a check on the spot."

"He must be pretty smart," Sarah said, impressed. "But Toronto is a long way from here. How did you get him to Brookmeade?"

"We didn't have a trailer then, so he was trucked by a commercial van. It was a long ride for Rhodes."

"If I ever have a horse, I hope he's as nice as yours," Sarah said.

Tim laughed. "If he hears you say that, he'll be getting a swelled head."

Sarah saw Paige leading Quarry from the lower wash rack back to his stall and went to meet her. The dappled gray's coat was wet from his bath, but on this warm afternoon he didn't need a cooler. Paige waved when she saw Sarah, and together they walked Quarry to his freshly bedded stall. Once inside, Quarry tugged against the lead shank, impatient to be free.

"I think he wants to roll," Paige said. She unsnapped the shank and removed his halter before quickly stepping out of the stall. Quarry circled once before dropping to his knees and rolling onto his back. He swung his body energetically from side to side, and when he scrambled to his feet, wood shavings were sticking to his wet coat.

"You look like a Frosted Flake, Quarry!" Paige said. She and Sarah laughed as Quarry shook himself and then turned to his hay.

"I guess I cut the lesson short for everyone," Sarah said.

"Oh, not to worry. It wasn't your fault. We were just about finished anyway. Before Jack left to find you, he told the rest of us to walk our horses up to the old orchard to cool them out. It was awesome! What a view from up there. You can even see Cobb's Cove and a few of the cottages at the beach."

Paige picked up a body brush from her tack caddy and went back into the stall. She began to brush the shavings off Quarry.

"Gray Fox was a real pain for me last week," Paige said, "but nothing like he was today! I hope Quarry stays sound so I never have to ride Gray Fox again."

"You're right about that," Sarah said. "Gray Fox is not an easy ride. I was glad I wore spurs and carried a crop."

At the sound of her cell phone ringing, Sarah stepped away and fished it out of her pocket. It was her mother. "I'm starting down the farm road. I hope you'll be ready when we get there."

Closing her cell, Sarah waved to Paige and hurried down the aisle to the front of the barn. Jack must have returned by now, and she wanted to check on Gray Fox before leaving. Passing the wash rack, she saw Lindsay hosing Gray Fox down to remove the dried lather from his coat. He stood compliantly as the cool water streamed over his back, ran down his legs, and washed soap suds down the floor drain. Then Lindsay used long strokes with a sweat scraper to remove water from his coat.

"How's he doing?" Sarah asked. "Does Jack think he's okay?"

"Jack said he's fine. We'll give him a bran mash with some oats tonight, and he should be his old self in the morning. But he'll have the day off tomorrow. It's too bad he was passing the tractor just when it backfired."

At the sound of a car coming into the parking lot, Sarah looked out the window and saw their SUV pulling up. Her mother gave the horn a soft tap.

"Gotta go, Lindsay," Sarah said, as she headed for the door. Seeing the SUV idling in the lot, she suddenly felt apprehensive about facing her mother and Abby. They'd want to hear how her lesson went, and that was one subject she really didn't want to talk about.

CHAPTER 4

The Proposition

"HOW DID YOUR TEAM DO today, Abby?" Martin Wagner asked, as the family gathered around the table in their country kitchen for dinner that evening. "Did you get any hits?"

Abby swallowed a mouthful of chili before beginning her account of the softball game. She was proud of the outcome and had monopolized the conversation on the ride home from Brookmeade Farm. Now she wanted to share the win with her father.

"I struck out twice, but in the last inning I hit a double that scored two runs! We won eight to five." She paused to help herself to a slice of French bread.

Sarah was glad the discussion revolved around something other than her riding lesson. Unable to shake the feeling she should have been able to stop Gray Fox before he ran away with her, she was reluctant to bring up the subject. She listened quietly, content to have her sister bask in the limelight. After Abby had given a complete rundown of the game, there was silence at the table, except for the sound of the occasional spoon scraping the side of a chili bowl.

"Sarah, you're on the quiet side tonight," her father said, as he added some dressing to his salad. When she didn't respond, he persisted. "How did your lesson go this afternoon?"

Sarah looked up to see three faces staring at her expectantly. Could she pretend nothing out of the ordinary had happened, that it was just another routine riding lesson? She decided she couldn't postpone telling them any longer. They would hear about it eventually.

"I rode Gray Fox today." Sarah hesitated for a moment as her family waited for more. "We went outside to jump on the hunt course." She took a deep breath. "Gray Fox got spooked when the tractor backfired right next to him, and he ran away with me. He was going at a full gallop, and I couldn't stop him."

Alison Wagner gasped while her husband and Abby stared in disbelief. This was far different from Sarah's usual account of her lessons.

"Where did he go?" Abby blurted out. "What stopped him?"

"He was running down the farm road when I remembered Jack telling us about a way to pull on the reins that will slow down a galloping horse—it's called the pulley rein. I tried it, and it worked. We were almost to Ridge Road when Gray Fox finally stopped."

Her father stared at her intently. "Sarah, can you start at the beginning, and tell us everything?"

Mrs. Wagner had inched to the front of her chair, leaning toward Sarah. "Yes, this sounds like a dangerous situation," she said. "We'd like to know exactly what happened."

Sarah reluctantly filled them in, from the ill-timed tractor

42

backfire, to when she finally halted Gray Fox, to the ride back to the barn with Mr. DeWitt.

"How fast do you think he was going?" Abby asked. "Like in the Kentucky Derby?"

Sarah shot Abby a look of disdain. "Yeah, right, Abby. As if Gray Fox could ever run like a Thoroughbred. But it was the fastest I've ever gone on a horse."

The telephone interrupted them, and Abby jumped up to answer it. She picked up the kitchen wall phone, and after a moment beckoned to Sarah. "It's for you."

Sarah recognized Jack O'Brien's voice. "Hi, Sarah. I thought you'd like to know Gray Fox appears to be fine after his escapade this afternoon. He was sound on the ride back to the barn, but to be on the safe side Lindsay rubbed his legs with a brace and put on support bandages for the night. Gus gave him a bran mash with his grain. I expect he'll be fine in the morning."

"That's good news," Sarah replied, relieved to have Jack confirm what Lindsay had told her was likely the case. "I guess it wasn't his fault the tractor backfired right beside him. Probably most horses would have done the same thing. But even when he was a long way from the tractor, he still wouldn't slow down. To tell you the truth, I think he liked running away with me."

"Knowing old Fox, I suspect you're right," Jack said with a short laugh. "But that's not all I'm calling about. Mr. DeWitt was here a few minutes ago. He asked if I could arrange a meeting tomorrow night at seven with you and your folks. He'd like you to come to the stable lounge by the office. Will that work for everyone?"

Sarah's grip on the receiver tightened. Something must be

wrong. Why would the DeWitts want to talk to her parents? Whenever this happened at school, it meant someone was in trouble. She turned and spoke in a voice so low her parents strained to hear. "It's Jack. He's wondering if we can come to the farm tomorrow night at seven. Mr. DeWitt wants to talk to us."

Sarah's parents saw the worried look on her face and heard the strain in her voice. Was there more to her story than she was telling them? What on earth could Chandler DeWitt want to see all three of them about?

"Gee, I guess so," her father said. He turned to his wife. "How about you, Alison?" She nodded slowly, a puzzled expression on her face. "It looks like we can make it," Mr. Wagner said. "But what's the reason for the meeting? Try to find out what Mr. DeWitt wants to talk to us about."

Sarah turned back to the telephone. After a moment she found her voice. "We can be there. But what's this all about, Jack?"

"Mr. DeWitt didn't say any more, so I can't help you. He wants me there too, so I guess we'll just have to wait and see."

Sarah frowned as she hung up the phone, rooted to the floor. Her parents and Abby waited for an explanation. "He doesn't know why," was all she could say.

It was quiet while they considered what this could mean. Finally Sarah spoke. "Maybe the meeting has something to do with the runaway today. Maybe he thinks I should have stopped Gray Fox sooner. Maybe he blames me that Fox was able to run away in the first place." Her voice faltered. "Maybe he's worried that having one of his horses run away with someone during a lesson will give the farm a bad name."

"Sarah, honey," her mother said, "I can't imagine that Mr.

DeWitt doesn't know the runaway was an unfortunate accident. It certainly wasn't your fault the farm tractor backfired just as your horse was going by it. I'm sure you did a fine job of riding to rein that horse in from a full gallop."

Her mother's words failed to reassure her. Sarah sat back down at the table, but no longer had any appetite. She pushed her bowl of chili away. "Maybe he doesn't think I should be in the Young Riders class—everyone else has been riding a lot longer. They all have their own horses, and they plan to go to shows this summer."

"That doesn't make sense, Sarah," her father said. "Don't overreact. The other riders can't be that far ahead of you."

"Oh really? Tim and Paige went to a two-phase event in the spring, and they're entered to ride in the Fair Pines Horse Trials. Rita's father is going to take her to lots of hunter/jumper shows. Kayla will compete with Fanny at the Quarter Horse shows. And then there's me. Where do I fit in?"

Sarah fought the tears that welled up and threatened to spill out. The events of the day had left her stressed and exhausted. Now this meeting with Mr. DeWitt seemed more than she could deal with.

"Look, Sarah," her father said, "Chandler DeWitt's farm is a business, and a business has got to make enough money to cover its expenses. I doubt that Mr. DeWitt makes a practice of discouraging steady customers like you. I think you're jumping to conclusions. Why don't we simply wait until tomorrow night to find out what's on Mr. DeWitt's mind?"

"You and Abby have both had pretty exhausting days," her mother added, as she got up from the table. "You'll feel much better after a good night's sleep. I'm just relieved you didn't get hurt, Sarah, and I hope Jack will put you on more reliable horses from now on. But you need to shower and hit the hay early, both of you."

The overwhelming sense of foreboding that had stayed with Sarah all day intensified when she and her parents arrived at Brookmeade Farm the next evening. She'd thought about little else except the meeting since she'd awoken that morning. She had come up with a number of possible reasons why Mr. DeWitt wanted to see them—none were good. When she told Kayla about the call from Jack, her friend was as baffled as she was. Both of Sarah's parents were quieter than usual during their early dinner, and even Abby didn't have much to say. *Well, here we are. We'll soon hear the worst*, Sarah thought.

They headed toward the stable lounge, a comfortable room with a large window looking out to the indoor arena. Turning a corner, there was the familiar scurry of paws from the DeWitts' Jack Russells. From the way they raced around Sarah, it was obvious Taco and Spin wanted to play. She bent down to pat them. The DeWitts followed closely behind their terriers.

Mrs. DeWitt spoke in her usual cheery voice. "Our two boys are very glad you're here, Sarah. They lobbied hard to come to the barn tonight in hopes they might see you."

"They're the cutest dogs!" Sarah replied, and for the first time that day she smiled. Taco raced away to pick up a small towel for playing tug-of-war and ran back to Sarah. "No time for fun and games tonight, Taco," Sarah said, as she rubbed him behind his ears.

Mr. DeWitt extended his hand to Sarah's parents, welcoming them to the farm. "I'm glad you could come on rather short notice." He held the door open, inviting them into the cozy lounge where a large flagstone fireplace was centered on the far side of the room next to hickory-paneled walls decorated with English foxhunting scenes. Bookcases on both sides of the fireplace held a collection of equestrian books supported by hunting horn bookends. During the winter, a warming fire often blazed here. Parents could watch their young riders during lessons, or boarders could kick back to read the horsey magazines that were scattered on the coffee table.

Jack rose from a chair near the door and also extended his hand in greeting. Mrs. DeWitt gestured toward the leather chairs and sofa. "Please make yourselves comfortable," she said. "Chandler and I are so pleased we can spend some time with Sarah's parents. She's one of our favorites, you know."

Sarah's mother placed her pronged cane in the corner before seating herself next to her husband on the sofa. When Sarah sank down on the braided rug at their feet, both Spin and Taco vied for space in her lap. She played with Spin's ears after both of the dogs got comfortable. Mrs. DeWitt settled into the rocking chair before drawing her knitting from a basket.

Chandler DeWitt cleared his throat and immediately everyone turned their attention to him. "I appreciate your taking time from your busy schedules to come here tonight," he began. "There's a matter Dorothy and I have been considering, and the time has come for us to talk to you about it."

Sarah felt her heart pounding. *Here it comes. He's trying to break it to us gently.*

Mr. DeWitt focused his steady gaze on Martin and Alison

47

Wagner. "All of us here at Brookmeade recognize the good qualities Sarah brings to our riding program. Her high work ethic is second to none, and when it comes to riding and overall horsemanship, she's a natural. Normally we would reserve places in Jack's Young Riders class for teens that have achieved a great deal of expertise and are either actively competing or about to start. But Jack recognized that Sarah is nearly at their level, even though she doesn't have a horse. He urged me to make an exception to our standard policy, and you know the rest. Since she entered the class, she's proven she belongs there. Jack tells me she's fast becoming an accomplished rider."

Sarah was puzzled by his words, but she began to breathe easier. Her eyes never left Mr. DeWitt as he continued.

"We're all aware of something that happened yesterday, something that firmly backs up Jack's recommendation. I happened to be at the stable when the school horse Sarah was riding was spooked by a sudden loud noise and bolted down the entry road. A terrified horse doesn't think clearly and can be difficult to stop. It's a dangerous situation for both horse and rider. Thank goodness Sarah rose to the occasion and was able to stop Gray Fox before he galloped right onto Ridge Road."

Dorothy DeWitt rested her knitting on her lap. "I think what Chandler is leading up to is that Sarah is ready for a horse of her own. For her riding to improve, she should be riding something besides our school horses, and she needs to ride more than once a week. I'm often here at the stable when Jack is teaching her class, so I see how hard she works, and how well her horses perform. She obviously has the potential to do far more, but having her own horse is essential."

Sarah looked up at her parents. She could anticipate what was coming next. The DeWitts would suggest her parents somehow come up with the money to buy her a horse, not realizing that it just wasn't possible.

The room was quiet until Chandler DeWitt spoke again. "We've made the decision to go forward with something we've never done before at Brookmeade Farm. We'd like to support a sponsorship program for a student we consider to have a lot of potential. In this case it's Sarah, and we want to help her get a horse."

Sarah couldn't believe her ears. The DeWitts were talking about something that for her had been an elusive dream. She had longed to have a horse of her own for as long as she could remember. What the DeWitts were saying now was almost too good to be true. Could this really be happening?

Mr. DeWitt began to tell them of an old college friend who some years before had gotten into Thoroughbred racing. He had retained a respected trainer who advised him on the purchase of a few well-bred broodmares at a Saratoga sale, most in foal to desirable stallions. He had also picked up some valuable bloodstock at a dispersal sale in Kentucky. Many of the colts and fillies from these mares became successful runners, and his racing stable grew by leaps and bounds.

"I had a call from Hank earlier this week," Mr. DeWitt continued. "He wants to cut back. He's decided to cull four horses currently in training at Raceland Park. All are geldings, so they wouldn't have any value as breeding stock, and for various reasons they aren't cut out to be racehorses. Hank and his wife Jean visited us here at Brookmeade last year, and they seem to think we know what we're doing. Hank feels this would be an ideal place to send horses to be retrained for something besides racing, and he'd rather these four become sport horses than be carelessly tossed aside."

Sarah sat mesmerized. What Mr. DeWitt was saying was almost more than she could comprehend. She looked up at her parents once more, and saw they were intently focused on the man before them.

Jack spoke up. "Unfortunately too many Thoroughbreds who fail to pay their way at the track don't get another chance. Many are unsound, and are bought on the cheap by the killers. They go to a rendering plant. I know it doesn't sound pretty, but the sad fact is that some perfectly good horses that can't run fast end up at a slaughter house." Sarah shuddered and hugged Taco a little closer.

"Your friend is doing a decent thing," her father said to Mr. DeWitt.

"I couldn't agree with you more," Mr. DeWitt said. "These four horses are all well-bred and supposedly sound. Hank thinks they are fine sport horse prospects, and has offered me the whole bunch for free. But we have two off-the-track Thoroughbreds here for training right now, plus a large number of boarders, so we really don't have stall space for four more."

Dorothy DeWitt didn't look up from her knitting when she spoke. "Of course we also have to consider there are only so many hours in the day Jack can devote to schooling green sales prospects."

"I'm not in a position to take them," her husband continued, "but this is where Sarah comes in. I'd like to offer her the opportunity to pick out one of the four horses and buy him for a dollar, just to make it a legitimate sale."

Sarah could hardly believe what she was hearing. A horse for a dollar! But then her mother entered the conversation. "Chandler, what you're proposing is kind and generous. But while I don't claim to know much about the world of horses, I'm aware there's a lot more than the purchase price to consider here. It must be incredibly expensive to support a horse, what with board bills on top of the cost of lessons. I regret that we must turn down your offer before you go any further. Our family can't possibly take this on right now."

Sarah hung her head and took a deep breath. She should have known this incredible idea of her getting a horse was totally off the charts. No way could it possibly happen. She'd reconciled herself to that reality a long time ago—all this talk now was just a cruel tease.

Mr. DeWitt responded quickly. "Let's talk this through, Alison. You see, if Sarah takes one of these horses, there will be a few conditions. First, the horse must be boarded here, at least for the first year. Now I'm aware a monthly board bill might be a stretch for your family's budget, especially after your car accident. So I'd like to offer Sarah the opportunity to work at the farm to help pay for her horse's board."

Mr. DeWitt sat back and crossed his legs before continuing. "Lucas is leaving for the summer, and Gus will need some help with chores here. Sarah would be what is called a 'working student.' She might clean stalls, sweep the aisles, fill water buckets, bring horses in and out from the paddocks, or help with feeding. At some point she could even be an assistant to Kathleen or Lindsay, helping with their beginner students. That would free them up to work with others. In exchange for her help, we're also prepared to offer Jack's continuing instruction, as Sarah's new horse learns what's expected of him." Mr. DeWitt paused and looked to his trainer. "Do you have any thoughts on this, Jack?"

Jack rose from his chair and moved slowly toward the fireplace, carefully choosing his words. He leaned his elbow on the mantle as he spoke. "Just this. We know a horse right off the racetrack will be green as grass, and 'twill take a bit of time for him to catch up with the others. But Sarah has done a good job when she's ridden French Twist, and I think she can ride another horse fresh from the track. For her age and experience, she has a good seat and excellent hands. But a lot will depend on the individual horse, so 'tis important she gets one that's levelheaded. She'll need some private lessons for a while, but eventually I can see her returning to my Young Riders class."

Chandler DeWitt nodded in agreement. "I'm glad to hear that. We'll figure out how many hours Sarah can work throughout the week over the summer, and of course she'll need to shift much of her schedule to the weekends once school is in session in the fall. We'll make allowances for times when she can't work, as long as she can make it up later."

Sarah listened carefully to every word being spoken, but she was becoming increasingly irritated by the conversation. Her mother had made it perfectly clear she wouldn't be getting a horse. Sarah didn't see her mother changing her mind any time soon. *It wasn't going to happen.* Why were they raising her hopes like this?

"Excuse me," Martin Wagner interrupted. "There's something else to think about here. Alison and I can only do so much chauffeuring. How is a high school student without a driver's license, or the wherewithal to support an automobile when she eventually does get a license, supposed to make frequent trips between the barn and home? I'm afraid transportation is a legitimate problem for us."

Mr. DeWitt's gaze shifted to Sarah. "Sarah, you live a few miles from Brookmeade Farm, not including the long farm road. Even when you get a driver's license, it sounds like having access to a car is not in the cards. How would you feel about riding a bicycle to Brookmeade and back home on a regular basis? It's a transportation choice that doesn't require fuel, and there's a bike lane on Ridge Road, so you wouldn't be at risk. We'll find a spot in the boarders' tack room for you to stash some things you otherwise would have to carry back and forth."

Without hesitation Sarah responded, "Mr. DeWitt, if I could have a horse of my own, I would ride my bike to the moon and back every day."

It was a relief to hear everyone laugh before Mrs. DeWitt interjected softly, "When Chandler proposed this wonderful idea, I began thinking about how Sarah could possibly ride her new horse if she has no tack or other equipment. So I decided to get into the act." Turning directly to Sarah, she continued, "In hopes you and your family would agree to this plan, I purchased a gift card for you from Atlantic Saddlery, the new tack shop that's going to open tomorrow down near the beach. You'll be able to get a saddle, bridle, and all the other things we riders need for our horses." She smiled warmly at Sarah.

Sarah was too stunned to speak—a shopping spree at a tack shop! But her father broke in again.

"I think we need to slow down here," he said. "This sounds like a fairytale come true for our daughter. It would add a wonderful new dimension to her life, one her mother and I cannot possibly provide on our own. But I'm afraid the plan won't work because Alison and I couldn't possibly repay you. Even with my school's health insurance plan, I have to admit we have a great deal of medical debt. And if the day ever comes we catch up with those bills, our next priority will be college for the girls. What you've proposed in terms of sponsorship will be costly, more than we could ever repay. I know it will break Sarah's heart to hear me say no, but I have to be realistic."

Sarah slumped and blinked furiously to keep the tears at bay. She had known all along it was too good to be true. Sensing something was wrong, Spin stretched to lick Sarah's cheek. The room was quiet.

Then Sarah heard Mrs. DeWitt's reassuring voice again. "Martin and Alison, you need to understand that Chandler and I are not expecting to be repaid. We're not offering to *loan* you a sum of money for Sarah to buy and maintain a horse. Rather, we're providing her with a horse along with a reasonable plan to support him and learn the skills she'll need to ride him. We feel it's important she work to pay for board and lessons. It will be more meaningful that way, and a little hard work never hurt anyone." Mrs. DeWitt looked at the Wagners almost pleadingly. "We *want* to do this for Sarah's sake. A young dedicated rider with lots of potential shouldn't be deprived of the opportunity to develop her skills. Let's not let money stand in the way."

Sarah looked up at her parents, who appeared deep in thought. She could see her dad was torn. He was a proud man who would hate to take a large handout from the DeWitts, but at the same time he knew what this opportunity would mean for her. He looked at his wife, who only nodded her head. Finally, he spoke.

"For some time Alison and I have wished Sarah could have a horse. Horses mean a great deal to her, and she'll only be a teenager for a few short years. Before we know it she'll be going off to college. You two have carefully thought through many angles of this proposal. On the condition she can defray a good portion of the horse's expense by working at the farm, we'll allow Sarah to accept your offer." He paused, looking at his wife and Sarah before turning back to the DeWitts. "And we want you to know we are profoundly grateful."

Sarah couldn't believe her ears. She had been so sure all the talk would be for nothing, that it would all come down to the Wagners' inability to come up with the money having a horse required. Now her father was accepting the DeWitts' offer!

Mrs. Wagner shifted uncomfortably on the sofa. "There's something else I feel must be said. As excited and happy as I am for Sarah, I also have some reservations. Sarah was run away with by a horse yesterday, a dangerous incident that could have had a tragic ending. And now she's going to be getting a horse from the racetrack? I need to be sure she'll be safe."

Chandler DeWitt fielded the question, glancing at Jack and Sarah as he did so. "Undoubtedly all of us in this room have the highest respect for Jack's equestrian knowledge and common sense. I think it's important that he help Sarah choose her horse.

With his counsel, I don't believe she'll come home with a horse that's an accident about to happen. We care too much about Sarah's well-being and the reputation of Brookmeade Farm to let her get a horse that's not appropriate."

Sarah continued to sit quietly, daring to hope against hope that her lifelong dream might actually be coming true. Her mother didn't appear completely convinced, but she said, "We'll go along with your plan, although Martin and I will need to keep close tabs on what's happening."

The DeWitts looked very pleased. "We should get moving on this as soon as possible," Mr. DeWitt said. "Hank's trainer would like all the horses to find new homes this month to make room for other young prospects from the farm. We need to get Sarah to Raceland Park within the next few days so she can make her selection and bring the horse back to Brookmeade. We're a little cramped for space until the crew finishes building the two new stalls, but we'll manage to find a place for him somewhere."

"Saturday is good for me," Jack volunteered. "Kathleen and Lindsay teach all the lessons in the morning, and I can arrange to reschedule the two I usually have in the afternoon."

Mr. DeWitt turned to Sarah's father.

"Does that work for the Wagner family?"

Sarah's father nodded. "I'm not working Saturday, and I think I can find a replacement for Sarah."

"Excellent," Mr. DeWitt said. "Hank's trainer suggested you arrive about nine, when most of the horses in his string will have galloped and cooled out. By then he'll have time to show you the available horses. Of course you're welcome to take the farm's pickup and horse trailer."

Mr. DeWitt stood up, signaling the meeting had come to a close, and everyone else rose with him except Sarah. She continued to sit with the DeWitt's two dogs, in a state of shock, as she tried to fully comprehend what had just happened. What had been impossible for years had become a reality in what felt like no time at all! She was actually going to have a horse of her own, a horse to ride, to care for, and to love. Finally, she got a grip on her emotions and gently pushed Spin and Taco aside as she rose to her feet, not knowing who to thank first—the DeWitts, for their outstanding generosity, or her parents, for agreeing to the plan.

As they were leaving the lounge, the adults shaking hands and Sarah floating along on a bubble of happiness, Mrs. DeWitt slipped something into Sarah's jeans' pocket.

"Here's the gift card, dear," Mrs. DeWitt whispered. "You have a lot of shopping to do!"

CHAPTER 5
The Tack Shop

IT WAS LATE FRIDAY AFTERNOON when Mrs. Wagner drove cautiously into the Atlantic Saddlery's crowded parking lot to drop off Sarah and Kayla. From the number of cars in the lot, it was obvious the shop was crammed with shoppers hoping to take advantage of grand opening specials. Sarah reached into her pocket, just to make sure the gift card Mrs. DeWitt had given her was still there, along with the list of things she wanted to buy for her new horse.

Mrs. Wagner excused herself from the shopping venture. "I wouldn't know a halter from a bridle, so I wouldn't be any help," she told Sarah. "But Kayla will have some good ideas. I'll be back in about an hour after I do some errands."

Sarah had never been more excited. In fact, all day it had been hard to think of anything other than the horse she'd be getting on Saturday and today's trip to the tack shop. She had always loved leafing through the pages of tack shop catalogs, but she'd never actually thought she would be shopping for things for her own horse one day.

Sarah and Kayla hopped out of the SUV and headed for the door where a stiff ocean breeze whipped red balloons on the sign that announced the shop's opening. Inside, they were met by the strong smell of leather and a dizzying amount of horse tack on display. Several bins of merchandise had signs announcing special bargains. At the far side of the shop, a woman wearing an Atlantic Saddlery polo shirt was celebrating the opening by serving complimentary punch and cookies while she chatted with customers.

"I'm sure glad you could come with me," Sarah said, as she picked up a shopping basket. "There's so much I need to buy. Jack gave me some ideas on what things I'll need right away, but I'm still not sure where to start."

"This is going to be a total blast!" Kayla said. "Do you remember when my mom took us to the tack shop in Bradley when I first got Fanny? Now it's *your* turn."

While Sarah's riding experience was limited to lessons at Brookmeade, Kayla had gotten her first pony when she was seven. Kayla's father had attached a modest two-stall barn to the back of their garage so her mother's horse could be stabled at home, and not long after the barn was finished, Kayla's first pony, Fuzzy, had moved in. When Kayla outgrew the pony, a small horse named Chubs took his place. She'd moved up to her Quarter Horse two years ago. The Romanos didn't have much land, just enough for a small turnout area and riding ring, but they lived close to an undeveloped land preserve where they could hack on miles of trails. Last year they'd invested in a horse trailer so Kayla could take Fanny to Brookmeade for lessons and go to a few horse shows.

"Are you sure you can't come with me to the track tomorrow?" Sarah asked. She studied Kayla's face closely, hoping for an encouraging response.

"I promised I'd babysit for the Nelsons almost a month ago, and I can't back out now. I wish I could. I'm coming right over to Brookmeade as soon as I get home."

"Oh, Kayla, I can't believe the DeWitts are doing this for me! I've dreamed of getting a horse for so long, and now it's actually going to happen."

"Yeah, it's awesome! It's been totally different for me," Kayla said. "Having a mother who rides makes a big difference."

"You've had your own horse for so long. Did you ever get a little bored with riding?"

"If I did, I knew better than to tell my mother. Actually, I remember getting tired of riding Chubs. He was fat and lazy, and it wasn't much fun taking him for a trail ride. My mother bought him because she thought he was a safe ride. He sure was—all he wanted to do was walk. Having Fanny has made all the difference."

"I always thought you had it made," Sarah said. "If you weren't my best friend, I'd have been pretty jealous."

"Now everyone at the barn thinks *you're* the lucky one!" replied Kayla with a grin. "But maybe they don't realize you'll have to work to pay for board and lessons. Just think, you'll get to choose from four horses! Before long we'll be able to go riding on the trails and maybe even go to shows together."

The girls moved out of the way of customers headed for the door, some with large bags. One woman struggled by them laden with a dressage saddle, a saddle rack, and a grooming caddy.

Kayla looked around. "It looks like this place has tons of stuff. You should be able to get everything you'll need right here. And maybe I can find a set of green polo wraps for Fanny."

"Green goes great with a chestnut," Sarah said. "But I don't even know what color my horse will be. Mrs. DeWitt said I should wait on some things, until I know more about the horse. She said that of the four horses, two are chestnuts, one's a dark bay, and the fourth is gray."

"Wow!" Kayla's hazel eyes widened as she looked at Sarah. "Maybe the gray will have dapples and a silver tail, something like Quarry. That used to be my favorite horse color until I got Fanny."

The girls moved to a display of wrap-around shipping boots. "You'll need a set of these for trailering the horse from the track. And the sign says they're half price!"

"They come in quite a few colors," Sarah said, hesitating.

"How about black?" Kayla suggested. "Black is good with any color horse. And that style gives great protection."

"Good idea," Sarah said, as she plopped a set into her basket. "Another thing on my list is a lead shank. Jack said that each horse at the track has his own halter, but not a shank. He said not to get a rope lead, but to find a leather one with a fairly long brass shank. It will last longer."

Kayla grinned. "Remember how Quarry chewed up Paige's rope lead when she left it in his stall? She said he turned it into a slobbery glob of strings." They laughed as they worked their way through a throng of shoppers to a rack of leather leads. Sarah looked them over for a few minutes. "The shank on this one looks plenty long enough," she said, choosing one and dropping it into her basket.

Taking Sarah by the arm, Kayla pulled her toward some bins that held various kinds of brushes. "Here's your grooming stuff."

Sarah glanced down at her list. "Let's see, for grooming equipment I'll need a stiff dandy brush, a soft brush, a curry comb, and a hoof pick."

"Don't forget a mane comb and a brush for the tail. And you'd better get a pulling comb if you want to keep his mane short and thin for braiding," advised Kayla.

"Well, it'll be awhile before I have to think about that."

"Hello?" Kayla said. "Even if you don't braid right away, you'll want his mane to look nice."

Sarah nodded as she put her selections into the basket, noticing it was getting heavy. She saw a number of grooming caddies stacked on the floor and considered the colors. As if reading her mind, Kayla picked up a red one. "Will this do?" she asked.

"Perfect," Sarah said. She looked down at her list. "What about hoof dressing?"

"That's a total no-brainer if you don't want your horse losing shoes." Kayla pointed to a pile of nested pails in the corner. "You're also going to need a wash bucket, horse shampoo, and a sponge, no matter what color the horse is!" she added. "And don't forget a sweat scraper."

Sarah laughed. "Slow down! At this rate, I won't be able to carry everything out of here."

Moving to another area of the shop, the girls spotted a collection of model horses on a cabinet by the window. The different breeds had been designed in fine detail, from high-stepping Saddlebreds to Appaloosas with spotted rumps. Kayla immediately picked up the Quarter Horse model.

"Look, Sarah. Except for the color, this Quarter Horse looks exactly like Fanny!"

"Cool. There must be a Thoroughbred here somewhere," Sarah said, her eyes running over the display. "Oh, here it is." She held up a finely molded model identified as the famous race-horse Seabiscuit. After looking at it carefully, she said, "I hope my horse looks just like this!"

Another model, so dark it seemed to be pure black, stood near the Thoroughbred. As Sarah looked more closely, she exclaimed, "It's a Dutch Warmblood, and it sure looks a lot like Chancellor. Rita's probably got one of these."

Kayla raised an eyebrow. "There isn't much Rita doesn't have."

"Yeah, it seems like all Rita has to do is mention she'd like something, and her father runs out and buys it for her," Sarah said. "And what a bragger she is. She's constantly telling every-one how much better Chancellor is than any other horse in the world. Give me a break!"

Kayla lowered her voice. "Judson told my mom why she's spoiled rotten. Did you know that Rita's mother died right after she was born? Mr. Snyder named Rita after her mother. He never got married again, so she's never even had a stepmother. Judson said that Rita's father is always trying to make it up to Rita."

"Gee, I didn't know that. I've wondered about her mother," Sarah said. "That's a tough break. And I guess it explains a lot of things."

They passed a section devoted to rider clothing, display-ing several styles of riding helmets, hunt coats, and boots. On their way to the saddle section, they passed the woman serving refreshments. She pointed to the table where jumbo raisin cookies were laid out on napkins. "You girls are doing quite a bit of shopping," the woman said. "Why don't you take a break with some punch and one of our super cookies?"

Kayla looked longingly at the cookies and then back at Sarah. "I've made up my mind. I'm going to lose five pounds before the summer show season begins. I guess I'd better skip the cookies."

"I guess I'll pass too," Sarah said to the woman. "But thanks."

"You're lucky you don't have to worry about your weight," Kayla whispered, as they moved out of the way to avoid some little girls and their mothers approaching the snack table. Just then they heard a familiar voice behind them.

"Hey, look who's here!" The girls turned to see Tim and Paige grinning from ear to ear. Both wore riding breeches, and Tim carried a navy blue sheet for Rhodes under his arm.

"I heard the DeWitts have some connections so you can get a horse from Raceland Park. Is that right?" Tim asked Sarah.

"Yeah," Sarah said. "We're supposed to go tomorrow. The DeWitts are being just super. They're letting us use the Brookmeade truck and trailer. But this is all happening so fast—I still can't believe it!"

"I hope you get a terrific horse," Paige said. "Just make sure it's not a confirmed runaway."

Laughing, Tim took Paige's arm as he started for the checkout. "Come on. We need to hurry if we're going to ride."

Paige waved to the girls. "Good luck, Sarah. I can hardly wait to see your horse!"

Sarah and Kayla watched them walk away. Kayla leaned

closer to say in a low voice, "I'll bet a lot of girls would love to date Tim. He's pretty cool. And guys would be interested in Paige if she wasn't already taken."

"I bet you wouldn't mind dating someone like Tim," Sarah said, looking for Kayla's reaction.

"I'd have to shed some pounds first," Kayla said. "And who would take a second look at someone with a face full of freckles?"

"Aw, you're too hard on yourself," Sarah said.

Kayla scowled. "If I could only be as lucky as Paige. She's skinny as a twig and her face looks like she's never had a zit."

"Well, Rita makes no secret of how she feels," Sarah said. "She'd like to give Paige a one-way ticket to Mongolia. As if Rita has any chance with Tim!" Her face sobered. "I just wish Rita would stop crowing all the time about how perfect Chancellor is!"

"Rita is weird," Kayla said. "She can be totally obnoxious, and then out of the blue she'll do something really nice. And sometimes she's so funny. You never know what to expect from her. She's an amazing rider, I must admit, and with that horse she'll be hard to beat."

The girls went down an aisle that seemed to have every kind of horse product imaginable, from shampoo to antibiotic ointments to fly spray. Sarah resisted the urge to pick up one of everything. She looked down at her overflowing basket and frowned. "I just hope my gift card will cover all this!"

As they headed to another wall rack loaded with bridles and bits, they saw Rita Snyder heading their way, squeezing between shoppers. Rita set her loaded shopping basket down when she got to them. She looked puzzled when she saw Sarah's basket. "Why are you getting all that stuff?"

"Sarah's getting a horse," Kayla said. "She'll be picking it up at Raceland Park on Saturday. Isn't that awesome?"

Rita's green eyes widened in surprise. "No kidding! From the racetrack? I guess you want something faster than Gray Fox to run away with you the next time," she said, grinning.

Sarah didn't know what to say, but Kayla came to her rescue. "He'll sure leave Chancellor in his dust."

Rita ignored the jab and turned to Sarah. "Tell me about this new horse."

"There are four Thoroughbreds this trainer wants to weed out, and I get to pick one of them. We'll bring him back to Brookmeade." Trying to change the subject, she pointed to the display of model horses. "There's a Dutch Warmblood here that looks a lot like Chancellor. Have you seen it?"

Rita sniffed. "I've already got two. My dad and my grandmother got their wires crossed and both gave me one for my birthday. She looked at Sarah's basket and frowned. "If you're getting a horse, you'll need more than that. I've got a whole closet full of stuff in my tackroom."

"If you have so much already, how come you're buying all that?" Sarah asked, pointing to Rita's full basket.

"Oh, I like to try different brands. And some of my stuff is getting tired." She paused a moment. "You know, since you're just getting started, Sarah, I'll bring a box of things to the barn for you. Maybe you'll be able to use some of it."

"Are you sure?"

"It will just go into the trash for Judkins to take to the dump. You might as well take it. But I gotta go," Rita said, as she picked up her basket. After she'd started for the checkout, she hesitated and turned back. "Any chance you guys would like to go to the beach with me? I want to check out the new shops that are just opening for the season. The Sweet Shop is supposed to be cool, and there's a new Abercrombie down there now."

Kayla and Sarah looked at each other and then back at Rita. "It doesn't work for me," Sarah said. "My mom will be getting back here pretty soon to pick us up."

"Another time," Kayla said. "Sarah will never carry all her stuff out of the shop without my help!"

When Rita was out of sight, Sarah said, "Offering me some of her stuff was the nice side of Rita."

"With the Visa card her father gave her, she can afford to be generous," Kayla replied.

Sarah scrutinized her list again. "I hope I'm not forgetting something important. I wonder how much all this will cost. The gift card has got to cover a bridle and saddle too, once I know my horse's size. And a winter blanket."

Seeing her friend's furrowed brow and her familiar anxious look, Kayla tugged at her sleeve. "There you go again, worrying. Will you ever chill out? Come on. Help me find some green polo wraps so we can check out before your mom gets back."

CHAPTER 6

The Racetrack

WITH JACK AT THE WHEEL, Sarah in the back, and her father sitting in the front passenger seat, the white Brookmeade Farm pickup nosed slowly onto Ridge Road, heading to the interstate. It was Saturday, and they were bound for Raceland Park. The Brookmeade Farm logo on the side of the horse trailer they were pulling was barely visible in the fog and the light rain that fell. The windshield wipers swished back and forth intermittently as the truck crept along the winding country road, its headlights making the fog seem even thicker.

Sarah held a tote bag filled with some of her purchases from the tack shop. She rummaged through it, running her hand over the smooth leather of the lead shank. Closing her eyes, she imagined leading her new horse into the barn at Brookmeade Farm. What would he look like? Would she end up with the gray, the bay, or one of the chestnuts? *Color isn't important,* she thought. *When I see my horse, I'll know he's the one.*

She leaned her head back and tried to envision the things she'd do with her horse. First she was riding him leisurely through the old orchard on the ridge, letting him eat a few apples along the way. Then they were galloping up the hill from the lower meadow, flying over the stone wall. Then they were performing a faultless dressage test, doing a flying change at X. Then they were....

Jack's voice brought her back to reality. "Sarah, have you given any thought to what you'll be looking for in a horse? It will help if you have some idea what's most important."

They were on the interstate now, and while the drizzle persisted, the fog had all but disappeared. The truck picked up speed as Sarah hesitated. Had she *given any thought* to what her new horse might be like? Where should she start?

"What do *you* think?" she asked, dodging the question.

"Well, an agreeable temperament counts for a lot. You don't want a horse that will battle you every step of the way, or one that's too excitable. And of course you don't want one that bites or kicks. I know the DeWitts don't want you to get an aggressive horse, one that might hurt you. Or for that matter, neither would your parents." Jack glanced at her father. "But then, I hardly think the trainer, Rudy Dominic, will show us a horse with a mean streak."

"Sarah, you must have *some* idea of what you want," Mr. Wagner said to his daughter.

Sarah thought for a minute before answering. "Most of all, I want a horse that will be my friend."

The men chuckled, but Jack replied, "Actually, I know what you mean, Sarah. You want a horse you can bond with. 'Tis true. Horses and riders can often tell what the other is thinking, and they come to trust each other. When I was competing Donegal Lad in Ireland and we were approaching a big cross-country obstacle, I might feel him hesitate slightly. That told me he wasn't sure he could jump it. I would sit deep and close my legs, using my body language to tell him it was a go, to be sure. That's all he needed to make good sport of it, because he trusted me. And it works both ways. If a rider is tense or nervous, his horse will pick up on that and might refuse."

Sarah's father swung around to face her. "I don't pretend to know much about horses, but I expect you'd like a horse that is good-looking and kind. How does that stack up?"

Sarah nodded, as she looked to Jack for his reaction.

"Looks are important," he said, "and we all like a horse we can feast our eyes on. But remember, a horse needs more than just a lovely face to perform well. If you want to compete someday, you'll be looking for an athlete with good conformation who'll be able to do his job while staying sound. He'll also need a good mind—character, I call it—to be brave but not too excitable. You don't want the nervous type."

He paused for a minute to let his words sink in. "And you'll not be wanting a horse with a vice, like weaving, cribbing, or stall walking. 'Tis hard to keep weight on a horse that has these bad habits. And why start out with a problem?"

"That makes sense," her father said. "But what about size? How big a horse do you recommend for a girl Sarah's age?"

"Sixteen hands would be a good size for you, Sarah, since you'll be growing a wee bit more. 'Tis important the horse is a good mover, with a long low stride that doesn't waste his energy. You'd best not pick out a high stepper or one who's lazy behind."

"What are the chances we'll find a horse that meets all those criteria?" her father asked.

"Well, we need to be realistic," Jack replied, "and not expect to find a perfect horse waiting for us. God has yet to put the faultless horse on earth. As we look at them, remember you'll always have to accept some things that are less than ideal."

Sarah sank back in her seat and thought about what Jack had said. She felt her excitement mounting. It wouldn't be long before she'd be seeing the horses and making her choice. Somehow she didn't envision it being a tough decision. Her horse was there waiting for her that very minute, and when she saw him, she'd know he was the one.

"Thanks for coming today, Jack," Mr. Wagner said. "This is a big step, not just for Sarah, but for our family. I know owning a horse is a big responsibility, and many things can happen. We'll just have to cross our fingers this horse will stay healthy. At any rate, we'll look to your judgment in helping Sarah make her choice."

"I guess you'll be losing a good worker at Seaside Creamery," Jack said.

"Yes, but her sister Abby is itching to take her place."

They drove steadily along the interstate toward the city and Raceland Park. Gradually the rain let up, and traces of brightening skies in the West promised sunshine later in the day. As they got closer, Sarah reached into her pocket again for the unsealed envelope Mr. DeWitt had asked her to give to Hank Bolton's trainer. She opened the letter to read it one more time:

Dear Mr. Dominic:

With the blessing of your employer, Henry Bolton, I have agreed to allow Sarah Wagner to choose one of the four horses *offered to me. Following her selection, the purchase price of $1 shall be paid to you as agent for Henry Bolton, after which the horse shall be transported to my farm and be examined by a veterinarian for health and soundness. Should the horse pass the pre-purchase exam, the sale will be final, and his Jockey Club registration papers shall be transferred to his new owner, Sarah Wagner. Should the horse not be approved by the veterinarian of our choice, the sale will be voided and the horse will be returned in like condition to you at Raceland Park. It is understood said horse will not be used for racing purposes.*

Chandler DeWitt's scrawled signature appeared at the bottom, along with the date. A second line was to be signed by the trainer, as agent for Henry Bolton, and there was a place for Sarah's father to sign as a witness to the transaction.

Traffic grew moderately heavy as they approached the city, with intermittent signs pointing the way to the racetrack. The truck started across a tall suspension bridge that gave them their first view in the distance of what looked to be a towering grandstand next to a vast parking lot. Beyond the grandstand, the white fencing of a circular track surrounded a grassy infield. Sarah carefully put the letter back in her pocket and gripped her bag more tightly. They were almost there!

"We'll be going to the backstretch where the horses are stabled," Jack said. "'Tis a little after nine, so we're right on time. We don't have ID cards, but Rudy will check us in. The security detail is pretty careful who they let into the stable area. Some of these horses are extremely valuable, and a lot of money is bet on races these days.

The truck went through an open gate designated as "Horsemen Only" and rolled to a stop in a paved lot next to a tall chain link fence. On the other side were the stables, off limits except to those who had official business. A uniformed guard manned a small admittance booth near a closed second gate.

Sarah saw long rows of rectangular barns, each identified by a single letter. The barns had stalls facing out on both sides, with roofs extending far enough beyond the stalls to form a sheltered walking area. "Hot walkers" were leading horses around these shed rows, circling the barns as the horses cooled out after their morning exercise and baths. Between the barns, other horses could be seen on machines that led them in a circle until they were cool enough to go back to their stalls.

After parking the truck and trailer, Jack approached the attendant in the booth. The guard looked up from reading *The Daily Racing Form*. "Can I help you?" he asked.

"Could you please page Rudy Dominic?" Jack asked. "We're picking up one of his horses."

"Sure thing," replied the attendant. He spoke into a microphone, which boomed his voice into the backstretch area. A few minutes later, a slightly built young man wearing chaps appeared.

"Rudy's busy," he told the guard. "He sent me to bring these folks in."

"Okay, Sam. Your word's as good as Rudy's. Just sign the slip."

Sam introduced himself quickly and motioned for them to follow him. He moved briskly, escorting them through the gate and toward barn M. At this hour, the backstretch hummed with activity, and Sarah could feel excitement in the air. Country music blared from an open tack room door and blended with the chatter of grooms, hot walkers, and exercise riders. Walking by one barn, they had to jump back quickly to avoid being side-swiped by a feed truck piled high with bales of hay and straw as it turned down a row. Golf carts ferried people back and forth to the track, where morning workouts were still taking place, and adding to the hubbub was the clanging of a blacksmith hammering horseshoes into shape. Several horses in a hurry to get back to their stalls pranced and jigged by them, chomping on their bits, their exercise riders keeping a tight rein.

"What do you do here?" Mr. Wagner asked Sam.

"I'm an exercise rider," Sam replied. "I get on horses that are going to the track for workouts in the morning. Then I help out with whatever the boss says needs to be done, and there's always plenty. Rudy checks with me about how the horses go. He likes to know if they pull and feel real strong, and if they don't seem right, he wants to know about it. He's got the stopwatch on them, too."

"It must take a long time to ride all of Rudy's horses," Sarah said.

Sam laughed. "Oh, I'm not the only exercise rider, and sometimes a few horses are galloped together in a set. Not all the horses go to the track every day, either. Some just walk in the shed row, maybe because they had a race the day before. Or maybe they have a strain or injury and need time rehabbing or just walking."

It seemed as if horses were everywhere, and Sarah thought they were all so beautiful. How she'd love to be an exercise rider!

A woman riding a Palomino in a Western saddle passed them, returning to the stable area leading a riderless Thoroughbred.

"How come no one is riding that horse?" Sarah asked.

"He's being ponied. It's just another way that horses go out in the morning. If a horse had an injury, sometimes it's better not to put weight on his back for a while."

A small man with slicked-back dark hair and wearing aviator sunglasses was standing just outside barn M, looking in their direction. As they drew closer, he walked forward, extending his hand to Sarah.

"I'm Rudy Dominic," he said to her. "You must be Sarah, and you're getting a new horse today. I hope you'll find one of ours to your liking." Sarah smiled back, suddenly feeling shy.

Rudy turned to the men. "Nice to see you again, Jack," he said with a nod to Sarah's instructor. Then he shook her father's hand.

"As riding horses go, these horses should all be fine. They just don't want to be racehorses, and we're tired of trying to get them to run well enough to compete. It costs a lot to have a horse in training, and these horses are just hay burners." He turned back to Sarah. "I don't mean to rush you, but let's get right to it. Are you ready to take a look?"

Sarah nodded her head vigorously. "Yes!" she said with her heart in her throat.

The trainer pulled a notepad from his pocket and looked down the handwritten list. He paused at one point, frowning. "This is the list Hank Bolton sent me—I apologize for not taking a closer look at it before now. It looks to me like three out of the four should be good prospects. Just so you know, the horses you don't choose will be sent to a dealer to sell with the condition that they go to good homes and not be raced."

Dominic waved an arm toward his barn. "Follow me. Let's start with Code of Honor. He cooled out a little while ago after doing a mile jog followed by an easy mile gallop." They walked along the shed row to the backside of Barn M. Grooms were sponging a number of horses from tall sudsy buckets while others rinsed them with a hose. Horses that had cooled out earlier were back in their stalls, most eating hay from nets hung by their doorways.

Sarah looked down the row of stalls, searching for a face to turn to her in recognition. Would she find *the one* here? Rudy led them to a good-looking chestnut whose only white marking on his face was a snip of white on his muzzle. He was nonchalantly eating his breakfast while keeping a watchful eye on everything going on around him.

"Sam, let's bring Code of Honor out for the folks to see."

Sam asked the horse to step out to the open area between the barns. Code of Honor balked at leaving his hay, but at Sam's insistence he came with him.

"This horse is pretty well bred, and Mr. Bolton had high hopes for him," Rudy said. "He's by Senior Diplomat, an excellent sire. But he prefers to gallop along behind other horses and let the rest of the pack compete for first place. There's nothing wrong with him, other than having a bad case of the slows. He's a nice medium-sized horse, as you can see, and for a Thoroughbred, he's pretty laid back. I guess that's part of his problem. He has only one bad habit, if you can call it that. He gets impatient when his oats are being dished up and he starts pawing up a storm by his stall door. It's a good thing we can use stall guards. If he had a solid door, he'd bang his knees."

Sarah had been inching forward while the trainer was talking, and now she was close enough to reach up to stroke the horse's neck. She felt his smooth chestnut coat, noticing how his pulled mane fell neatly on his right side. He immediately thrust his head toward the carrot in her hand, and Sarah let him bite off sections until it was gone. He looked for more, but she stepped back. "You can't have them all, boy."

"We call him Cody around the barn," Rudy continued. "He doesn't give anyone any trouble. I think he'd be a great kid's horse."

"Could we have him walk away from us in the open area and jog back?" Jack asked. "I'd like to see how he moves." Jack had carefully positioned himself so he could observe the horse moving straight away and coming back. Cody calmly walked and jogged, showing he didn't interfere or even travel close. Jack observed the horse's attractive topline and commented to Sarah that his shoulders and pasterns followed the same pleasing sloping angle. Bending over, he ran his hands expertly down the horse's front legs, feeling his knees, tendons, and ankles. They were tight and cold.

"Cody is a Kentucky-bred, four years old," Rudy volunteered. "Mr. Bolton bought him at the Keeneland Yearling Sale and expected a lot from him. It's always a big disappointment to have a horse not show any ability after you've put so much time and money into him. But this horse is clearly better suited for the show ring or a hack in the woods."

"He seems quiet enough," Jack commented, "and looks like

a good prospect. If the others are as nice as this horse, it will be a hard choice, Sarah."

"Let's go see Sun Worship," Rudy said. "He's also a chestnut, and while not as classically bred as Code of Honor, his sire, Sun Venture, has sired a lot of useful runners."

They walked down the shed row to where a smaller chestnut gelding stood at the stall door but showed no interest in his hay. He had a pretty head with a blaze running down the length of his face. Jack immediately noticed telltale teeth marks on the wooden lip of the horse's feed tub in the corner of the stall. Rudy saw him looking at it and commented, "He cribs once in awhile, so most of the time he wears a cribbing strap around his neck to discourage it." Jack gave Sarah a knowing look as she stepped forward to offer a carrot to Sun Worship.

"In case you don't know what cribbing is," Rudy continued, "it's when a horse grabs a hard surface with his teeth and pulls back while he swallows air. Unless a strap around his throat stops him from cribbing, he gets air in his stomach and doesn't digest his food well. This horse is also a little on the nervous side, which hasn't helped. Between that and his cribbing, he's not an easy keeper. I think he'll do better away from the racetrack, where he can be turned out regularly and may be more inclined to relax."

"That makes sense," Jack said. "But I think Sarah and I agree she'd best avoid a horse that has a vice from the get-go." When she nodded her approval, Jack added, "Let's move on and take a look at the gray."

"He's on the other side," Rudy said, as he led the way. Sarah looked at each horse as they passed, thinking how magnificent each was. As they rounded the corner, they saw a big-bodied steel-gray horse being led into his stall. His groom circled him to face the stall door and his hay net. The horse wasted no time diving into the hay.

"This is Cut Glass, and I have to be honest—he can't outrun a fat man," said the trainer. "He's a full brother to a stakes winner, but you'd never know it. He just doesn't have class. It goes to show you that sometimes well-bred horses can be pretty common. He's definitely one that Mr. Bolton needs to weed out. But he should be a great riding horse for you, young lady," he said, smiling at Sarah.

Jack, Sarah, and her father sized up this third horse in their lineup. Jack's knowledgeable eyes saw that the horse toed in with his left front leg, and his narrow chest placed his front legs close together. Sarah stroked the gray while he quickly devoured the carrot she offered him.

Just then Rudy's cell phone rang and he excused himself. "I'm expecting an important call," he explained.

Jack slipped into the stall and continued to evaluate the gray horse, noticing his rather long back and that his rump was higher than his withers. When Jack emerged from the stall, he looked at Sarah and her father, shaking his head. "This horse will be unsound sooner rather than later," he predicted. "His poor conformation puts a lot of stress on his body. I don't think you want to take this horse, Sarah."

Sarah nodded. It certainly made sense. The gray was not going to be the one.

"The first horse we saw seems like an exceptional prospect," continued Jack. "What do you think, Sarah? Will Code of Honor be the horse for you?"

"I like him a lot. He's beautiful. But isn't there a fourth horse for us to see?"

Her father looked to the end of the shed row where Rudy was talking on his cell phone. "Let's ask Rudy," he said.

When the trainer rejoined them, Jack posed the question. "What about the fourth horse that Hank Bolton had on your list?"

Rudy hesitated before answering. "Yes, there is another horse Mr. Bolton has decided to cull, but honestly, I was surprised to see him on the list for you folks. It's a four-year-old that has never started in a race because of training problems."

Rudy leaned back against the shed wall and went on to tell them about a homebred out of Mr. Bolton's champion, Northern Princess, a well-bred mare from a brilliant family who had won several Grade I stakes races. Before Mr. Bolton owned her, the mare had produced a horse that won the Preakness several years before, and he was able to afford her only because she was getting along in years. "As an older mare, it was questionable she could carry a foal to term, or even get in foal, but Mr. Bolton took a chance on her," explained Rudy. "After being bred to a stallion that had won the Kentucky Derby—Emperor's Gold—Northern Princess foaled a colt my boss had great hopes for. The colt was named Crown Prince."

Sam came around the corner and stopped to listen.

"That colt was a beauty from the start," Rudy continued. "He was big, too, and very correct. I understand he dominated the other colts on the farm and won every spontaneous dash across the fields. He was broken to saddle late in his yearling year, as is customary, and as a two-year-old came to me to begin serious training."

"How well I remember." Sam said. "Crown Prince was a real eye-catcher as a two-year-old. He turned a lot of heads every time I took him to the track. He was quite a mover, too. Very well balanced. People around here thought he was a prospect for the Breeders Cup Juvenile, so of course Mr. Bolton was high on him."

Jack, Sarah, and Martin Wagner listened, spellbound, as Rudy continued the story. "All went well for a while. We did slow gallops at first, taking our time, not rushing him. One day Sam told me he thought the colt didn't feel quite right. We had Doc Greene go over him, taking X-rays and checking his blood. Doc determined that being a big growthy colt, the bones in his knees hadn't closed completely. He hadn't finished growing. Doc said he should be turned out for at least six months, so he was shipped back to the farm in Florida."

They moved off the shed row to give plenty of space to a horse prancing toward them, pulling against his hot walker. Sam moved to the outer wall of the feedroom as he picked up the threads of the story. "I remember what he looked like when he came back as a three-year-old," he said. "He was close to seventeen hands, big and strong, and he knew it. When I tried to do slow gallops to gradually condition him for faster work, the horse wouldn't buy it. He fought me constantly. The way he leaped and whirled in the air, it's a wonder I could stay on him."

"Yes," Rudy agreed. "His antics continued to get worse, and we knew we were getting nowhere. Finally I told Mr. Bolton I thought the horse should be gelded, even with his impeccable breeding. He could have been one heck of a valuable stud prospect, but gelding usually calms down male horses. It looked like this was the only way to salvage him as a racehorse. We hoped that as a four-year-old, he would have matured and be more trainable. So again he went back to the farm."

"Did it make a difference?" Jack asked.

"I'm afraid when he returned to me last February he was even bigger and his attitude hadn't improved." He gestured to his exercise rider. "Sam, tell them what he was like when you were on his back."

"It's hard to believe, but the last time I rode him, he was worse than before. A few times I thought he was going to take me through the rail. Funny thing, though, in the stall and walking on the shed row, he's always been a puppy dog, quiet, although at times a little spooky. It will always be a mystery to me."

"Finally Mr. Bolton agreed he just wasn't going to be the racehorse we'd hoped for," Rudy said. "It was time to punt. In this game you have to be prepared for disappointment. But as I said, I'm surprised he added him to this list. Crown Prince certainly isn't a quiet ride for a young girl."

"From what you've told us, I would agree," Jack said. "The chestnut horse, Code of Honor, looks to be our best choice, so let's get back to him. Does that sound like a plan to you, Sarah?"

Sarah nodded, although she couldn't help being curious about Crown Prince. Where was he? What did he look like? She wished she could see him.

"Okay," answered Rudy. "I understand you have a letter from Chandler DeWitt I need to sign, and I have a folder of information on Cody to give you, medical records and such. I'll also write up what we've been feeding him, so you can gradually change him over to whatever your farm uses for grain and hay. Let's go to my office to take care of the paperwork."

CHAPTER 7
The Choice

SARAH WISHED SHE COULD go back to Cody's stall, but she grudgingly followed the men down the shed row to the trainer's office. She really didn't want to be cooped up inside "doing business" when there were so many beautiful horses here to see.

Rudy opened the door and gestured for them to enter. For someone who had been a longtime leading trainer at Raceland Park, his office was surprisingly "no-frills." The room was sparsely furnished with a desk and an older computer. A few straight-backed chairs sat beside two metal file cabinets, and the only other piece of furniture was a drop-leaf table near the door, where a bulging scrapbook was displayed. Except for a large chart mapping out the training program for each horse in his string, the paneled walls were bare.

Rudy began looking for Code of Honor's file in one of the cabinets. One Thoroughbred racehorse could accumulate a lot of paperwork, with a record kept of every shoeing, every visit from the vet, and a lifetime of training schedules. The successful horses' files also included listings of their racing wins, any newspaper clippings, and printouts from websites and racing blogs.

"His Jockey Club registration papers are over in the Racing Secretary's office, and I'll forward them to you once he's passed the vet exam. They verify his age, breeding, and ownership history. Unfortunately, you won't find anything in the races won column."

Jack opened the scrapbook on the table to a newspaper article, faded and yellowed over time, with the headline, "Best Beau First in Raceland Handicap." The scrapbook was filled with other clippings and magazine articles about some of the notable horses Rudy had trained and the important races they'd won. Sarah's father joined Jack, and soon the two men had tempted Rudy to regale them with the highlights of his impressive career and the horses he'd trained. Rudy seemed to have story after story to tell.

They don't need me here, Sarah thought. She wanted to get back to the horses. Quietly she slipped out the door and went to Code of Honor's stall, where the chestnut gelding was still eating hay from his net. Sarah brought out her last carrot, and as before, let the horse have small bites. She stroked his face as he chomped on the carrot. When it was gone, he strained over his stall's webbing to nudge her with his nose, asking for more. "Sorry, Cody, that's it," Sarah said, showing him empty palms.

A groom walked by carrying a bale of golden straw that he plunked down by the next stall. He paused to look at Code of Honor and Sarah. "Cody's a nice horse," he said. "I've been his groom all year, and he's been a peach. I've never had to watch my back with that one. You're going to like him a lot."

"Will you miss him?" Sarah asked.

The man shrugged. "Horses come and go. I rub four horses

and that keeps me too busy to notice, really. I hear there's a nice two-year-old coming from the farm to take the first open stall. Maybe he'll be the 'big horse,' with speed to burn. You never know. It's great to groom a horse with class, if you're lucky enough."

"How about Crown Prince?" she asked. "Can you tell me where he is?"

"Oh, that one?" He looked at her curiously. "You're interested in him? Well, he's around here somewhere. Maybe on the other side," he said, gesturing down the shed row. With that he cut the twine on the straw bale and went to work in the stall next to Cody's, shaking the straw out with a pitchfork.

Sarah looked up and down the aisle. Somehow she couldn't get Crown Prince out of her mind. Rudy had painted the horse as a hard-to-manage rogue. Could he really be that bad? She wanted to see for herself. Slowly she worked her way along the shed row, looking at each horse as she passed. Most had returned to their stalls, and grooms were busy filling water buckets, doing up legs with support bandages, and carrying off muck baskets to the manure bin. Many of the horses wore halters with nameplates. She checked the names on each one, but saw no sign of Crown Prince. Rudy Dominic hadn't given any clues to his whereabouts. Where was the mystery horse?

At the end of the shed row Sarah neared the darker area by the barn's feedroom, where the extended roof blocked the sunlight. As she started past what appeared to be an unused stall with both its top and bottom doors shut, she heard a faint noise. She stopped in her tracks and stood still, listening. There it was again, the sound of a rustle in straw that seemed to come from inside the stall.

Turning back, Sarah cautiously opened the stall's top door and peered inside. When her eyes grew accustomed to the darkness, she could make out the silhouette of a horse against the far wall. He was like a giant statue, his head high and alert. Maybe this was Crown Prince! It was strange to find him shut up in his stall like this when all the other horses' top stall doors were open. Had Rudy hoped to keep them from seeing him? She couldn't imagine why else the big horse would be kept in the dark.

Sarah stood quietly watching the horse. There was no movement as he stood facing the far corner, ignoring her. She clucked softly, but there was no response. Her hand dug deep in her pocket in hopes of finding one more carrot, but it was empty. Nothing was left, except perhaps…yes, in her other pocket she felt a peppermint candy, which she withdrew and slowly unwrapped. In response to the crinkling of the cellophane, a slim finely chiseled head turned her way, his ears pricked forward. He wore a halter, but was too far away for her to read the nameplate. She placed her outstretched hand with the peppermint over the stall door and spoke softly, "Prince, come Prince."

Slowly the horse turned from the rear wall and cautiously moved toward her. As he got closer, she felt delicate nostrils blow gently on her hand and then the slender muzzle lifted the peppermint away. He studied her as he chewed the candy slowly and deliberately.

He was big. Except for the enormous draft horses she had seen in pulling competitions at the state fair, this horse was larger than any Sarah had ever seen, including Chancellor. The only horse who might possibly match his size was Donegal Lad. But this horse possessed such refinement his size wasn't readily evident until he was close. In the dimly lit stall his dark bay coat looked almost black, and his only marking was a small white star in the center of his forehead. The deep straw bedding hid any possible white markings on his legs.

For several moments Sarah and the horse stood looking at each other. Then she lifted the stall door's latch and let herself inside. As Crown Prince retreated to the corner, she reached back over the door to lower the latch back into position. Slowly she approached the horse, all the while talking softly. "Good boy, good Prince," she repeated. Once by his side, she reached to touch his long neck and stroke it gently. His coat felt like sleek satin. He turned his head toward her, seeming to know she meant him no harm.

Now she was close enough to make out his halter plate. Sarah read the name in large block letters: CROWN PRINCE. Below it in smaller print his sire and dam were listed: Emperor's Gold – Northern Princess. Yes! This definitely was the horse with the reputation of an untrainable rogue.

"You beautiful Prince," she murmured. As Sarah stroked his neck and continued to speak in hushed tones, she felt the horse become more relaxed. His head dropped down to her and gradually his eyes softened, as he clearly enjoyed her touch and gentle voice. He offered no resistance as she gently pulled his head closer and rested her cheek on his muzzle. It was so soft. With his head lowered, she caressed his forehead, tracing the white star, and gently tugged on his ears. She felt as if she had known this horse forever.

Sarah had no idea how long she had been in the stall with Crown Prince when she became aware of a presence outside.

"Sarah, what are you doing! We've been looking all over for you." It was her father's voice. She turned to see him looking in at her, along with Jack, Sam, and Rudy Dominic. Worry and concern were written all over their faces.

"I'm fine, Dad. Don't worry. This is Crown Prince. And he's the horse I want."

Her father's jaw tightened as his eyes met Jack's before he turned back to Sarah and the dark bay horse standing beside her. Crown Prince surveyed them all curiously, the picture of refinement and nobility. Mr. Wagner observed the horse's beautifully shaped head, which tapered from small ears to large intelligent eyes down to a refined muzzle. His white star contrasted sharply with his deep mahogany coat. Sarah's father shook his head, acknowledging the horse's beauty, but anxious for his daughter's safety.

Rudy Dominic pointed to the horse. "Isn't he just like I said?"

Jack was too absorbed to answer. He opened the stall door and joined Sarah to get a closer look. He had seen some impressive horseflesh in his life, but this one ranked up there with the best of them. His eyes traveled from the powerful hindquarters to the pleasing topline and nicely sloping shoulder.

"Have you got a shank right there, Rudy?" Jack asked. "I want to get a better look at this fellow outside the stall."

Rudy nodded to Sam, who left, returning in a few minutes with a lead shank and let himself into the horse's stall. "Come on, big horse. Let's show off for these folks." As he started to attach the lead to Crown Prince's halter, the horse playfully grabbed the brass shank with his teeth. "Oh, no you don't," Sam said, as he pulled it away. He ran the chain through the halter's side ring, over the horse's nose, and attached it to the other side. Turning to Sarah, he said, "If he decided to put his head to the sky, as a short guy I'd be in trouble. But he knows me. He's not a bad horse around the barn. It's only when you sit on him he gets rank. I'll bring him out so you can have a look-see at a real horse."

Jack opened the stall door, and Sam led the horse to the open area between the barns. The backstretch was quieter now, since most grooms had finished caring for their horses and were having a late breakfast in the track kitchen. Crown Prince walked with a stately dignity and halted when asked, his coat gleaming in the sun's rays.

Jack moved around him, thinking out loud. "Strong hindquarters, nice length of back, pronounced withers, good bone, and a lovely long neck." He moved to stand directly in front of the horse before speaking to Rudy.

"His conformation is quite correct. No toeing in or out, good width of chest, nice head. They don't come any better than this. But I'd like to see him move."

Rudy motioned to Sam. "Walk away and then jog him back, Sam. But be careful. He hasn't been to the track to gallop in awhile, so keep a tight hold on him."

Rudy turned to Sarah and her father. "I'm always surprised at how well behaved he is except when there's a rider up. Then he becomes a lunatic."

Jack positioned himself to get a good view before Sam led the horse away from him. Coming back, Prince trotted agreeably beside Sam and stopped when they reached Jack. "He's a good mover too, well balanced," said Jack, "and his ground manners can't be faulted."

Sarah's father was standing back but listening carefully. "He *is* a beautiful animal. It's too bad his reputation takes him out of the running for being a horse for Sarah," he said firmly.

Sarah, who up to now hadn't taken her eyes off the horse, swung to face her father. "Dad—I don't believe he can be as bad as Rudy says! He deserves a chance to be a different horse when he gets away from the racetrack and comes to Brookmeade Farm. Maybe he wasn't meant to be a racehorse, but I think he will be a wonderful horse for me. I just know it!"

Mr. Wagner was quick to respond. "Sarah, this is a large and powerful animal. Above all else, I won't let you be in harm's way. From what I've heard today, this horse is dangerous. We mustn't be so taken with his splendid appearance that we lose sight of the big picture. I can't have you getting hurt by a horse."

Sarah could see her father was totally serious. He was thinking only of potential disaster. She had to change his mind.

"We can start working with him on a longe line, Dad, until he knows what's expected of him. I can turn him out in the big pasture where he can run off some energy. He'll come to trust me. I promise I won't even think about riding him until Jack gives the okay. You can see he's well behaved. He's a special horse, Dad, and he should have another chance."

"But what about the handsome chestnut horse you like so much?" her father asked, motioning toward the other end of the shed row. "Don't you think Code of Honor will be the perfect horse for you? And don't you want a horse you can ride? Who knows how long it will be before you can get on this horse, if ever."

Sarah looked at her father, her dark eyes pleading. "Dad, I

know you want what's best for me. But this is supposed to be *my* decision. Please don't stand in the way. You've got to trust me. I want to take Crown Prince back to Brookmeade Farm more than I've ever wanted anything in my entire life. I *know* he's the right horse for me. He's the one I've been waiting for."

Jack, who had been quietly studying Crown Prince, turned to them. "'Tis for sure we have a grand animal here. Who knows the heights he and Sarah might reach if we can turn him around. Sometimes Thoroughbreds are completely different when they get away from the racetrack." Jack walked over and placed a hand on Crown Prince's shoulder. He stroked the horse, deep in thought.

After a few moments he turned back to Sarah's father. "I tell you what, Martin. Perhaps we can give this horse a trial run. If we could arrange to take him for a month, I'll pledge to be deeply involved in his handling, and I mean every part of his care and schooling, to make sure Sarah is safe. I won't allow her to get on him until I've tested those waters myself. I'll know in thirty days if he will be a suitable mount for her. If by then we've made no headway and I decide he's not the right horse, we'll notify Hank Bolton and return him to you, Rudy," Jack added, looking at the trainer. "If this trial scenario is acceptable to you and Hank Bolton, let's give it a shot." He paused and looked intently at Sarah's father. "Martin, I'm willing to make this commitment to ensure your daughter's safety."

Sarah stood quietly, her gaze never leaving her father. He was solemn, as he stood deep in thought. She knew he was worried, that above all else, he didn't want her hurt. Mr. Wagner looked hard at Jack for a few moments before speaking. "Without your encouragement, I would never even consider letting Sarah take a horse with the shady past this one has. But if you can assure me you'll stay on top of things and manage everything that's done with him, I'll go along with your proposal. But remember, this is a trial. At some point in the next month I will look to you, Jack, for an answer. If Sarah is at risk at any time, the horse must go."

Sarah threw her arms around her father. "Dad, you're the greatest! I'll always remember this, that you gave Crown Prince a chance."

"And let's not forget he will have to pass a vet exam," her father said. "Depending on how it goes, the horse may be coming back here sooner rather than later. I want that to be clear."

Jack wore a pleased expression, happy at the prospect of bringing such an exceptional horse back to the farm. Crown Prince might be difficult, but now the horse would be dealing with someone who had retrained many bad actors. And for such a striking animal, it certainly was worth a try. Jack was more than ready to give it his best go.

Jack looked at his watch. "It's getting late, and we should be back on the road soon. So let's do what has to be done."

Rudy beckoned to Mr. Wagner. "I need you and Sarah to come back to my office while I make the changes to your paperwork. I'll need your signature for Sarah, since she's a minor. The trainer started down the shed row, but stopped after going a short distance and turned back to Jack. "After Sam puts the horse away, why don't you guys go to the ingate and ask Smitty to let you bring your rig back to my barn. We'll load him here."

Back in Rudy's office, Rudy offered some advice as he opened his file cabinet again. "You'll want to have your blacksmith or farrier replace Crown Prince's aluminum plates with regular horseshoes, or perhaps just pull the racing plates and let him go barefoot for awhile. He's got a decent foot, so that shouldn't be a problem." His face was serious as he spoke to Sarah. "If this is going to be *your* horse, you need to start thinking about these details."

Sarah drew Chandler DeWitt's letter from her pocket and gave it to the trainer. Rudy promptly pulled a pen from his desk drawer and signed the appropriate spaces. "He's all yours now, Sarah," he said, handing it to her father to witness. "I just hope he works out."

Sarah beamed. The horse she had always dreamed about was hers! At least for now....

"There's one thing we almost forgot," Martin Wagner said, pulling his wallet from his back pocket. He pulled out a dollar bill and laid it on the desk. "We need to pay our way here, just to make it 'legal.'" They both laughed, as Rudy took the letter back and made note of the payment.

Sarah and her father were almost back to Crown Prince's stall when the Brookmeade truck and trailer pulled up in front. Sarah hurried to the truck and grabbed her tote bag from the back seat. Jack nodded at the wraparound shipping boots she pulled from the bag.

"Chances are he hasn't worn anything like these before. At the track they use bandages and cottons for shipping, so the heavier material and velcro will seem a little strange to him. But they'll provide good protection if he becomes rambunctious in the trailer. I'll hold him while you put them on."

Sarah looked up in surprise. "Are you sure? I've never done

this before." Jack took the lead shank. "Now that you have a horse, there will be many new things you'll be doing. 'Tis time you'd be learning how."

Under his watchful eye, Sarah wrapped a boot around each leg, making sure the Velcro straps were going in the right direction and the boots were taut but not too tight. Crown Prince was wary of the large shipping boots, sensing the difference in height and weight. He shook his head nervously and tried to move away.

"Whoa, son," Jack said, holding the shank firmly.

When Sarah had finished, Jack held out the lead shank to her. "We're ready to load—let's go," he said. "Take him up the ramp, and once he's on we'll close the bar behind." Sarah gulped, but took the lead from Jack. It seemed as if he was testing her. Even though she had never loaded a horse on a trailer before, she was determined to do whatever he asked. Besides, she'd seen Kayla load Fanny tons of time.

The ramp was down and a full hay net hung in the front. They were ready for the journey back to Brookmeade Farm. Sarah spoke once more to *her* horse and gently stroked his neck. "Come Prince. We're going home." Her father swung the stall door open and she stepped onto the shed row, leading Crown Prince to the trailer. Feeling the weight of the heavier shipping boots, he hiked his hind legs high for a few steps and kicked out with one hind leg as he left the stall. A few steps later he was moving normally. Walking beside him, Sarah looked up at his withers. Crown Prince towered over her—by comparison, Lady Tate would seem like a cob!

Sarah remembered a few loading battles Fanny had waged when Kayla first got her. The mare had a deathly fear of horse trailers and refused to go on. Once, when Fanny dug her toes in and resisted going forward, Kayla turned to face the mare, but Mrs. Romano quickly corrected her. "Have you ever seen anyone backing their way up a ramp?" she'd asked Kayla. "Of course you haven't—and this mare hasn't either. When Fanny sees you turn to face her, she thinks you're not going any farther." Being trailered every week to the lessons at Brookmeade helped Fanny overcome her fear, and now she loaded onto the Romanos' trailer as willingly as she walked into her stall.

As he approached the Brookmeade trailer, Crown Prince hesitated. In the past he'd been transported on huge horse vans more like barns on wheels. He looked warily at the trailer and stopped abruptly, planting his feet in front of the ramp. Sarah waited a few moments, giving him time to lower his head to sniff the ramp, while she continued to face the inside of the trailer and apply tension to the lead shank. As she clucked loudly and began moving up the ramp again, Jack placed a hand on the horse's hindquarters to urge him forward. Crown Prince took a few tentative steps and then strode up the ramp. Jack snapped the butt bar in place behind him. "Well done, Sarah," he said, as he and Rudy lifted up the ramp and fastened it securely.

"Good boy, Prince," she murmured, stroking his neck and attaching the trailer tie to his halter. She offered him her last peppermint, but he was too distracted to have any interest in the candy. He looked nervously out the trailer's side door, tossed his head, and pawed the trailer floor a few times. Jack read her anxious mind. "Don't be worrying, now. He'll be all right. But the sooner we get started the better, to be sure."

Sarah dug in her pocket for her cell phone and quickly took a picture of Crown Prince as he looked out the trailer door toward her. Once they started down the road, she'd send the pic to Kayla. Sarah could hardly wait to show her friend what her new horse looked like.

"I'd like to ride with him in the trailer," Sarah said. "Maybe he won't be so nervous with me beside him."

"Absolutely not!" her father exclaimed. "I don't like that idea one bit."

"Furthermore, it's against the law," Jack added, as he closed the side door to the trailer. Sarah sighed and dropped her head as she resigned herself to riding in the pickup. What if he got upset in the trailer on the ride back?

"I have to leave you now," Rudy said. "I have a horse running in the first race this afternoon, and we need to get him ready. But I want to wish you luck with Crown Prince."

Jack reached out to shake the trainer's hand.

"Thanks for giving us a big part of your morning, Rudy. We'll be in touch to let you know how the vet exam goes and how we make out with the horse."

"Yes," Mr. Wagner said. "And I appreciate your willingness to take him back if he doesn't work out. You'll be hearing from us in a month, one way or the other. Maybe sooner."

As the truck made its way out of the stable area and toward the main highway, they met a steady stream of traffic funneling its way through entry roads to the parking area in front of the grandstand. On a day that featured a stakes race, the lot was filling up with racing fans and those with money to bet.

Sarah sat in the back, twisting against the seat belt to watch

Crown Prince. She was grateful there was a window in the front of the trailer that allowed her to see his every move. His head was up and his ears pricked, apparently watching the cars and tractor trailer trucks through the front window. He showed no interest in the hay in the net.

Sarah's mind raced. So much had happened in the last few hours, things that would change her life forever. Or so she hoped. She knew her father would return Prince to the track in a heartbeat if he thought the horse would prove to be dangerous. And her mom would nix the arrangement if she suspected Sarah was over-mounted. She might even veto the decision to let Sarah have Crown Prince in the first place, even if it was only a trial.

Sarah clenched her fists. Now that Crown Prince was hers, she was determined to keep him.

CHAPTER 8

The Homecoming

THE MORNING FOG HAD burned off completely by the time the Yardley exit from the interstate came into view, and it had become warm and humid. From the exit ramp the truck bringing Crown Prince to Brookmeade Farm headed north on Ridge Road toward the rural part of town. The truck slowed considerably after turning onto the farm road, as Jack maneuvered around the road's rough spots.

Sarah had hardly taken her eyes off her horse during the ride back to the farm. But as they drove along the road, she turned to watch the antics of the three foals turned out with their dams. She noticed how fast the babies were growing, especially the black colt, a striking contrast next to his dam. This was Ice Sculpture's sixth foal, and over the years the once dappled gray mare had turned almost white. As they passed, the colt reared before galloping in a big circle around the pasture.

The men in the front seat also turned their attention to the foals as they passed. "I suspect the black colt is going to be a standout," Jack said. "And as dark as he is now, it looks like he'll be gray like his dam. I noticed a few white hairs on his forehead the other day."

"That's cool," Sarah said. "I wish the foals didn't have to leave here. They don't come back, and we never see them again."

"Yes," Jack said, "after they've been weaned from their mothers, they go to Hyperion Farm, Hank Bolton's place in Florida. Horses can be turned out year-round down there, and bad weather doesn't hold them back. The farm has a training track where they begin to learn to become racehorses."

"Who knows," Sarah's father said, with a grin, "perhaps someday we'll see one of them on television running in a big race for the glory of Brookmeade Farm. But seriously, Jack, it sounds like somewhere along the line you've been involved with horse racing. Actually, it seems there's not much about horses that you don't know."

Jack laughed. "Horses are almost sacred in Ireland. I was on the back of a horse from the time I was a wee lad. Later on I trained them and rode in all sorts of competitions. Throw in a little foxhunting, and I even rode in some steeplechase races—plus my father always had a few broodmares on the farm."

He slowed as they approached two riders headed in their direction, probably going to the trails on the other side of Ridge Road. The riders guided their horses into the meadow, giving the truck a wide berth. When Sarah saw it was Tim and Paige, she waved and gave them a thumbs up as they passed. They waved back. Sarah was glad they were around—they could come see Crown Prince after their ride.

When the truck rolled to a stop in the parking area next to the barn, Gus Kelso came out to meet them. The barn manager's burly frame was slightly bent from a lifetime of lifting bales and pushing wheelbarrows, and as usual his face was shaded by a red baseball cap that covered much of his disheveled gray hair. Gus wasn't particularly friendly, and no one at the barn warmed up to him right away. But most boarders felt blessed to have him in charge of their horses once they saw the excellent care he gave them. Now Gus approached the truck, his face stern and unsmiling.

Jack climbed out of the cab and called to him. "We've got Sarah's horse, Gus. Do you know where he's going?"

"He'll have Medina's stall for now. Mrs. DeWitt said we should move her mare to the carriage shed for a few days. Medina will bunk down with the broodmares until the carpenters finish the new stalls here."

Sarah's father shook his head in amazement as he, too, exited the truck. "Incredible! Mrs. DeWitt is letting Sarah's new horse have her own horse's stall?"

"Yes, but she's not just being generous," Jack said. "There's more to it than that. A new horse could carry viruses that might cause the mares to abort the foals they're carrying. We don't want Crown Prince anywhere near them for a while."

Sarah grabbed her lead shank from the seat beside her and hurried to the trailer's side door. When she pulled it open, Crown Prince thrust his head out, his ears flicking in all directions as he took in his new surroundings. His eyes were wide, showing the whites, and when Sarah climbed up to run her hand along his neck, she noticed it was damp with perspiration. He must have been nervous on the trip, or maybe it was just the warm day. "It's okay, boy," she said softly as she stroked him.

Jack moved to the rear of the trailer. "When you're ready, Sarah, we'll let the ramp down and you can back him off. Don't let him come too fast, though. Take him right into the barn to Medina's stall."

Sarah once again tried to remember everything she had learned from watching Kayla unload Fanny. She ran the lead shank through the rings on Prince's halter, and after unsnapping the trailer tie, released the breastplate. She tried to sound confident as she called out, "I'm ready."

Jack let the ramp down slowly and unhooked the butt bar before stepping to the side. "Okay, back him out."

Sarah pressed her hand against Prince's chest and clucked softly, asking the horse to move away from her. He began backing slowly, but as he started down the ramp, Prince suddenly rushed backward, an alarmed look in his eyes. Sarah, gripping the lead shank tightly, was pulled off the ramp. She fought to keep her balance when Prince whirled to face two horses being led across the parking area. He whinnied loudly to them, his nostrils quivering, his noble head held high.

Gus was leaning on the barn door, watching. He whistled softly. "It's a good thing he's got the end stall. It's plenty big, and it looks like he's gonna need it."

"Come on, boy," Sarah urged, putting pressure on the shank as she started for the entrance. Prince turned to walk beside her with quick mincing steps, but at the doorway he again balked, not sure what was inside.

Sarah spoke to him again. "It's okay, Prince, it's okay. This is your new home." After hesitating a moment he followed her into the barn and down the aisle toward Medina's stall. The horses along the way heard his aluminum racing shoes ringing on the cement and came to the front of their stalls to eye the newcomer. Two girls who boarded their horses at Brookmeade were carrying saddles out of the tack room and stopped in their tracks to watch the large stunning horse walk by.

Once in the stall, Sarah circled Prince back to the door and snapped a stall tie to his halter. Prince tossed his head fretfully, but otherwise he stood quietly as she removed his shipping boots and nested them near the door. Jack and her father stood outside, watching through the bars.

"He'll settle down after a bit," Jack said to Sarah, "and 'twill help if you stay calm. Take deep breaths. The horses near him are relaxed and that will help. But now he needs some time alone."

Sarah sighed resignedly as she stretched up to remove Prince's halter. She picked up the shipping boots and eased out of the stall. After hanging his halter and shank on the stall door, she stood by the bars watching her horse move uneasily around the stall, stopping occasionally to paw the deep bed of fresh shavings. The high side walls kept him from seeing Wichita in the next stall, but he paused a few times to listen when he heard his neighbor moving about.

"Do you suppose he's always had straw bedding?" Sarah asked. "He acts like he doesn't know what to make of the shavings."

Jack turned to watch the horse. "You could be right. From his pawing, I expect he'll be rolling soon. And don't be surprised if he doesn't clean up his grain tonight." He gave Sarah a firm look. "But he'll be fine. You needn't be worrying. He can see other horses across the way, and that should steady him."

Sarah's father turned to leave. "I'll be off now, Sarah. Call when you're ready to come home. And be careful." He looked intently at Jack. "I guess I don't have to remind you that I have reservations about this horse, and Sarah's mother certainly will, too. The only reason he's here is that I know you'll stay on top of things." With that Mr. Wagner made his way down the aisle.

Jack watched him go, and then walked to where Gus was working his way from stall to stall using a long hose to fill water buckets. "Gus," he said, "I don't know if Mr. DeWitt has mentioned it, but Sarah's going to start helping out here, taking Lucas's place. She's now a working student. Maybe you could show her the hay routine later today."

Gus spun around to face Jack, the water from the hose spraying loudly against the side of the bucket. "What? It's the first I've heard of it! I knew someone would be helping out after Lucas left, but a girl?"

Jack had learned to ignore Gus's customary fuming when he first heard someone else's plan. In time he always simmered down. "I think you'll find Sarah's a good worker. You'll not be disappointed," Jack said firmly.

Gus shut off the water spigot with a quick jerk. "What does she know about taking care of horses? Never had one of her own," he grumbled.

Sarah couldn't help overhearing the conversation, and she cringed at Gus's words. It was obvious he didn't like the idea of her working at the barn.

"She'll be fine, Gus. Just give her a chance. I hope you'll be having a few moments tomorrow morning to help set up her work schedule. Can you drop by the office, say at nine o'clock? It won't take long."

Gus shrugged his broad shoulders. "I guess so," he muttered, as he went back to watering the horses. Jack left for the office.

A few minutes later, Tim and Paige arrived to see Prince, who was still moving nervously about the stall. "Wow!" Paige exclaimed. "He's big and beautiful, Sarah. He makes Quarry look like a shrimp. What's his name?"

"Crown Prince, but just Prince will do."

"Well, whatever his name is, he's awesome," Tim said, moving away from the bars.

"I texted Kayla and Rita and told them where to find us," Paige said. "Rita's going to pick up Kayla and come right over. How long will you be staying?"

Before Sarah could answer, the sound of hooves crashing against the stall wall caused them to turn quickly. Crown Prince was down in his stall. He had rolled too close to the rear wall, and his hind legs had struck the sides with a loud crash. Startled by the noise, he leapt to his feet and shook himself. He nervously circled the stall a few times before finally dropping his head to nibble on some hay.

"Your horse will be getting the royal treatment from the Brookmeade hospitality committee," Tim said. "Everyone who rides here will want to check him out. It was the same when Rhodes first arrived. I'm surprised the DeWitts aren't here."

The hum of a car coming right up next to the barn caused them to stop talking and listen. The sound was surprising, since the parking area was on the other end of the building. Paige darted to the window and then looked knowingly at Sarah and

Tim. "It's Rita's Mustang," she said. "She must have driven right over the lawn."

A minute later Rita and Kayla were hurrying up the aisle toward them. They lost no time going right to the stall to peer in at the horse.

"Gee," Kayla said, "he really is gorgeous!" She gave Sarah a hug. "You've been waiting a long time for this, kid." She turned to Rita. "Isn't he something?"

Rita had been standing quietly, her face stony as she stared into the stall. "At least he's good-sized. Maybe not quite as big as Chancellor, but he's kind of cute. Congrats, Sarah."

Kayla turned back to Sarah. "This is so exciting! Tell us everything."

The small crowd listened as Sarah told them about the racetrack, describing the backstretch and the other three horses they'd looked at. She caught herself as she was about to tell them more about Crown Prince's background. Maybe best *not* to mention his checkered past. There was no need to influence their opinions so soon, before he had a chance to make a favorable impression. And besides, coming to Brookmeade Farm was going to be a new beginning for Prince. Now he was *her* horse, and things would be different.

"It's so cool you had your choice of four horses," Paige said. "And Cody sounds like he's amazing. What made you pick this one?"

"I believed I'd know my horse when I saw him. That I'd *know* he was *the one*. And that's what happened. He was the last horse I saw, and I knew he'd been waiting for me."

Rita listened with a slight smirk on her face. "My dad had

three equestrian agents looking for the right horse for me," she said. "We didn't need to look into a crystal ball to know Chancellor was *the one*."

Just then Taco and Spin roared down the aisle, ushering in the DeWitts. Sarah reached down to pat Spin, rubbing his side and stroking his ears. Taco, not to be ignored, whimpered and pawed Sarah's arm.

"Oh, Sarah," exclaimed Mrs. DeWitt, walking quickly toward them, "we just talked to Jack, and it appears you have found a horse. We can't wait to see him!" She and Mr. DeWitt joined the audience looking in at Crown Prince through the bars. "My goodness," Mrs. DeWitt gasped, "he's a giant of a horse! And so beautiful, too! He almost takes my breath away!"

"Mrs. DeWitt, thanks for letting Crown Prince stay in Medina's stall," Sarah said. "I hope Medina doesn't mind being in the carriage shed."

Mrs. DeWitt laughed. "Don't give Medina another thought, my dear. She absolutely loves a change of scene once in awhile, and she seems quite taken with the foals. But tell us about this lovely creature."

"Well, he's a four-year-old Thoroughbred who never raced. He's very well bred. His mother, Northern Princess, was a stakes winner, and his father is Emperor's Gold—he won the Kentucky Derby. I guess Prince just didn't want to be a racehorse."

Chandler DeWitt stood quietly observing the horse before him, noting his quality and excellent conformation. Over the years he had cultivated a keen eye for a well-put-together horse, going back to his foxhunting days with Hank Bolton in Virginia. They'd both relished the sound of the huntsman's horn and the baying of hounds as they raced over the countryside, jumping everything in their path. As their friendship deepened, Bolton had taught him a great deal about good conformation and what to look for in a horse.

Mr. DeWitt found much to admire in this newcomer to his barn. He also knew that Northern Princess was Bolton's best broodmare, a great producer from an outstanding female family. And Crown Prince was sired by a Secretariat-line stallion, the Derby winner Emperor's Gold. With that breeding, it was hard to believe that this horse hadn't been tried on the track. Chandler DeWitt wondered why Prince was offered as part of Hank Bolton's plan to cull the losers from his stable. Something had to be wrong—either the horse was unsound, or there were behavior problems. Mr. DeWitt resolved to talk to Jack. If that didn't shed some light on the matter, he'd get in touch with Hank Bolton directly.

Dorothy DeWitt continued her conversation with the group of young riders, wanting to hear how all their horses were performing. She always delighted in any progress they reported. She noted how she hoped they would all be able to compete in a few local shows or events close enough so she and Chandler would have a chance to watch them ride. "I will be very disappointed if you don't keep me abreast of all your competitions, girls. And that goes for you, too, Tim," she added with a smile.

While the group chatted, Chandler DeWitt walked back to the office where Jack, Kathleen, and Lindsay were discussing the day's lessons. "Jack, I'm sorry to interrupt, but I wonder if I could have a few words with you," Mr. DeWitt said. "Let's go to my office."

"We were just finishing up," Kathleen said. "We've been hearing about the terrific horse Sarah picked out, and Lindsay and I are about to go take a look for ourselves."

The men walked to Chandler DeWitt's private office. It was decorated much like the lounge but looked out on the hunt course rather than the indoor. Mr. DeWitt flicked on the overhead lights and motioned to Jack to sit down in the straight-backed chair opposite his desk. He didn't waste any time getting to the point.

"Sarah has picked out what appears to be a spectacular horse. His breeding is superb, and he's an exceptional individual. But I'm baffled why this horse wasn't tried on the racetrack. Do you know how he happened to be among the four horses Hank offered me?"

"Yes, there is rather more to the story than what Sarah is saying. Rudy Dominic gave us the scoop—and he didn't appear to be holding anything back." Jack went on to relate the difficulties in training the horse, how he became unmanageable under saddle, even though he was otherwise well-mannered. He mentioned the decision to geld the horse, despite the likelihood that with his impressive pedigree he would be a valuable stallion prospect even if he didn't earn a superior race record.

"They finally had to admit that the horse was a rogue and they should give up on him," Jack said. "I guess they figured that his bad behavior would eventually get him ruled off the track. So he was offered to you." Jack thought back to their conversations with the trainer. "Rudy had definite reservations about the horse going to a teenage girl, and he talked down the horse when we asked about him. But Sarah found Crown Prince and immediately fell in love with him. He seems to respond well to her, too."

"After hearing so much negative talk about the horse, I'm surprised Martin didn't put his foot down on her choice," Mr. DeWitt said.

"Well, he did at first. But it didn't make sense to me that the horse could be a maniac under saddle and yet a cream puff in every other way. I suggested we take him on a one-month trial, so I could see just how bad an actor he is, and decide if there is hope we can turn him around. I assured Martin that at no time will I allow Sarah's safety to be at risk, so he reluctantly agreed."

Chandler Dewitt sat deep in thought, considering the information. Finally he spoke. "There's something else to consider. I scheduled a pre-purchase exam with our vet for Monday morning. Wes Reynolds will be coming to give shots to a boarder's horse, and he said he could fit in the exam. We need to be sure this horse is sound before we go any further. Just because he's not off doesn't mean there's nothing wrong with him."

"Right you are," Jack replied. "I also need to set up a work schedule for Sarah. I mentioned to Gus that she would be helping out. He was surprised and far from happy that Lucas's replacement is a girl. But I think he'll come around once he sees her doing a good job. We'll have to find out when Sarah can be here and how she will be most useful. She can adjust her barn visits to go along with Gus's work plan. I just hope he won't be too difficult. Gus can be a wee bit cantankerous these days."

"Time will tell," Mr. DeWitt said, "and keep me posted. Particularly in regards to this horse."

Jack nodded. "And I'll let Sarah know about the vet's visit. She'll need to be here."

When the last of her friends and well-wishers had left, Sarah sighed in relief. Finally she had her horse to herself. She entered the stall where Prince was nibbling on some hay. He seemed to like it when she stood by his side, talking softly and stroking him. She pressed her face against his neck, breathing deeply and loving his distinctive horsey smell.

Sarah was so engrossed with Prince she didn't hear Gus's approach, and she was startled when he spoke to her from outside the stall. "It's time to feed the hay," he said gruffly. "Come along, if I'm going to show you." Without waiting for a response, he started down the aisle for the stairs to the loft.

Sarah hesitated for a moment before exiting the stall and following Gus down the aisle. She had often seen him doing farm chores when she came for lessons, but until now she hadn't had any occasion to speak with him. She climbed the stairs quickly, hurrying to catch up, and when Gus opened the door to the loft, they were met by the sweet aroma of the newly cut hay. The greener bales were stacked on the far side of the loft, with the seasoned hay pulled to the front.

"Over here," Gus said in a clipped voice that clearly conveyed irritation. "If I have to train you, pay attention, and don't get things mixed up."

After using a hay hook to pull out an older bale of the alfalfa and timothy mix the horses thrived on, Gus went to a shelf along the wall and picked up a pair of wire cutters. The sound of a bale being dragged overhead brought a chorus of nickers and deep-throated neighs from the horses below. They knew what was coming. Gus cut the wire on the bale, and then with his rugged hands he pulled the sections apart. He used a pitchfork to toss two flakes through the opening over Max's stall.

"Now be careful you don't fall through. I don't need to be dealing with that!" Sarah was taken aback by his unpleasantness and wasn't sure how to respond.

"Each horse gets two flakes morning and night," Gus continued, "and one more at noon, in the paddock if they're turned out. I take care of that. The ponies get one flake three times a day."

Sarah felt intimidated by his crotchety manner, and fought the urge to retreat back down the stairs to get away from him. But she knew she would have to prove herself over time, and she wanted to reassure Gus. "I'll work hard to do a good job," she said. Gus didn't reply, but pulled another bale out of the pile in silence. "I'll try to do everything the way you show me." Gus didn't acknowledge she had spoken, but continued his instructions.

"Remember, you won't be feeding any of the green hay until I tell you it's ready. Hay has got to cure for a while, or it'll make a horse sick. Now don't forget that!" His manner of speaking prompted Sarah to step back, putting some distance between them. Turning toward the end of the loft, he pointed to the opening over Prince's stall. "You can throw two flakes down to him now," he said, as he thrust the pitchfork her way.

Under Gus's watchful eye Sarah continued to distribute the evening hay to all the horses. When necessary, she used hay hooks to drag a bale to a new location. The bales were heavy, but she tried not to let Gus see that moving them was hard work for her.

Sarah saw another chance to reassure Gus. "I'll come tomorrow morning to help feed, if you want me to."

He eyed her. "All right, but you'd better be here by seven." He turned abruptly and retreated down the stairs. Sarah put the tools away and hurried from the loft, glad to have the encounter with Gus Kelso over with. She knew there'd be hell to pay if she ever made a mistake!

When Sarah reached the foot of the stairs, she found Jack waiting for her. "Sarah, you know that your horse must be vetted soon. Mr. DeWitt made an appointment with Dr. Reynolds for Monday morning at nine. 'Tis important that you be here."

"Sure. Of course. With school out, that's not a problem."

"Good. As for tomorrow, I won't be doing anything with your horse. Hedgerow and French Twist both need a jumping school and I have lessons in the afternoon. But I'd like you to walk Prince in the indoor for a half hour or so in the morning and then again in the afternoon."

Sarah brushed some hay chaff from her jeans. "How about putting him in one of the paddocks?" she asked.

"'Tis been awhile since he was turned out. We don't want him being too rambunctious and doing something that might make him sore for the vet exam. 'Tis best to just hand-walk him. And be sure you have the shank's chain over his nose, so he won't pull you around." As he turned to go, Sarah called after him.

"Jack. Wait." He stopped, looking back. "Thanks for your help today," Sarah said, trying to keep the emotion out of her voice. "My father wouldn't have let me take Prince if it hadn't been for you."

Jack paused to choose his words carefully. "You've got a grand horse, Sarah. Now 'tis to be seen if you can keep him." With that he walked away.

Sarah hurried back to Crown Prince. Slipping into his stall, she hugged his neck and felt his warmth as she thought about the events of the day. She could still see his image when she'd first opened his stall door at the track, a giant dark silhouette against the wall.

What would tomorrow bring? The thought of the pre-pur-chase exam on Monday brought up storm clouds in her mind. Her face sobered. What if the vet found something wrong? Unless it was very minor, she knew she wouldn't be able to keep Crown Prince. She took a deep breath and closed her eyes. That was a possibility she didn't want to think about.

CHAPTER 9

The Visitors

AFTER A NIGHT OF FITFUL SLEEP, Sarah was up and out of the house early the next morning. She was anxious to check on Crown Prince after his first night at the farm. As she peddled fast down the bike lane on Ridge Road, bad scenarios ran through her mind. Could he have gotten cast in the stall? What if he had colicked in the night! She pedaled faster. Soon she was on the farm road, speeding by the fields dotted with patches of fog, and finally coasting down the last hill on her way to the barn.

Several cars were in the parking area when she arrived, surprising since it wasn't quite seven. But then Sunday was the day of the week when most of the Brookmeade Farm riders showed up at the barn, and at the beginning of summer quite a few liked to ride before the day got hot. She took the shortest route to Prince's stall in the back of the barn by riding her bike to the side door.

Hurrying down the aisle, her heart warmed when she saw her horse facing the door with his ears pricked, almost as if he was watching for her. The white star centered on his forehead showed prominently against his dark bay coat and black fore-lock. He nickered softly when he saw her. *He knows me already!*

Sarah slid the stall door open enough to slide through and went to her horse. She had been in a hurry when she left the house and so had forgotten to bring carrots, but there were peppermints in her rear pocket. She removed the cellophane on one, and Prince quickly took the candy, just as Paige and Tim appeared outside the stall.

"Hey, guys," Sarah said, "how come you're here so early?"

"We decided to ride when it's cooler," Tim replied, walking closer to the stall to get a better look at her horse.

"You must be getting ready for the Fair Pines event," Sarah said, stroking Prince's neck.

Tim nodded. "I think we'll do some hill work up near the orchard today."

"Quarry has a fitness edge from once being a racehorse," Paige said, "but he still could use the hill work." She pressed her face to the bars to look closely at Crown Prince. "Your horse must have been relaxed enough to lie down last night," she said. "He has shavings on his side."

"Yeah, and he cleaned up his grain. I guess that's a good sign," Sarah said. She reached for Prince's halter and put it on him, stretching tall to pull it over his ears. After clipping him to the stall tie, she beckoned them into the stall. "Come on in and see him up close."

Prince turned to look curiously at Paige and Tim as they joined Sarah. "Wow! This stall is a lot bigger than Quarry's, but it seems small with your horse in it," Paige said.

"Medina is the queen, and her stall is the biggest in the barn,"

Sarah said. "She'll be coming back here when the new stalls are finished and Prince has moved into one of them. I hope it will be big enough. It would be horrible if he got cast."

"Don't worry. That doesn't happen very often," Paige said, as she ran her hand down Prince's shoulder. She stepped back. "Feel his coat, Tim. It's like crushed velvet."

Tim put his hand on Prince's side and nodded. "Yeah, he does have a nice coat."

"Did you give him a bath with fabric softener?" Paige asked. She grinned as she turned to leave. "I better go back to Quarry before he gets uneasy on the cross-ties."

"I have to hay the horses now anyway," Sarah said. "Lucas already fed the grain. Have a great ride, guys. Rhodes and Quarry will have hay in their stalls when you come back."

Paige and Tim weren't Prince's only visitors that day, and most everyone remarked that he was a beautiful horse. On her way to the back of the barn to get Snippet ready for a private lesson, Lindsay came to see Prince.

Sarah was surprised when Nicole Jordan and Kelly Hoffman stopped to look at Prince on their way to the tack room. They boarded their horses at Brookmeade and used to ride with Sarah in one of Jack's classes. A year ago they had both asked to move up to Jack's Young Riders class, but he felt they needed more experience before making the change. When Sarah started riding with the more advanced group, Kelly's mother complained bitterly. "That girl doesn't even have her own horse!" Ever since then Kelly and Nicole had made it painfully obvious they didn't like her. Sarah braced herself for their comments, expecting the worst.

"Where did you get him?" Kelly asked, as she looked in at Crown Prince with narrowed eyes.

"He's off the racetrack," Sarah said.

"Oh, so he's green." Nicole raised a pierced eyebrow. "Will you ride him in your lessons?"

Sarah took a deep breath, not sure how to answer. She decided to play it safe. "Eventually. But like you say, right now he's green. It will be up to Jack."

Nicole stepped closer to the stall to get a better look at Prince, who was checking his feed tub for any oats he might have missed.

"How is Jubilee going these days?" Sarah asked her. Ignoring the question, Nicole turned away, and the two girls walked toward the tack room, talking quietly to one another. Sarah could just imagine what they were saying.

Gus kept his promise and came to the office at nine to talk about Sarah's work schedule. Earlier, when she had finished feeding the hay, Sarah noticed a broom leaning against the wall. Gus hadn't mentioned sweeping the loft, but she took a few minutes to push the loose hay into one of the stalls. *Gus will probably never mention my sweeping*, she thought. *He just plain does not want to find anything to like about a girl working here.*

As they began discussing the tasks she'd be responsible for, Gus said, "You can start feeding the morning grain Tuesday. Monday is Lucas's last day here."

For the summer, Sarah was to work at the barn every morning, feeding both hay and grain. Saturday would be her day to scrub and fill water buckets. While Gus would attend to sweeping the aisles on other days, she would put in additional time on Sunday, his day off, sweeping the aisles, feed room, and tack rooms. She'd also be responsible for cleaning Prince's stall every day and bringing in new shavings by wheelbarrow from the storage shed as they were needed. As Sarah thought about it, she was glad she would be doing most of her chores early, which gave her the rest of the day to spend with her horse. In the fall, her schedule would have to change—she'd only be able to work after school and on weekends.

Sarah was expecting her parents and Abby to come see Prince at the barn that morning, and she was grooming Crown Prince when they arrived. "Here's something for all that new stuff you bought at the tack store," her father said, lowering a large black trunk in front of the stall. "I found it in the basement and thought you might be able to use it."

Sarah left the stall to get a closer look. "Awesome, Dad!" she said, as she lifted the top of the trunk and looked inside. "I like these compartments and drawers. I was wondering where I would put my stuff." The trunk would look old-fashioned compared to the newer models in the tack room, but at least she had a place to store her horse equipment.

Sarah went back into the stall to finish grooming Prince, answering their questions as she worked. She wanted to give his coat a dazzling shine for her parents to see. Except for being a little touchy when she rubbed his underbelly with the rubber curry, Prince didn't seem to mind being groomed. He willingly lifted his feet for her to pick out, and stood quietly as she combed his mane and ran a soft brush over his body. Prince seemed to bask in all the attention, and clearly liked having his face brushed. The hardest part was reaching his topline. Even when she stood on tiptoes, his hindquarters and withers were a long way up.

With her family watching from outside the stall, Sarah was relieved that Prince was behaving so well while she worked on him. She couldn't forget the conversation she had overheard the night before. As she tossed and turned trying to get to sleep, her mother's elevated voice drifted up the stairs and into her room.

"How could you let Sarah come home with a horse no one at the racetrack could handle! And you tell me they decided to get rid of the horse because it can't be ridden." Her mother's voice had grown louder. "How is Sarah supposed to be safe with a horse like that?"

Sarah heard her father's attempts to reassure her mother in his usual calm tone. "Alison, we've got to trust Jack and place some responsibility on his shoulders. He tells me that sometimes a horse can make a complete turnaround once it's away from the racetrack. He assured me he will not let Sarah be in harm's way. We agreed the horse will go back in thirty days or even less if he has any misgivings—or if we do." Their voices became muffled as they moved to a different part of the house, and finally Sarah had drifted into a worried and restless sleep.

Now, as they watched her groom the horse, neither of her parents appeared less uneasy. For one thing, the horse was awfully big. Sarah had always been tall for her age, but standing next to Crown Prince she looked petite and fragile. Would she be able to control such a large animal? Mrs. Wagner was torn. She didn't want to be overdramatic or unsupportive, and only wished she could give the horse the benefit of the doubt. She seemed a little less nervous after seeing how well behaved Prince was while Sarah was grooming him. "He shines like polished mahogany," her mother said. "You do a good job, honey."

Though he said little, Sarah's father also watched closely. Was the decision to allow Sarah to take Crown Prince for a one-month's trial a terrible mistake he would come to regret?

When Sarah put her brushes away, Abby came into the stall with the bag of carrots Sarah had left at home. "Just keep your hand flat when you feed him," Sarah warned. "He might think one of your fingers is part of the deal." Abby didn't usually take an interest in horses, but she seemed to like Crown Prince. With Sarah at his head, Abby stayed for a long time stroking him while he nosed her pockets for more carrots. The Wagners had errands to run, and finally it was time for them to leave.

Later on Mr. DeWitt came back to the stall. His eyes went over every inch of the horse as they talked. Seeing him a second time confirmed DeWitt's initial impression that this was one well-put-together animal. But he reminded Sarah that even if Crown Prince passed the vet exam, he would still have to prove he was safe for her to ride. "We don't need another runaway at Brookmeade Farm," Mr. DeWitt said with a smile. He appeared to be joking, but she knew he was dead serious.

Sarah felt jittery at the prospect of hand-walking Prince in the indoor arena, even though he was more relaxed now than he had been when he first arrived at the farm. She remembered Prince's trainer saying he could be a tad spooky. Perhaps the indoor was a completely new experience for him, and a lot of horses freaked out until they got used to the loud creaking noise the metal roof made when it was windy, or to the sound of snow sliding off the roof in winter. Even Lady Tate had been known to leap in the air when barn sparrows swooped down from overhead.

Sarah ran the lead shank through the halter rings and over

Prince's nose before leading him from his stall and down the aisle to the entrance to the indoor arena. As they got closer, Sarah could hear that something was going on inside. Kathleen was longeing Hedgerow at the far end of the indoor. He trotted around her at the end of a long line as she called out vocal commands in firm voice.

Once inside, Prince looked around nervously. Even with another horse nearby, he was tense. He walked briskly beside Sarah with his head high, occasionally prancing and pulling on the shank. When they reached the long side of the arena, he snorted and jumped back at the sight of his own image in the mirror that ran the length of the wall. Further along, he shied away from a set of jump standards and painted rails stacked in a corner, taking her with him. She was relieved that the next time around he took a long look at the jumps but didn't spook. Sarah talked softly to him, and occasionally reached up to give him a pat. Once she thought she saw Jack watching from the lounge, but the next time she looked, he was gone.

"Congratulations on getting such a nice horse," Kathleen called out. "He's handsome, to be sure."

"Thanks, Kathleen," Sarah said. "He's a little nervous. I'm glad you have Hedgerow in here to keep him company."

"We're just about finished. I hope Prince won't be upset when we leave."

Sarah gripped the lead shank tighter when Kathleen led Hedgerow toward the outgate, and Prince's head came up when he saw them leaving the arena. *I should keep on walking as if nothing is happening,* Sarah thought. Suddenly Prince whinnied loudly and pulled against the shank, his body turning sideways beside her. *Thank goodness the shank is over his nose,* she thought. She could feel his power through the shank. "Easy, boy," she said, while tweaking the pressure of the shank on his nose. Remembering what Jack had taught them to do when a horse got too strong under saddle, she turned Prince off the track and led him on a small circle. He whinnied once more and then seemed to quiet down, so she took him back out onto the track that went around the arena. A few minutes later he was much more relaxed.

After the light exercise session, Sarah brought Prince back to his stall. She thought about all the visitors they'd had that day. It was good to have some time alone with her horse, even with the noise the carpenters were making. They were under pressure to finish building the two extra stalls and had consented to work over the weekend.

Prince cleaned up his hay and sniffed his feed box one more time before coming to stand beside her, nuzzling her pockets. Sarah spoke softly and gently stroked him. As he had done on their first meeting at the racetrack, his eyes softened and half closed. He lowered his head to lean on her shoulder. "What a good boy you are, Prince," she murmured, continuing to stroke him. His first full day at Brookmeade had gone so well. Now they just had to get a clean bill of health from the veterinarian tomorrow.

CHAPTER 10

The Vet Exam

IT WAS BARELY LIGHT the next morning when Sarah rolled over and glanced at her clock radio. As her head cleared, she remembered. This was Monday, the day of Prince's vet check! Gus would be furious if she wasn't at the barn by seven to feed the horses, and the last thing she wanted was to be late. She sprang out of bed, splashed some cold water on her face, and slipped into her jeans and a T-shirt. She ran a brush through her hair and put it in a ponytail before hurrying downstairs.

The house was quiet, not surprising, since her father wouldn't be going to the Creamery until mid-morning. She was glad she could bike to the barn without waiting for a ride. If she hurried, there was time for a quick breakfast. She poured a glass of orange juice and a bowl of Cheerios. While she was eating at the kitchen table, Abby appeared in the doorway, still in her pajamas. Her blonde hair was tousled, and it was obvious she hadn't been awake very long.

"I thought I heard someone down here," she said, her voice scratchy. "Are you going to the barn pretty soon?"

Sarah nodded, continuing to eat her cereal. "Prince is being vetted today," she said between mouthfuls.

"You wouldn't need any help with that, would you?"

Sarah frowned. This was a surprise, coming from a girl who had never shown much interest in horses. On this most important day, Sarah didn't want to deal with having her younger sister at the barn.

"Look, Abby, it's going to be a long day. I have to hurry to get Prince ready for Dr. Reynolds. I'm going to be busy, and there won't be much for you to do. What makes you want to come to the barn now?"

Abby stared at the floor for a moment, fiddling with a button on her pajamas. When she looked up, her face mirrored her disappointment. "I thought maybe I could help you," she said in a low voice.

Sarah saw she had hurt her sister's feelings, like the time Abby had wanted to go with her to a pool party at Rita Snyder's last summer. "No one else will be bringing a little sister," she'd complained to their mother, who seemed to understand.

Sarah thought for a moment before answering. "Abby, Dad will be going to the Creamery today. Don't you want to work there in my place?"

Abby's face brightened. "Oh, that's right! He said I could!"

"Do you want my Seaside Creamery T-shirts?" Sarah asked. "They're in my bottom drawer."

"Cool!" Abby said, starting toward the stairs. As she stopped to look in the hall mirror, her nose scrunched up. "Bed head," she muttered before hurrying up the stairs.

Sarah was relieved her sister had given up the idea of coming to the barn, though at the same time she couldn't help feeling a twinge of guilt. But there was no time to dwell on it. She rose from the table, mentally checking the things she needed to take with her. She quickly stuffed the sandwich she'd made the night before and her water bottle into her backpack. She took two carrots from the refrigerator, and as she headed for the door, grabbed some peppermints and stuck them in her jeans pocket.

Easing the screen door shut behind her so it wouldn't slam, Sarah walked quickly to the tool shed where her bike was stored. After adjusting her bike helmet, she pulled her bicycle out of the shed. The morning sun had gotten a head start and was high above the horizon, but the grass under her feet was still wet with dew. With a running start, she was on her way. Pedaling fast down the bike lane, she was glad she wore a sweatshirt against the early morning chill. She'd timed it yesterday. If she hurried, it was about twelve minutes to the Brookmeade entry road and another six to the barn.

Just like the day before, Prince was clearly glad to see her when she arrived. What an awesome horse! She stroked his head and gently tugged on his ears. When she stepped back to pull one of the carrots out of her sweatshirt pocket, Prince reached out to take a large bite.

A glance at her watch told her it was time to feed hay. With a kiss on his velvet nose, Sarah left the stall and headed for the hay loft. Gus would be back on duty today, and she didn't want to give him any excuse to be critical. It would be great if she didn't meet up with the cranky barn manager at all. Coming up to the loft, she breathed deeply the sweet aroma of the newly cut hay before pulling out several seasoned bales. She carefully followed Gus's instructions, which she'd gone over and over in her head, as she distributed hay to the horses, and again did a quick sweep of the loft before rushing back to Prince's stall, stopping by the tack room on her way to get her grooming equipment. She brushed him while he ate his hay, stopping only when Jack stopped by to remind her of the veterinary appointment.

"If I have time, should I walk him in the indoor before Dr. Reynolds gets here?" Sarah asked.

"Good idea. 'Twill loosen him up a bit. But have him in the courtyard at nine sharp." Jack started to leave but turned back. "Mr. DeWitt wanted me to tell you not to worry about the cost of the vet exam. He said he and his wife got you into this deal, and they are prepared to pay for the pre-purchase."

Sarah gulped. She hadn't even thought of this extra expense.

Paige was again at the barn early to ride Quarry. She poked her head around the corner when Sarah had nearly finished brushing Prince's tail. "Hey, good luck with the pre-purchase. I hope he passes." She stepped closer to look at Prince. "Gee, Sarah, your new brushes are getting quite a workout." She grinned. "How many times have you groomed him so far? When you finish this time, your horse will either have the shiniest coat in the barn or no coat left."

Sarah laughed and thanked Paige for her good wishes. "What are you doing with Quarry today?"

"We need a dressage school. There's a lot to improve on before Fair Pines. But since we did a conditioning ride yesterday, I'll probably just school Quarry for a bit then take a short hack with Tim when he gets here."

"I hope Prince and I can go with you on a trail ride one of

these days," Sarah said, imagining the three of them cantering along wooded paths.

"It will definitely happen!" Paige assured her. "Gotta go... See ya."

After Paige left, Sarah led Prince out of the barn toward the indoor riding arena. Today the cavernous indoor was deserted. They didn't have long to walk before the vet appointment, only a few minutes, and thankfully Prince didn't seem to mind being there without another horse. He was much more relaxed on his second visit. They had gone around only once when Jack appeared in the doorway. He appeared tense.

"Sarah, Dr. Reynolds is here. He's a little early, but he wants to start with your horse right away. So hurry along." Sarah gripped the lead shank tighter as she left the arena, heading toward the courtyard near the front of the barn. *This is it*, she thought. So much depended on the exam.

A man with a buzzcut, glasses, and wearing a stethoscope around his neck stood next to a capped pickup talking to Jack and Mr. DeWitt. As Sarah drew nearer, the veterinarian turned to look at her horse. "This must be Crown Prince," he said, "and you must be Sarah."

Sarah's throat felt scratchy, and all she could manage was a rather feeble, "Yes," as she asked Prince to halt.

Dr. Reynolds walked around the horse, sizing him up with an experienced eye that immediately recognized an extremely fine equine individual. The horse was the picture of health, his smooth coat gleaming in the rays of the morning sun, and his legs showed no signs of injuries. Typically horses the vet saw coming off the racetrack had blemishes—big ankles, popped knees, bowed tendons— but this one's legs were clean. The vet also noticed that the horse carried more weight than was typical for fit racehorses.

"You want to give me the story on this horse?" he asked.

Jack spoke up. "He's a four-year-old Thoroughbred that came to the farm on Saturday from Rudy Dominic's barn at Raceland Park. He never started."

The vet raised his eyebrows. "Do you know why he was retired without ever running in a race? Does he come with any soundness or health issues you're aware of?"

"We're hoping you can answer that question," Mr. DeWitt said. "We need to know if there are underlying problems."

Dr. Reynolds scratched his head and thought for a moment. Looking toward the barn, he picked up his medical bag and said, "Before we check him for lameness, let's put him in his stall where conditions aren't so bright. It will be a better place to check his eyes and vital signs."

Sarah turned her horse and began walking him to the barn's side door, with the three men following behind. When they reached Prince's stall, Dr. Reynolds went into the stall with Sarah and her horse while Jack and Mr. DeWitt stood outside watching through the bars. Sarah was relieved that Prince didn't appear to question Dr. Reynolds's presence. The horse didn't resist when the veterinarian inserted a thermometer, and Prince continued to stand quietly when the vet leaned over to listen to his heart and lungs with his stethoscope. After righting himself, the vet removed the thermometer and read it.

"Nothing out of the ordinary so far," Dr. Reynolds commented, as he lifted Prince's upper lip to check for the tattoo found there on all racing Thoroughbreds. "He must have been a long way from a race when they gave up on him," the vet said, "or he'd be tattooed. The question is why." He reached into his bag for a bright flashlight and spent several minutes looking closely into Prince's eyes, shining the flashlight into each one.

Stepping back, Dr. Reynolds paused for a few moments, looking intently at Crown Prince. He turned to Jack and Mr. DeWitt. "His eyes look normal. Now we have to consider the possibility he could have developed a wind problem. Have you heard him making any breathing noises when he's been exercised or turned out?"

"We've not had an opportunity to observe anything like that," Jack said. "Except for hand-walking in the indoor, he's been in his stall since he came to the farm on Saturday."

"That being the case, I'm going to check his throat first," Dr. Reynolds said. "I'd like to avoid sedation if possible, since we still have to see if there are lameness issues. But if I detect any sign of unusual tissue, I will sedate him and take a look at his larynx. He left to return to his truck for a speculum, a metal device designed to hold a horse's mouth open.

Sarah couldn't stop the feeling of doom that was settling over her. Would they find something in Prince's throat that would take him away from her?

When Dr. Reynolds returned and entered the stall with the speculum, Prince was immediately apprehensive. Sarah tightened her hold on the lead shank when he began tossing his head and attempted to move away.

Dr. Reynolds beckoned to Jack. "We'll need some help keeping him steady," he said. Jack entered the stall and placed a strong hand on Prince's halter. Under a tight hold from both Jack and Sarah, Prince's jaws were forced open and the speculum inserted. Sarah watched, almost holding her breath, as the vet played a flashlight in Prince's mouth at different angles and peered inside.

"Holy smoke!" Dr. Reynolds suddenly exclaimed, as he pushed the flashlight closer to get a better look. After a few moments he stepped back and turned to them. "I've never seen anything like this in my life. This horse has a large and grossly misshapen wolf tooth. It extends forward over the bars on the right side of his mouth."

Jack and Chandler DeWitt looked at each other incredulously. Both had enough experience to immediately comprehend what this discovery could signify. It could very well explain why the horse had been unruly when he was under saddle. The bit would have been constantly banging against that wolf tooth, possibly causing Prince extreme pain.

The veterinarian beckoned to them as he held out the flashlight. "Here, Jack, I want you to take a look. You, too, Chandler."

Crown Prince had come to accept the speculum in his mouth, and he stood fairly quietly while the two men took turns shining the flashlight into the horse's mouth. "'Tis amazing how big that tooth is compared to his molars," Jack said. "Sarah, I want you to see this."

Sarah had never looked inside a horse's mouth before, but even to her, the guilty tooth looked grotesque.

"Did the people at the track say he ever had a problem accepting the bit when he was bridled?" Dr. Reynolds asked. "A wolf tooth of that size would almost certainly cause a lot of discomfort to a horse when a bit was in his mouth." Again Jack and Mr. DeWitt looked at each other.

"I guess you've quite possibly solved the mystery, Wes," DeWitt said, shaking his head in disbelief. "This is a well-bred Thoroughbred that had the potential to become a top racehorse, except he became so fractious in training they finally gave up on him. Having him gelded didn't help. He was offered to me along with three other geldings being culled from the string for various reasons."

"I can certainly believe he would react violently when ridden," Dr. Reynolds said. "The minute a rider put any pressure on the reins, he likely experienced jarring pain in his jaw. I would expect him to be unruly, and I'm really surprised his mouth was never checked. But then, most racetrack vets focus on horses' legs, where the problems usually lie."

Mr. DeWitt thought on this a moment. "Both Hank Bolton and his trainer are knowledgeable horsemen, so I admit it does seem surprising. It appears they left it up to a veterinarian to check the horse without specific direction from them—and that vet made a huge omission when he or she didn't look at Crown Prince's mouth."

"Because they interfere with the bit, in Ireland wolf teeth are routinely pulled before horses are broken to saddle," Jack said.

Dr. Reynolds nodded. "I would say about half of all horses develop wolf teeth. Some lie undeveloped below the gum. But I've never seen one this size." He took back the flashlight.

Sarah stood next to her horse, spellbound by what she had heard. She didn't understand all the details, but she knew this could very well explain her horse's rowdy behavior. Her mind raced. No wonder he'd acted so badly on the racetrack! This was the reason he would behave well in his stall and on the shed row, but turn into a maniac out on the track with a rider on his back. The whole thing made perfect sense. He didn't have a mean streak after all, and once the tooth was removed, he'd be the horse of her dreams. She'd be able to keep him!

"Well, Sarah," Mr. DeWitt said, "it looks like you and your horse got a lucky break. I suspect the tooth's removal will be a fairly simple procedure. With that gone, Crown Prince just might ride as quietly as a hobby-horse." He raised his hand. "But we mustn't get carried away," he said. "We still need to check him for lameness. Shall we move our operation to the indoor? It shouldn't be busy on a Monday morning."

Prince shook his head and worked his jaws rapidly when the speculum was removed from his mouth. "I'll exchange the speculum for my hoof testers in my truck and meet you there," Dr. Reynolds said.

Once the veterinarian had joined them in the indoor arena, he proceeded to pick up each of the horse's feet and squeeze the testers to put pressure on all the parts of the hoof. When Prince did not react, the vet put the testers down. "Well, he's not footsore," he said.

Next Dr. Reynolds went over each of Prince's legs, his experienced hands carefully feeling for heat or swelling. He stood up and looked at the horse again. "It isn't often you find a horse coming from the track as clean-legged as this one is," he said. "There isn't a pimple on him. Let's do some flexion tests to see if there are any soundness issues with his joints."

He addressed Sarah. "I'm going to hold up his leg for a short time, and when I say okay, I want you to immediately move him off at a brisk trot." As the vet hoisted Prince's near hind leg into a cramped position, Sarah gripped the lead shank tighter and prepared to run forward, hoping Prince would follow. When the vet released the leg and said, "Go," she sprinted off, Prince trotting fast by her side.

"He didn't show any lameness there," Dr. Reynolds said. "Let's try it on the others."

The exercise was repeated on the other three legs, and on each attempt Prince trotted off soundly. "Your horse appears to be sound," Dr. Reynolds said, as he picked up the hoof tester. "The next step is to remove that oversized wolf tooth. I recommend you make an appointment to bring him to our clinic where we can radiograph the site to see what the root of that sucker looks like. Then we can sedate him and remove it."

Sarah was about to explode with relief and happiness. Noticing her huge smile, Dr. Reynolds said, "It looks like you've got yourself a spectacular horse, young lady. But now I need to find my next client," he said, heading back to the barn.

Jack and Mr. DeWitt were also pleased with the results of the vet exam. Having the wolf tooth removed might be a simple way to turn the horse's unruly behavior around.

"Would you like me to call Rudy Dominic and tell him the good news?" Jack asked.

Chandler DeWitt didn't reply right away. His face was suddenly serious. Finally he turned to Jack. "I think we need to be careful here."

Sarah was stroking her horse, basking in the discovery of the tooth and what it could mean. It was the best of news! But when she heard Mr. DeWitt's comment and saw his expression, Sarah froze, her excitement quickly changing to alarm. She knew immediately what Mr. DeWitt was implying. Prince's former owner would also realize why the horse had been so difficult, and when he found out, of course he'd want Prince back. A small knot of fear began to grow in the pit of her stomach.

CHAPTER 11

The Sales Receipt

SARAH FELT PANIC RISING as she looked back and forth between Jack's and Chandler DeWitt's faces, searching for their reactions to this latest news. Did finding the probable cause of Crown Prince's bad behavior mean Mr. Bolton would want to take him back? Was there reason to fear he *could* reclaim Crown Prince? Was there reason to hope he couldn't? The men knew what she was thinking.

Without a word to her, Jack followed Mr. DeWitt to his office where they could talk privately. They sat down in the leather chairs, both mulling this latest development. "What do you think, Jack?" Mr. DeWitt asked the younger man.

Jack didn't hesitate. "Up until now, we worried that Crown Prince would be too much horse for Sarah. Now those fears may be groundless. After the wolf tooth is removed, the horse may be perfectly quiet and well-mannered under saddle, without all those shenanigans. But I fear his racetrack connections will reach the same conclusion."

"Exactly," said Mr. DeWitt. "Hank Bolton and Rudy Dominic may want to give him another try. Hank will be upset that the wolf tooth was never found. He'll be kicking himself and bemoaning the loss of a potentially outstanding racehorse." Jack nodded in agreement.

It was apparent Mr.DeWitt was torn. He surely didn't welcome the prospect of having to return the horse Sarah had chosen and clearly bonded with. Yet he must also have a sense of loyalty to his longtime friend and desire fairness to prevail. While he could stretch the truth by omission, saying only that Crown Prince had passed the vet exam, in the long run he probably wouldn't feel comfortable doing that. He wasn't the type of man to be less than honest with his old friend.

Jack understood his employer's dilemma. "Where do we go from here?"

Mr. DeWitt leaned back in his chair, strumming the desk with his fingers as he considered the alternatives. Finally he spoke. "It's best to keep Rudy Dominic out of this. Of course he'll want to have a talented runner in his barn. But I'm going to e-mail Hank and let him know what the vet found. I want to be open and I want a paper trail. Let's hope he's moved on and already set his sights on another horse, so things won't get messy." He met Jack's solemn gaze before turning to his computer.

Jack rose from his chair and left the office. When he got back to Crown Prince's stall, he found Sarah standing close to her horse, her face troubled. "They won't make us bring him back, will they?" she asked him.

"I wish I knew what to tell you," Jack replied quietly. "We have to leave this in Mr. DeWitt's hands. But I can tell you one thing—he'll do everything in his power to keep the horse with you." Sarah took a deep breath. It was good to hear that Mr. DeWitt was on her side. After all, the DeWitts had made it possible for her to get Crown Prince in the first place. Why would they take him away?

Jack thought it best to move on to a different subject. "Since we don't have to be concerned with soundness now, Prince can be turned out in one of the paddocks. Not a large one, though, where he might get up a head of steam. He hasn't been turned out for several months, it's likely, and he's probably going to run."

Sarah felt a surge of excitement that helped eclipse her anxiety. She looked forward to seeing Prince in action when he was turned out. "Why would it be bad for him to gallop?" she asked.

"We don't want him running so fast he goes through a fence or hurts himself. The small paddock near the hunt course will probably be best, if it's not occupied."

Sarah's face brightened. "That's where Quarry usually goes, and I don't think Paige has finished riding." She quickly put on Prince's halter and attached the lead shank. Leading him from the stall, she followed Jack to the white-fenced paddocks near the barn. Gus kept these turnout areas well maintained, alternating their use so they didn't become dust bowls from over-grazing. This particular morning some of the school horses that had been used for a number of lessons over the weekend were enjoying some time together in the largest paddock. Tim's horse, Rhodes Scholar, was grazing along the fence line in the turnout next to the small paddock.

"I probably don't have to tell you that we always turn boarders' horses out by themselves," Jack reminded her. "Lots of injuries can be avoided that way, mainly from kicks and sometimes from bites. Horses play rough at times."

Sarah pointed to the school horses grazing in the largest paddock. "How about them?" she asked.

"'Tis too bad we don't have enough individual turnouts for the schoolies, but so far we've been lucky. Some of them, like Gray Fox, need to be separated. The two ponies get along, and they have their own paddock."

As Prince walked eagerly beside Sarah, he raised his head to look at the horses enjoying their time outside. He seemed to know what was going to happen, and tossed his head impatiently, sending his mane flying. After leading him inside the small paddock, she circled to face the gate and pulled it nearly shut. Quickly she unsnapped the lead shank and slipped outside. It took Prince a few moments to realize he was free. At first he put his head down to crop from a patch of grass near the gate, but suddenly his head shot up. He hesitated only briefly before he wheeled, and with a snort bolted off at a full gallop. It reminded Sarah of how Gray Fox had taken off with her.

The horse was beautiful to watch, his motion effortless and graceful. He was almost at the end of the paddock in half a dozen strides, and Sarah's heart was in her mouth, afraid he would crash into the fence or try to jump it. Instead of slamming on the brakes, he adroitly swung sharply to the left and circled the paddock, although his mad dash was now a more controlled canter. As he passed the gate the first time, he swerved to the inside, stopped in the center, and reared so high his body was almost perpendicular to the ground. In an instant he had whirled and with lightning speed was galloping in the other direction.

In the next paddock Rhodes stopped grazing and also began to run. He had more room to stretch out, so he could gallop faster. His rapid pace spurred Crown Prince to take off again, circling his paddock as fast as he could manage. Farther away the horses in other paddocks became excited by the two galloping horses, and they began to run as well. Even the school horses decided to join the gallop and began running in their paddock.

All the commotion didn't go unnoticed by Gus, who came storming out of the barn. When he saw Crown Prince running in the small paddock, he strode toward them, his face reddened and a stubby finger stabbing the air. He hollered at Sarah. "Look what your horse is doing to the rest of them! They'll get all lathered up! Stop him!" Sarah flinched at the harsh words, wishing she could sink into the ground.

"Just a minute, Gus," Jack said, walking toward the man. "This won't last long, and none of them will have to be brought in. Just relax." Gus watched with them, scowling, and true to Jack's prediction, after another round of the paddocks, first the school horses and then the others slowed, came to walk, and finally went back to gazing. Prince was the last to stop running, but finally he, too, settled down and lowered his head to graze.

"You'd better have that horse out of there when Quarry is ready for it!" Gus snapped at Sarah as he turned and marched back into the barn.

Sarah held tears back as she watched him go. Jack saw how Gus's performance had affected her. "His bark is worse than his bite, you know."

Sarah took a deep breath, trying to shake off the effect of Gus's tirade. "I guess I have to learn to deal with him. I have no choice, if I want to keep Prince." She looked back at her horse and saw he was still grazing contentedly.

"Gus's temper tantrums are short-lived," Jack explained. "He's probably forgotten all about it by now. I hope you can, too."

"I'll try, but sometimes he scares me. He's such a grouch!" Sarah admitted.

"That he is," Jack replied. "I may have to have a word with him."

"Oh, please, don't!" Sarah pleaded. "If you do that, he'll really have it out for me!"

Just then Paige came around the barn riding Quarry, a dressage whip in her hand. She had been schooling in the outdoor dressage ring, but Quarry's concentration had ended when he heard the horses running. He pranced toward them, looking around for the horses he had heard galloping and no doubt would like to join.

"What's all the hubbub about?" Paige asked, pulling him up. "It sounded like a cavalry charge! Quarry heard the thundering hooves, and that's all he could think about."

"The horses were showing their frisky sides, that's all," Jack said. "How did your school go?"

"Okay, I guess, until we had to quit just now. I'm working on Test 2, the one Tim and I'll ride in the event. It's only two weeks away. We're kind of shaky in places, especially on transitions."

"We'll work on parts of the test in your lesson this week," Jack said.

"Do you want to turn Quarry out now?" Sarah asked Paige.

"Oh, not for awhile. I'm going to pull his mane before Tim

gets here. He's working this morning, but we're going for a short hack later."

"Is Tim working at the hardware store again this summer?" Sarah asked.

Paige nodded. "It helps pay for his car and his horse. I'll be working at Dad's restaurant again for the same reason. Well, it's mane-pull time for Quarry," she said, as she rode off.

After Sarah put Prince back in his stall, she checked her cell phone. There was a text message from Kayla, *call me,* and she immediately dialed her friend's number. "What's up, Kayla?"

"How did the vet exam go?"

"You'll never guess what Dr. Reynolds found! Do you know that horses have wolf teeth?"

"Yeah," Kayla said. "I think they're usually pulled, but I'm not sure why. Does Prince have one?"

"He has a huge one! The vet had never seen anything like it. Here's the best part. He probably was in a lot of pain when he had a bit in his mouth. Once the tooth is pulled, he should be fine when he's ridden!"

"That's totally awesome!" Kayla squealed. "If he's not lame, that means you can keep him. Did the vet find anything else?"

"No. Dr. Reynolds said he doesn't often find a horse off the track as clean-legged as he is."

"Great news, kid." Kayla paused. "Here's something else: Next Sunday is the Riverbend Quarter Horse Show. I'm taking Fanny. Can you come? We had a blast last year."

Sarah thought a minute. She loved going to horse shows with Kayla. She was Kayla's groom and cheerleader at the same show last summer when Kayla and Fanny had impressed the hunter judge and been awarded a third-place ribbon in the large hunt seat equitation class.

Sarah suddenly realized how limited her free time would be this summer, especially now that she was working at Brookmeade. She'd have to say no to things she liked a lot, and this was one of them. Gus would probably have a hissy fit if she asked to have Sunday off by working extra time on Saturday. And besides, there was too much going on with Prince right now.

"Kayla, I can't. I have to work on Sundays now, and I can't ask for time off so soon. You know I'd love to groom for you like I did last year. I loved being your cheering section."

"Well, that's no fun. I really wanted you to come," Kayla said, her voice conveying her disappointment.

After Sarah snapped her cell shut and put it back in her pocket, she started for the office. She wanted to talk to Jack about scheduling an appointment with the vet hospital. She was surprised to see Mrs. DeWitt hanging up the office phone just as she stepped inside. Taco and Spin were curled up on a horse blanket in the corner.

"Hello, Sarah. Chandler told me all about the vet exam. I'm thrilled your horse is absolutely fine except for a tooth that needs to come out." She saw a worried look suddenly appear on Sarah's face. "Why the frown, Sarah? Having a horse of your own is supposed to bring smiles."

"I'm afraid Mr. Bolton will want him back," Sarah said. "Prince is such a special horse. I don't know what I'll do...." Her voice trailed off.

"Don't you worry, dear. We folks at Brookmeade Farm don't throw in the towel easily. I've reminded Chandler that we have a sales receipt on our side, the one Rudy Dominic signed. You have that paper at home, don't you?"

Sarah swallowed hard. Back at the track her dad had pulled a dollar bill from his wallet as a token payment for the horse. All she remembered was him putting it down on the table. The paperwork—had he picked up the letter along with the horse's records in the folder? He must have!

"My dad took care of that," she said, hoping she sounded more confident than she felt.

"That's good. You need to know that we stand firmly on your side. I just made an appointment for Crown Prince to have the wolf tooth removed. He'll go to the vet hospital Wednesday morning. They squeezed you in," she said with a smile. Then seeing the downcast look still on Sarah's face, she called to Spin and Taco. "Come on, boys. I think Sarah needs some cheering up."

Later that afternoon, with Jack's blessing, Sarah took Crown Prince to an area near the hunt course to hand-graze him where the grass grew tall along the fence line.

"He's had his run, so he should be quiet enough on the shank," Jack had said. "But he's not had much green grass for a while, so don't let him graze more than ten minutes."

Sarah tried to enjoy the time in the sun with her horse, but her mind raced as she watched Prince greedily snatch mouthfuls of the clover, blossoms and all. If only she could be sure her father had saved the sale agreement. Sarah was so preoccupied she didn't see Paige coming across the lawn, and was startled when Paige spoke. Paige saw the worry lines on her friend's face as she grazed Crown Prince.

"What's up, Sarah? You look a little down in the dumps. I heard that except for the wolf tooth Prince got a good report this morning."

"I'm just afraid something will go wrong," Sarah said, turning toward her. "If he's in such good shape, maybe the man who owned him will want him back."

Paige bent down to pull a long shaft of Timothy from the tall grass, and leaning back against a fence post, she chewed the end thoughtfully. This was not a time for her usual witty comments.

"I hope you didn't have to go through anything like this when you got Quarry," Sarah said.

"I was lucky. My grandmother made it possible for me to have a horse. I've always been horse crazy. She realized that if I had to wait for my parents to come up with the cash, a horse would be a long time coming."

"Where did you find Quarry?" Sarah asked.

"He had been off the track about a year, and the girl who owned him before me had worked hard so she could show him. She trained under Jeffrey Davis and showed in equitation classes."

"Wow," Sarah said. "I've heard of that trainer. How did the girl and Quarry do at shows?"

"She had the same problem with him rushing fences. But he's getting better, thanks to Jack."

"Is that why was he was for sale?" Sarah asked.

"No, the girl was going away to college. I was one of the first to see the ad and call about him. When I saw his dappled gray color and big dark eyes, I wanted him so bad! I was just lucky that my grandmother liked him, too! She bought him for me after he passed the pre-purchase exam."

"I wish getting Prince was that simple."

"Don't get stressed out with worry, Sarah. I just know you're going to keep him. Once that wolf tooth is out, you'll be on your way. Try to chill."

Sarah moved closer to Prince as she brought his head up. "I think he's had enough grass for today. But thanks, Paige. I hope you're right."

She started back to Prince's stall, all the while thinking about the letter. For once she didn't want to be at the barn—she just wanted to go home and track down that piece of paper. It was actually a sales contract, and Rudy Dominic had signed it. She needed to see it in front of her, the proof that Crown Prince was hers. When her father returned from the ice cream shop, she'd know. Maybe sooner. She pulled her phone from her pocket and hit the speed-dial button for her father's number. *Darn!* she thought when the voicemail cut in. His cell was off, which meant he was busy, so he probably wouldn't be calling her back anytime soon.

The bike ride home seemed to take forever. When she finally pulled into the driveway, only her mother's car was in the garage. Her father must still be at work. She wasted no time putting her bike away and bounding up the porch steps. After removing her paddock boots, she moved quickly through the mud room and into the kitchen, where her mother was standing at the kitchen counter making hamburger patties. Sarah offered only a quick, "Hi, Mom," before hurrying up the stairs two at a time.

Where would her father have placed the yellow piece of paper? Most likely it would have landed on the top of his bureau, where the contents of his pockets usually came to rest. She'd heard her mother complain about the clutter many times. If the paper was there, she'd have it immediately. But her heart sank when she entered her parents' bedroom and saw only some loose change and an extra set of car keys on the bureau. As she scanned the room, searching for any clue, she heard her mother's footsteps laboring slowly up the stairway.

"What's going on, Sarah?" her mother asked when she came into the bedroom.

The words tumbled out of Sarah's mouth, barely intelligible. "We need the letter Rudy Dominic signed. The DeWitts are afraid that once Hank Bolton finds out about the wolf tooth, he'll want him back."

"Slow down a minute," Mrs. Wagner said, lowering herself into the bedroom's easy chair. "What are you talking about? What in the world is a wolf tooth?

Sarah looked at her mother intently. "I just need to know if Dad kept the paper that says we bought Prince fair and square. Mrs. DeWitt says it is really a sales contract. I was hoping it would be here."

Her mother's gaze went to the bureau and then back at Sarah. "You mean to tell me you're worried that *your father* might have thrown it away?" She rolled her eyes at the ceiling and then looked at Sarah. "How can you have so little faith in your father?" her mother asked, her voice slightly raised. "He's the most organized person in the world! Surely you must know he would never have thrown something that important away."

Sarah hung her head, realizing her mother was probably right. Of course her father would have it. Maybe not here, but he'd have it in a safe place. Of course he would!

Back downstairs, Sarah set the table for dinner while she told her mother about the vet exam and counted the minutes until her father got home. When she heard the sound of car doors shutting, she went to the window. Her father and Abby were heading toward the house. The minute they came through the door, Abby started telling Sarah all about her first day at Seaside Creamery. Sarah raised her hand to interrupt her sister.

"Abby, I'm sorry, but there's something really important I have to ask Dad. *Right now!*" Turning to her father, she blurted it out. "Dad, the letter, the sales contract for Prince. Where is it?"

Her father was tired from a day at the Creamery, and he could do without the third-degree interrogation. He scowled. "Why do you need that now? What's going on?"

"If Mr. Bolton decides he wants Prince back, the DeWitts say we'll need that paper to prove we bought him free and clear. It's got to be legal." Sarah paused to take a breath. "I just need to know you have it, Dad."

"Of course I saved it," her father said in a tone of annoyance. "I wouldn't discard something as important as a bill of sale. It's in a folder in my file cabinet."

Sarah felt as if a heavy load had been lifted. Her mother had been right. She was so thankful her dad was her dad.

"Can you calm down long enough to tell me what this is all about?" Mr. Wagner asked. "And how did the pre-purchase exam go?" Before Sarah could answer, her mother interrupted.

"Dinner is almost ready. You two wash your hands and come to the table. Sarah can tell you the whole story. Wolf tooth and all. And we want to hear about Abby's first day at the Creamery, too."

CHAPTER 12

The Deal

TUESDAY MORNING DAWNED OVERCAST with a fine mist falling. Sarah knew she'd need the waterproof poncho she'd stashed in her closet, and she rummaged around to find it. It wasn't raining hard, so with the poncho she'd stay pretty dry on the bike ride to the barn. She placed the envelope with the precious letter inside the zippered pocket on her sweatshirt.

Her father was up early, too, and having coffee in the kitchen when she came downstairs. She sat down with him while she ate her cereal. "How's Abby doing at the Creamery?" she asked.

Her father laid down the newspaper. "Just fine for a beginner, and she'll get better. She's not happy she can't wear flip-flops on the job, though."

Sarah smiled. "I miss the ice cream, especially the chocolate chip."

"Do you have that sales receipt with you?" her father asked after taking a sip of coffee. When she nodded, he said, "I don't have to remind you how important it is to get it to a safe place. Be sure you give it to the DeWitts right away."

"Thanks, Dad. Believe me, I will."

A few minutes later Sarah had gathered her things for the day and was out the door. The soft, warm rain wasn't unpleasant as she pedaled down the bicycle lane on Ridge Road. Her unprotected face and hands got a bit wet, but the poncho kept the rest of her—and the all-important letter—dry. She thought of the encounter ahead with Gus, when he showed her the routine for feeding grain. She was trying so hard to do a good job. Would he ever learn to appreciate it?

Sarah arrived a few minutes before seven and immediately saw the familiar figure with the red baseball cap at the end of the long aisle uncoiling the hose in preparation for filling the water buckets. Gus stopped what he was doing when he saw Sarah and looked at his watch. *He's checking to see if I'm on time,* she thought. She took a deep breath and started up the aisle toward him.

Trying to sound positive and sincere, she spoke up as she got closer. "Good morning! I'm ready to help with the grain, if you want me to."

Gus didn't answer, but he put down the hose and with his chin motioned her toward the feed room. He pulled a key on a buffalo-head key ring from his pocket and unlocked the padlock on the extra wide door. Once inside, he flipped on the switch, and a large overhead light flooded the windowless space.

Sarah had never been in this part of the barn, and she was met with the pungent aroma of grain and molasses. A pull cart loaded with blue plastic pails sat in front of a blackboard that listed each horse's grain ration. Each pail had a horse's name in block letters taped on it and was filled with grain. Without saying a word, Gus grabbed the cart's handle, and with Sarah following, started for the aisle. He stopped by the first stall, and hastily tossed the contents of one of the pails through the opening above French Twist's feed tub.

The sound of the grain being dished out was met with a chorus of neighs as horses showed their eagerness for what they knew was coming. A few whirled around in their stalls, some pawed, and others just tossed their heads as they waited impatiently for their breakfast.

"Don't just stand there. Start feeding," Gus barked. They were now near Gray Fox's and McDuff's stalls, and Sarah obediently searched for their pails. They made their way down both aisles, feeding the grain as they went. Crown Prince was waiting by his stall door and offered a low nicker as she came closer.

She paused to speak softly to him. "Here's what you've been waiting for, Prince." She noticed that his grain was different from the others, mostly oats with some pellets and sweet feed mixed in. Prince shoved his nose into the feed tub as Sarah moved on to the next horse. The ponies were the last to be fed, and they got less than half the grain the horses did.

Gus turned, pulling the grain cart back in the direction of the feedroom. Once inside, he pointed to where the silo let grain into a deep wheelbarrow. "Now we fill the pails for the next feed." A motor started when he pushed a green button on the silo, and a mixture of pellets and sweet feed began falling into the large wheelbarrow. When it was nearly full, Gus turned the motor off and began scooping grain into the pails. He paused to point to the black board on the side wall. "That's how much each horse gets."

Sarah looked at the board and noticed that Crown Prince

was the only horse getting oats in addition to the other grain. As if he could read her mind, Gus continued, "Horses coming off the track get weaned off oats a little at a time." He pointed to the corner. "The oats are in that bin over there."

After measuring out a few grain rations, Gus retrieved the key on the buffalo-head key ring from his pocket and handed it to Sarah. "Lock up when you're done, and whatever you do, don't lose that key! If a horse ever got loose and found his way into the grain room, there'd be hell to pay. Most horses would eat so much they'd colic and die." Gus paused, but seeing she had no questions, he went back to the aisle to fill the water buckets.

Relieved to be free of Gus, Sarah finished dishing up the grain. She stepped out of the feed room, locked the door, and carefully put the key deep in her jeans pocket. What if she lost it? Maybe she'd put the key on a sturdy chain—she had one at home—so she could wear it around her neck when she came to the barn.

Feeding hay was next. Sarah made her way down the aisle and climbed the stairs to the loft. After cutting the wire on several bales and tossing two flakes into each stall, she began to sweep the loose hay toward the opening above the closest stall, McDuff's. From the vantage point of the loft's second-story window, she could see the O'Briens' bungalow and the outlines of the mares and foals in the pasture.

Something unusual caught her eye, and she moved closer to the window to get a better look. In addition to Jack's pickup, two cars were parked in the narrow driveway. She recognized Mr. DeWitt's red Blazer, but she had never seen the other vehicle. Even from this distance she could tell it was a late model sports car, shiny and black. She couldn't see if it had out-of-state plates, but her stomach tightened. Was something going on that might involve Crown Prince?

Sarah went back to the hay detail, while considering what to do next. She should get the bill of sale to the DeWitts right away. She looked at her watch. It was early, so Mrs. DeWitt would probably still be at home. Sarah had never had any occasion to go to the rambling farmhouse that looked down on the farm from atop a low hill, but it would only take a few minutes to walk there. Maybe she should drop off the bill of sale while Prince ate his hay.

The light mist had stopped when Sarah started up the sloped driveway. She caught glimpses of the white farmhouse with its wraparound porch through the large shade trees that surrounded it. As she got closer, shrill barking erupted, and Taco and Spin came streaking ferociously down the driveway toward her. As they got closer, the terriers recognized the would-be intruder. They stopped barking and ran even faster, their short tails wagging furiously. Sarah laughed as she reached down to pet the little dogs. "Did you think I was public enemy number one?"

Hearing the commotion, Mrs. DeWitt appeared on the porch, standing next to the pots of red geraniums that lined the steps. She waved to Sarah, beckoning her to hurry. There was no sign of her usual sunny smile. Her mouth was drawn, and her brow was creased by worry lines.

"I'm glad you're here, Sarah," she said. "Chandler just called me." There was an edge to her voice. "We've had some unexpected company. Hank Bolton is meeting with Chandler at Jack's bungalow right now. And I'll bet you can guess what they're talking about."

Sarah stiffened. "He wants Prince back, doesn't he?"

"I'm sure that's being proposed. Chandler asked me to get the sales receipt that Rudy Dominic signed and bring it to him right away. I hope and pray that after our discussion yesterday you brought it with you this morning." She looked expectantly at Sarah, and appeared relieved when the girl fumbled in her sweatshirt pocket and came up with the envelope.

"My dad had filed it. When he heard what happened with the vet yesterday, he thought I should bring it to you." She handed the envelope to Mrs. DeWitt.

"You precious girl," Mrs. DeWitt exclaimed. "I'll take it right over to Chandler." She started toward the garage, but suddenly stopped and turned back to Sarah. "I have an idea. I think Hank should probably meet the girl who is now the proud owner of Crown Prince. Yes, I think that would be an excellent move."

Sarah was taken aback. What would she say to the wealthy man who had once owned her horse and now wanted to take him away?

Seeing the hesitant look on her face, Mrs. DeWitt put her hand on Sarah's shoulder. "Now, now, it will be fine. I think you should come along. We need to show Hank that the horse is in good hands."

"But he didn't come here to see me," Sarah protested. "I really don't want to butt in."

Mrs. DeWitt's voice took on a more serious tone. "I know you're prepared to do everything you can to keep Crown Prince. I think you should come with me." She called to Taco and Spin, as she started toward the garage. "The boys think so, too."

A few minutes later Sarah and the terriers were in Mrs. DeWitt's Mercedes for the short drive to the O'Brien's bungalow. As anxious as she felt, a nervous laugh escaped Sarah when Taco crawled into her lap and lapped her cheek. But her heart raced faster as they got closer. With Hank Bolton's Porsche filling the driveway, Mrs. DeWitt parked on the side of the gravel roadway, finally rut-free after the road crew had done their work the day before.

"You boys can wait out here," Mrs. DeWitt said to her dogs as she lowered the windows a few inches. "On a cool day with no sunshine, they'll be fine," she said to Sarah, and together they walked to the entrance.

Kathleen must have been looking for them, because she opened the door before they could ring the bell. "Come in," she said in a hushed tone. She ushered them into the O'Brien's cozy living room, where Jack, Chandler DeWitt, and Hank Bolton talked as they drank from steaming mugs of coffee. Mr. Bolton sat his mug down and rose from an overstuffed chair when they entered. After exchanging pleasantries with Mrs. DeWitt, he was introduced to Sarah. He smiled broadly as he shook her hand.

"So you're the little lady who wants to ride the big horse." A stocky man with expensively cut gray hair and heavy dark eyebrows, he had the easy confidence and self-assured manner of a man of privilege who was accustomed to calling the shots. He observed her closely, causing Sarah to shift self-consciously under his gaze. She smiled shyly, feeling her cheeks growing warm in the presence of this powerful man.

"Thank you for Crown Prince," Sarah said." He's awesome."

"Yes, I must agree with you on that, Sarah," Mr. Bolton replied in a voice designed to reassure her.

After they were seated, Mrs. DeWitt gave the envelope to her husband, who opened it immediately. After reading the contents, Mr. DeWitt handed it to his friend. "Hank, I think this sale contract that I wrote is pretty clear that acting on your behalf, Rudy accepted one dollar as payment in full for the horse," Mr. DeWitt said.

The room was quiet as Mr. Bolton took his time reading the document. At last he looked up to their expectant faces, taking a moment to choose his words carefully. "I'm not an attorney, but I can recognize an open-and-shut case when I see one. There's no doubt in my mind that this is a sales receipt, which legally transferred the horse's ownership with a one-dollar binder."

The DeWitts, Jack, and Sarah sank back in their chairs, all seeming to breathe a sigh of relief. It appeared there would be no legal battle over Crown Prince.

But Mr. Bolton hadn't finished. "I, of course, am disappointed that a horse with Crown Prince's breeding won't have a chance to be tried on the racetrack to see what he can do, especially when he showed so much promise. I'm particularly disappointed that our track vet never discovered the cause of the problem, which I understand is an overgrown wolf tooth. The fact that neither the veterinarian nor my trainer ever checked the horse's mouth is appalling." Mr. Bolton rose and walked a few paces, pausing to look out the window, momentarily lost in his own thoughts. Turning back, he looked at them again. "I'm also saddened that there will be no more foals from Northern

Princess. We lost her and the filly she was carrying in a difficult foaling when Crown Prince was a yearling. So he is her last foal."

Mr. Bolton stopped to look intently at Sarah. "I have a proposal for you to consider, Sarah, one that might work out for everyone concerned. I'm going to offer you what I think is an extremely good deal. You'll be needing money for college in a few years, and I have a way you can fund your education: If you return Crown Prince to me so I can put him back in training, I'll split any earnings he might realize right down the middle with you."

There were gasps in unison heard around the room, as everyone considered this extraordinary offer.

"Furthermore," Mr. Bolton continued, "should the horse, for whatever reason, have no earnings in purses in excess of this amount, I will pledge that for each year he's in training I will deposit $40,000 into a college savings account for you. And I also promise that when Crown Prince's racing days are over, he will come back to you, Sarah." Mr. Bolton paused to let all he had said sink in, waiting a few moments before launching one more piece of what he hoped would be an irresistible offer that couldn't possibly be refused.

"In the meantime, I'll provide you with another horse, Code of Honor, as a free lease until Crown Prince retires from the track. Cody is a wonderful horse, and I know you'll come to love him dearly." Mr. Bolton stooped to open his briefcase. He removed an embossed white envelope and presented it to Sarah. "This is a serious offer, one I've put in writing so you can understand the terms precisely. I'd like you to discuss this with your parents, Sarah, and let me know your decision as soon as possible."

Everyone in the room was shocked by the enormity of Mr. Bolton's proposal. Sarah sat in stunned silence, the blood drained from her face. She knew immediately that this savvy business-man had played the ace card in his strategy to get Crown Prince back. She silently took the envelope Mr. Bolton offered.

Chandler DeWitt cleared his throat and commented on his friend's generosity in what was, for everyone, a difficult situation. "I can only speculate on how the Wagner family will respond to this. The decision is theirs."

Later Sarah wouldn't remember leaving the bungalow. She wouldn't remember riding with Mrs. DeWitt back to the barn, and she wouldn't remember going immediately to Crown Prince in his stall. The only thought that filled her mind was Mr. DeWitt's parting words: …the Wagner family—*the decision will be theirs*. Prince was finishing his hay, and he raised his head when Sarah entered the stall. She flung her arms around his neck while she fought back tears. He stood quietly, seeming to understand her sadness.

Why was Mr. Bolton doing this? She wouldn't give up Crown Prince for any amount of money, but she knew it would be a dif-ferent story for her parents. Would they think she'd lost her mind to even consider passing up an opportunity for a free ticket to a college education? And all for a horse she had known for less than a week? Mr. Bolton's offer would create a huge wedge between them, she just knew it. She would have to give them the letter Mr. Bolton had prepared, and there would be a terrible argu-ment. Her father would use logic to try to convince her to accept the offer, and her mother would be angry, ranting about money. Abby would be on the sidelines, wide-eyed as she took it all in.

Sarah pressed her face against Prince's broad cheek. "They can never love you the way I do," she whispered. She stood by her horse for a long time, trying to collect her thoughts, and jumped when her cell phone rang. It was Kayla.

"My Mom's going out to do errands and will drop me off at the barn, if you have time to hang. Does that work?"

"Sure. How soon can you come?" she answered, her voice breaking.

"Sarah, what's the matter?" Kayla asked. "I can tell something's wrong. Are you okay?"

"Just get here," was all she could say. As Sarah closed her phone, she saw Mrs. DeWitt and the terriers making their way toward Prince's stall. Mrs. DeWitt had changed into jodhpurs and paddock boots, but the serious expression on her face said she had something besides riding Medina on her mind.

"Let's go sit down outside," Mrs. DeWitt said, as she neared Sarah. "I'd like to talk to you." Sarah followed her out the side door to the wrought-iron bench under the maple tree where she usually ate her lunch. They sat in silence for a few moments. Finally Mrs. DeWitt spoke. "Sarah, my dear, what do you think of all this?"

Sarah held back a moment, not sure she should unload her feelings on Mrs. DeWitt. She clenched her fists, obviously angry and upset. Then it all spilled out, her words coming fast. "Mr. Bolton is used to getting whatever he wants with his money. He must think that everything has a price. But I've waited a long time for this horse, and I won't give him back, not for a free college education or all the horses in the world!"

"What about your parents?" Mrs. DeWitt asked, her voice low and measured.

"I don't know if I can make them understand." Sarah paused to wipe a tear starting down her cheek. "The worst part is they'll probably decide I'm selfish, thinking only of myself." She lowered her head into hands, and a sob escaped through a gush of tears. "Maybe I am."

Mrs. DeWitt offered a tissue from her pocket as she slipped an arm around the girl's shoulders. She spoke softly. "There, there. Your parents won't be one-sided. They know how much Crown Prince means to you. But they also care about you deeply and want what's best for you. That would include having the money to pay for a college education."

Sarah wiped her eyes as she turned to face Mrs. DeWitt. "But going to college isn't the only thing in this world that matters. For as long as I can remember I've wanted a horse more than anything, and now I have Crown Prince, and he's wonderful." Her voice broke, and she lowered her head again, weeping quietly.

Mrs. DeWitt waited a few minutes before speaking. "Sarah, there's something you might not be aware of, and you should have it in the back of your mind. I understand your Dad teaches at the community college in Bromont. If that's the case, you may be able to go there tuition-free. Did you know that?"

Sarah's head snapped up, and she stared at Mrs. DeWitt. She thought for a moment. Yes, now she remembered her mother saying that no matter how great their medical debt, the girls would always be able to attend Bromont Community College.

"You're right. But my parents will still want me to have a

choice, to be able to attend an even better school." Sarah wiped her eyes. Would she be able to persuade her parents to let her turn down Mr. Bolton's money because there was always the option to attend her father's college after high school? She didn't know if it was possible.

"It's your decision to make," Mrs. DeWitt said. "No one will be critical, no matter what you decide. But you should be aware of all the facts. Then you and your parents can decide what's best."

"Mrs. DeWitt, how can I ever thank you and Mr. DeWitt for all you've done for me?"

Mrs. DeWitt stood up. "Don't worry about that, dear. I'm going to the carriage shed now to tack up Medina, but Jack wants to see you. He has some thoughts on what you should be doing with Crown Prince today. He's schooling Hedgerow in the outside ring."

Sarah sat for a few minutes trying to collect her thoughts before getting up from the bench. As she started across the courtyard to find Jack, she saw Kayla in the parking area climbing out of her mother's pickup. Kayla hurried over to her. She looked worried. "What's up, kid?" she said.

"Do you remember me telling you about Hank Bolton, the man who used to own Crown Prince?" When Kayla nodded, Sarah continued. "Well, he knows about the wolf tooth, and now he wants Prince back. He's offering tons of money to pay for my college if I'll give him back."

"You've got to be kidding!" Kayla exclaimed. "So what did your parents say?"

"They don't know yet. But there's no way I can't tell them.

This guy will call them himself to make the deal, I just know it."

A car horn sounded behind them. Rita Snyder was driving toward them in her racy green Mustang convertible. The top of the fast-moving car was down, and Rita's long black hair was whipping behind her. Even from a distance, the sound of her blaring music seemed to invade the farm.

"She's driving kind of fast," Kayla observed.

"What else is new," Sarah replied. The car slowed as it neared them and came to a stop beside the barn.

Rita reached to turn the radio volume down. "How's your new horse?" Rita asked Sarah. "Have you gotten on him yet?"

Sarah hesitated. She really didn't want to deal with Rita right now, but there was no way out. She took a deep breath before answering.

"Jack hasn't mentioned riding Prince yet. He was vetted out yesterday."

"How did that go?" Rita asked.

"The vet found a huge wolf tooth. He's going to the hospital tomorrow to have it pulled."

"Really?" Rita exclaimed as she tossed her hair back, showing her large hoop earrings. "I want to hear more about this. I'm going to park my car, but I'll be back in a minute."

Sarah and Kayla walked toward the outside ring, where Jack had Hedgerow trotting a figure eight pattern, asking the horse to stay on the bit and adjust his bend as they frequently changed direction. When Jack saw them, he brought Hedgerow to a walk and then halted by the rail.

"Good morning, girls," he said. "Sarah, you can turn Crown Prince out again this morning. 'Tis likely he won't be as full of himself as he was yesterday. I asked Gus to leave Quarry in his stall until later so your horse could have twenty minutes or so in the small paddock, where the grass isn't very tall. After lunch I want to introduce him to the longe line. Sound like a plan?"

"Cool!" she said, the excitement she felt helping to push her worries aside for the moment. Prince's training was about to begin, regardless of Hank Bolton's interference.

"I'll be at his stall at two o'clock." With that Jack turned Hedgerow and resumed trotting. The girls stayed to watch him and the beautiful horse he was riding. In a few minutes Rita joined them.

"Hedgerow has put on weight since he came here, don't you think?" Kayla asked.

Yeah," Sarah agreed. "He was a little ribby at first. They don't stay that way long at Brookmeade."

Rita looked closely at the horse. "They're always pretty skinny coming from the racetrack. My Dad wouldn't have a horse that thin in our barn," she said matter-of-factly.

Sarah ignored the comment. She had learned that it was better not to respond to much of what Rita had to say. "I need to turn Prince out. Want to come?" she asked.

The three girls turned from the rail and walked across the closely mowed lawn toward the barn. "By any chance is Tim here today?" Rita asked casually. Kayla gave Sarah a knowing look, as she tried to hide her smile.

Sarah thought a moment. "I think he rode this morning," she said. "He and Paige usually hack early before it gets hot."

Kayla couldn't hold it back, and a snicker escaped even as she covered her mouth. Rita looked at her with blazing eyes, her dark brows pinched together. 'Excuse me?" she said. "What's so funny? I've got a bit he wants to borrow for Rhodes, that's all."

Managing to keep a straight face, Kayla said, "Maybe you could leave it with Sarah to pass on to Tim, or just leave it on Rhodes' stall door."

Rita frowned. "I'm not taking the chance somebody might swipe it." She turned to Sarah. "You're here every day. Would you give it to him when you see him?"

Sarah nodded her head. "Sure. No problem."

Rita pulled a Dr. Bristol snaffle bit from her jacket's large side pocket and gave it to Sarah. "Just tell Tim I'm in no hurry to have it back."

"What's going on with Chancellor?" Kayla asked Rita, changing the subject. "Do you have any shows lined up this summer?"

"My dad wants to start out with the Rally Round Farm unrecognized show in a few weeks, because it's close to home. After that, there's a hunter and dressage show at the State Fair. We'll be there a few days, and I'll go in a ton of classes."

Sarah turned to Kayla. "Any chance you might show Fanny at the fair?"

"I don't think so," Kayla replied. "It gets pretty expensive when you have to pay for stabling on the grounds, stay in a motel, and eat out a lot. I don't think my parents are ready for that."

Rita broke in. "My dad says he might get one of those huge trailers that have living quarters included. That would be totally cool! Dad will have to get a new truck to pull it." Sarah wished Rita would just shut up.

As an afterthought Rita said, "The van can hold four horses."

She turned to Kayla. "Maybe we could travel to a show together, and stay in the van."

Kayla didn't answer, but Sarah could tell she found the invitation interesting.

"So what are *your* plans for showing, Kayla?" Rita asked.

"We're going to the Riverbend show this Sunday. It's for Quarter Horses only, but it's still pretty big."

"What classes are you going in?" Rita asked.

"The Novice Hunter division, and this year I'll do both the flat and over-fences classes. This will be the first time I've ever jumped Fanny anywhere except here at Brookmeade, so I don't know what to expect."

"Well," Rita scoffed, "you'll be up against just Quarter Horses, so don't worry. You'll do great. I'll have all kinds of Warmbloods and Thoroughbreds in my classes, but I know Chance can beat them all. That's why my dad bought him."

Rita was starting to really irritate Sarah. "You seem awfully sure of yourself," Sarah said. "There will be some tough competition at the shows you go to."

"I'm not worried," Rita said confidently. As they approached the side door, she looked at her watch. "Listen, I've gotta go. It's later than I thought. I'm supposed to be at Atlantic Saddlery in fifteen minutes to be fitted for new custom boots. Can I give you a lift home, Kayla?"

"My mom's picking me up later. But thanks."

Sarah and Kayla walked to Prince's stall, where he was nosing through his bedding for bits of hay. The girls both knew what the other was thinking. Finally, with no one else around, they could talk.

"I'd be freaking out if I were you," Kayla said. "First everyone was afraid your horse might be dangerous. Then you were worried he might not pass the vet exam. Now Mr. Bolton wants to take him back, and he's offering you so much money your parents might make you give him up. When are you going to tell them?"

Sarah looked over at Prince, who was drinking from his water bucket. She turned back to Kayla. "As soon as I can," she said, a lump forming in her throat. Tonight."

CHAPTER 13

The Decision

JACK DIDN'T MENTION Hank Bolton's visit to Brookmeade Farm when he arrived at Crown Prince's stall promptly at two o'clock. "This horse has been in limbo long enough," he said. "'Tis time he went to work." Sarah and Kayla watched as he entered the stall with a longeing cavesson and a coiled longe line draped over his arm. Prince noticed the equipment and began backing away.

"'Tis like a bitless bridle, Prince," Jack said, moving with him and stroking his long neck. "You'll not be minding it." He deftly slid the cavesson around the horse's nose and over his ears before Prince knew what was happening. In many ways it seemed like a bridle, something he'd come to hate, and he tossed his head in annoyance. But with no bit to bring jarring pain to his mouth, after a few minutes he quieted down. Jack buckled the straps and attached the longe line to the ring on the front of the noseband. "Let's go, son," he said, leading Prince out of the stall and picking up the longe whip with its long lash.

Sarah and Kayla fell into step with Jack as they walked

toward the outside ring on the opposite side of the barn from the indoor. The weather had cleared, and the gray clouds of earlier in the day had been replaced with sunshine. Prince's coat gleamed as he moved eagerly beside Jack. This was the first time he had been to this part of the farm, and he held his head high, looking around.

"'Tis always an advantage to longe a horse before you ride him," Jack explained. "'Twill get rid of any pent-up energy, and he'll be forming the habit of listening to you."

"How soon can he be bridled after the tooth is out?" Sarah asked.

"We'll see what Dr. Reynolds has to say about that. But in the meantime, much good can come from longeing. It will help him become better balanced while he learns to work with you."

The two small riders Lindsay had been instructing on Pretty Penny and Snippet were just leaving the ring. "It's all yours," Lindsay called out. Sarah waved a greeting to the DeWitts' granddaughter, Grace, riding Pretty Penny. Grace smiled back, and then with the heels of her laced paddock boots she prodded her pony to keep up with Snippet.

Sarah and Kayla found a good vantage point outside the white board fence to watch. Just as they got comfortable, a low rumble announced a vehicle's approach, and the girls turned to see the Romanos' pickup coming down the hill.

"I hope Mom isn't in a hurry," Kayla said. "I want to watch this."

A few minutes later, Mrs. Romano joined Sarah and Kayla by the rail. Wearing jeans and a straw hat, she was an athletic-looking woman in her forties with short hair a deeper auburn shade than her daughter's. Like Kayla, her face was splashed with freckles. Mrs. Romano seemed as interested as the girls in what was happening.

"I came at just the right time," she said softly.

Jack brought Prince to the center of the ring, and after asking him to halt, began to slowly rub the longe whip over his body. "Why is he doing that?" Sarah whispered.

Kayla's mother leaned over to the girls and replied in a hushed tone, "Jack's making sure that Prince has no fear of the whip. He'll be using it to urge him forward and keep him out on the circle. Prince should respect it but not fear it."

At first Prince tried to move away as Jack slowly rubbed the whip lightly against his hindquarters and sides. Jack moved with him, all the while talking reassuringly. When Prince seemed more relaxed, Jack led him forward. While pointing the whip at the horse's hip, Jack slowly uncoiled the longe line and moved away from him. Now with a gentle flip of the lash he asked the horse to continue walking around him, keeping his distance on the circle.

"Before I ask him to trot, 'tis important he learns to halt on command," Jack called out to them. "It's a break you'll be needing." Jack then distinctly said "halt," as he gave a few soft tugs with the line and pointed the longe whip in front of the horse. Prince stopped and looked toward Jack, not quite sure what was being asked of him. Jack repeated it a few more times until Prince seemed to understand the voice commands.

Then Jack used a new word. "Trot!" he said crisply, as he gently flipped the lash toward the horse's hindquarters. As Jack clucked, Prince somewhat hesitatingly broke into trot and continued moving on a circle, gradually going forward more confidently. *He's so beautiful!* Sarah thought, watching her horse trot smartly around Jack. He moved with an air of nobility, his long strides floating above the ground. He was the horse of her dreams!

Mrs. Romano leaned toward Sarah and whispered, "Your horse seems pretty easy-going. He's gorgeous, and what a nice mover! You got lucky, Sarah, and I certainly hope he works out for you."

Sarah nodded without taking her eyes off Prince and the man in the center. "Thanks," she said.

After doing a number of transitions, Jack asked Prince to halt and went to his head. "It's your turn, Sarah," Jack said, beckoning her into the ring. Sarah hadn't been expecting this, and she froze momentarily. She knew nothing about longeing. Did Jack expect her to start right now, training a green horse right off the racetrack?

"Come, come," Jack insisted. Sarah reluctantly ducked through the fence boards and went to him. "You need to learn to do this. Now follow the same routine." With that he showed her how to hold the longe line and whip before he retreated to the outside rail. Sarah tried to keep the contact with her horse through the longe line while pointing the longe whip toward his hip.

"That's good, Sarah," Jack said. "Now gently use the longe whip and your voice to ask him to walk."

Sarah spoke the word distinctly, as she'd heard Jack do. "Walk!" When Prince didn't move forward right away, she clucked and slowly swished the longe whip behind him. The horse turned to look at her for reassurance as he began walking forward. "Good boy," she instinctively called to him.

With Jack making helpful comments from the rail, soon Prince was doing all the things he'd learned from Jack. After a number of transitions from walk to trot and back, Jack said, "He's not ready to canter on a small circle, so I think that's enough for one session. Ask him to halt and immediately go to his head. Don't allow him to come to the center—always go to him."

After Sarah had followed Jack's suggestion, he said, "This is also the way you will change rein on the longe, by asking Prince to halt and then going to him and moving him out in the opposite direction. Next time you'll work him equally in both directions."

Mrs. Romano clapped her hands. "A wonderful start," she called. "But I have to drag Kayla away now. I'm glad I came at a good time to see your new horse, Sarah."

Kayla gave Sarah a thumbs-up. "He was awesome, kid!"

"Thanks," Sarah said. "And good luck at the show. I wish I could come with you."

"Call me later!" Kayla called out as she and her mother headed for the parking area. Sarah knew what Kayla would want to know. She'd be anxious to learn how Sarah's parents reacted to Mr. Bolton's offer.

Sarah reached up to stroke her horse. "You were a star, Prince." She led him to the gate that Jack opened for them.

"By the way, Sarah," Jack said, "don't forget we have an appointment tomorrow morning at the vet clinic. It won't take us long to get there. You'll have him ready to load at nine?"

She nodded. "Of course. I'll be here before seven to feed."

"Good. And don't forget his shipping boots."

Sarah led Prince back to the barn, where she saw Gus cleaning stalls. He stepped into the aisle as they approached and held up his hand to stop her. It was unusual for him to seek her out, and Sarah immediately became uneasy. Had she done something wrong?

"The carpenter says he's just about finished with the new stalls in the ell," Gus said. "Your horse is going to have the outside one with the window. It's bigger. I'll tell you when to move him."

"Thanks, Gus!" Sarah said enthusiastically. *To think, he actually started a conversation with me!* she thought. Gus paused to scrutinize Crown Prince as the horse walked by, but he had seen many handsome horses before this one and seemed to see no need to comment.

Once back in the stall, Sarah looked her horse over before removing the longeing cavesson. Despite the warm afternoon, he hadn't broken into a sweat. Prince went immediately to his water bucket, drinking deeply. *He's happy here,* she thought. *Brookmeade Farm is the best place for Prince, not the racetrack.* But it was getting late. Her dad would be home soon, and while she didn't look forward to the conversation she had ahead of her, she needed to get it over with.

After giving Prince a final pat, she scooped up Jack's longeing equipment and headed to the office. Lindsay was talking with a student and her parents in the hallway, but the office was empty. Sarah coiled the longe line and hung it along with the cavesson on a hook on the wall where Jack kept it before going to get her bicycle.

On the ride home her mind raced. She braced herself for the

confrontation that was sure to come. Mr. Bolton's letter was in her jeans pocket, ready for her to give to her parents. She steeled herself for their reaction, determined to stand her ground. Could she make them understand how much her horse meant to her? Would they recognize that no amount of money would tempt her to part with him? It should be *her* decision and no one else's. It was *her* life. And *her* horse.

Soon she was turning into the driveway by their white shuttered Cape-style house. Both garage doors were down, which meant her father was already home, and her mother was probably in the kitchen preparing dinner. Abby would be there too, most likely talking on her phone or texting friends.

Sarah put her bike away and walked toward the house. Before starting up the back steps, she paused a moment. So much rested on her parents' reaction to the deal Hank Bolton was proposing. When she stepped into the mudroom, she was struck with how quiet the house was. No music was playing, no noise from the television, and no voices.

Sarah was sitting on the deacon's bench removing her barn shoes when Abby appeared. Even her sister was uncharacteristically quiet, as she bent over to whisper in her ear. "They know," was all Abby said. She cast a knowing look before retreating back into the kitchen. Abby had to be speaking about Mr. Bolton's offer—what else could she mean? Sarah stepped into the half-bath off the mudroom to wash her hands, her thoughts whirling. How had they learned about it? She walked into the kitchen where her mother was slicing tomatoes for a salad.

"Hi, Sarah. Did you have a good day?"

"Yes, Mom, it was a great day. I actually longed Prince for the first time. But there's something important I need to talk to you and Dad about. Do you have time now?"

Her mother put the knife down and wiped her hands on a kitchen towel. Her face was noncommittal. "Yes, Sarah, of course we have time. Your dad's in the den."

Martin Wagner was working on some papers at his desk, but he swiveled his chair to face them. He looked equally serious. Sarah sat down on the loveseat in front of the Franklin stove while her mother settled in a nearby chair.

"Sarah," her mother began, "an unusual letter was left in our mailbox. It had no postmark, so it must have been hand delivered. It's from Hank Bolton. Do you know anything about it?"

Sarah's throat felt tight and dry. She sat up straight and took a deep breath before answering. "If it's from Mr. Bolton, then yes, I do. He was at Brookmeade today and gave one to me, too."

Her parents exchanged glances before Mrs. Wagner continued. "Well, then we don't have to go over the contents of the letter. We all know that Mr. Bolton is prepared to reward you with a lot of money if you return Crown Prince to him." She paused again, looking at her husband before continuing. "We can appreciate what a difficult position this puts you in. It forces all of us to consider some tough questions and think about our priorities."

"I know what's most important to me," Sarah shot back defiantly. "Sure, I want to go to college someday, but not if it means giving up the horse I've been waiting for all my life. It makes me mad that Mr. Bolton is trying to use his money to force me to give up Crown Prince. It makes me even madder that he's trying to get you on his side."

She wasn't surprised when her father's response was calm and considered, and she struggled to remain patient while he spoke. "We know how much you've always loved horses," he said, "and now you have one of your own, a horse that everyone seems to think is pretty special. But Hank Bolton has come up with a lucrative offer for the return of Crown Prince, a plan that includes a replacement horse. You say you're angry he made this proposal, and you don't want to accept it. But are you being reasonable? Can keeping Crown Prince really be worth sacrificing a gift card for your college education?"

It was so like her father to want her "to be rational," as he always phrased it. Sarah's back stiffened, and her dark eyes remained resolute and determined. "I won't give Prince back for a hundred college educations!" she blurted.

Her mother's mouth was set in a grim line. "Do you know what's at stake here? You're a smart girl who should go to college. An education will open up a whole new world for you. Do you think you can spend the rest of your life doing barn work at Brookmeade Farm to support a horse?" It was clear from her mother's rising voice and flushed face that she was upset by Sarah's response. Mrs. Wagner rose from her chair and walked as quickly as she could to the bay window, her back to them.

Sarah's father stepped in. "Hank Bolton isn't offering you a paltry sum, Sarah," he said. "We're talking serious money here. Do you know what that could do for you?"

Her mother turned around to face Sarah. "We won't let you ignore your future!" she said, her words terse and clipped. "This is a once-in-a-lifetime opportunity. We don't want you to make a terrible mistake you'll someday regret."

When Sarah didn't respond, her father spoke up. "Think about all the things you could do with the amount of money Hank Bolton is offering. Pick one of the top colleges. With your grades, you'll be able to get into any of them, and the money to make it happen has just fallen out of the sky. Your mother and I want to be sure you fully understand the big picture. Don't make a bad choice in haste."

Sarah clenched her jaw. For a moment she pictured what would happen if she went along with Mr. Bolton's plan. A van would show up to take Prince back to the racetrack. A stranger would lead him up the ramp, and off he would go, out of her life. She'd probably never see him again. He'd forget her and his time at Brookmeade. She squeezed her eyes shut against the image. It must not happen!

"I know you want what's best for me," Sarah said, her voice cracking. "But even if I keep Prince, I'll still be able to go to college. After I graduate, I can go to Bromont Community for free, because you teach there, Dad. I'll study to be a teacher like I've always planned. And I can get a part-time job while I'm in school." Her voice failed completely, and she whispered, "Somehow I'll find a way to keep Prince." And then a tear started down her cheek. "Please don't make me give him back."

Mrs. Wagner started for the door. "My casserole is ready to come out of the oven. I think we could all use a hot dinner." She looked back at Sarah. "But we haven't finished discussing this."

Sarah got up to leave, but her father motioned her back. "Sarah" he said, "please don't dig in your heels. Think this through carefully and keep an open mind."

There was little conversation during the evening meal; a

cloud of tension hung over the table. Abby tried to make small talk without much success. Sarah's stomach was in knots. She poked at the food on her plate before finally asking to be excused before the others had finished. She went to the welcoming quiet of the den and tried to get comfortable in the wing chair. She picked up the new issue of *Practical Horseman* that had come in the mail and leafed through the pages, but it was hard to concentrate.

When she heard dishes being stacked in the kitchen, Sarah went to help with the nightly chores. Abby chattered about her day at the Creamery as she cleared the table. Sarah listened half-heartedly, glad to have her sister fill the void as Sarah rinsed the dinner dishes and loaded them in the dishwasher. She was relieved when she could escape back to the den and an article on teaching horses to jump. She had just sat down when suddenly the quiet was broken by the shrill ring of the doorbell.

Sarah looked out the window facing the driveway. Her heart leaped when she saw Hank Bolton's Porsche parked in front of their garage. He was here! He was pulling out all the stops to get Crown Prince back, coming right to their house. She bit her lip in anger. What a nerve! What should she do? Her mind was racing. She didn't know whether to confront him at the door or hide in her bedroom.

The front doorbell rang once more, and Sarah heard her mother speaking. Then Mr. Bolton's distinctive voice carried from the front room to the den. "I hope you received the letter I left here earlier."

He was so slick. He was probably wearing the same impressive suit and winning smile that had gotten him money and power throughout his life. What if he convinced her parents that she should go along with his plan? Sarah felt her anger rising. At once she knew she had to speak for herself. She rose from the chair and strode into the front room.

Hank Bolton turned when she entered, smiling broadly as he stretched out his hand. Ignoring the gesture, Sarah struggled to be anything close to civil. The rage she felt consumed her. When she spoke, her words came in short, clipped bursts with an intensity that surprised even her.

"Mr. Bolton, I listened to you this morning. Then I read your letter. I'm sure you're here to try to convince my parents and me to accept your offer. But I can tell you my answer. It's no. Absolutely no." She heard her voice grow louder, and she struggled to stay in control. But the words came gushing out.

"No matter how much you try to change my mind, I will never give up Crown Prince." She paused to catch her breath. Was this really Sarah Wagner speaking? Her parents must be shocked to hear a girl who was usually quiet and even a little shy talking this way to an adult. But she went on, her fists clenched by her sides. "He's *not* going to be a racehorse. He's mine now, and I won't give him up, not for anything. Not for your money, and not for another horse."

Mr. Bolton was clearly taken aback. He looked beyond Sarah to her parents, his eyes pleading, asking them to use their better judgment. Could they possibly agree with their emotional teenage daughter? How could they refuse his offer? Always the skilled negotiator, Mr. Bolton decided to sweeten the deal. "I'm willing to up my proposal to $50,000 a year toward college. Isn't that more than generous and fair?"

The Wagners turned from his gaze, and an intense look

passed between them. There was a long moment of silence before Sarah's mother turned back to Hank Bolton. "Mr. Bolton, we appreciate your generous offer, and we are not ignorant of its amazing benefits. We've had a chance to discuss it with Sarah, but as you heard, her mind is firmly made up. She wants to keep Crown Prince." Mrs. Wagner's eyes met Sarah's. "And we must respect her wishes."

Sarah felt dizzy. Her parents would stand behind her! They were taking her side. She wanted to shriek for joy. Hank Bolton looked away for a moment. He seemed to be absorbing the fact that although he'd done everything he could, he'd lost. When he looked back at them, the smile was gone and there was no warmth in his voice when he spoke. "It's clear you're determined to keep Crown Prince, and it doesn't look like I can change your mind."

Her fierce resolve showed on Sarah's face. Her arms were folded across her chest and her mouth was pressed into a grim determined line as she shook her head unwaveringly.

Mr. Bolton spoke to Sarah's parents. "You can't imagine how sorry I am that you won't accept my offer. Crown Prince may be one of the best horses I ever bred, but I guess we'll never know. I suppose I should take comfort knowing that he's in good hands in my friend Chandler's barn and cared for by a dedicated young rider."

"We certainly appreciate your understanding," Mr. Wagner said.

"I'll be on my way," Mr. Bolton said, turning to Sarah. "But not before I wish all the best to you and Crown Prince. I only wish I had been as loyal to him as you are." With that he turned, and with his head slightly bowed, he retreated out the door and down the steps to his car. Moments later they heard the engine start and the car pull out of the driveway.

Sarah turned to her parents. How could she express the love she felt for them? Her gratefulness knew no bounds. "Mom, Dad, thank you, thank you." Her eyes were moist as she rushed to hug them both. Mr. Bolton's money hadn't swayed them. They had let *her* make the choice!

Abby skipped into the room to give Sarah a high five. "You were wicked good, Sis!" she cheered. "You really told him off!"

Sarah's parents remained serious. "What a gracious man," her mother said. "I only hope you won't come to regret your choice as he has come to regret his."

Her father nodded. "Well, he's gone," he said, turning to Sarah. "You made your decision, and now you must live with the consequences. But there's something else we should make clear. You've always worked hard to be a good student, and we expect that to continue. If you become so involved with this horse that your grades start to slip, the horse will have to go. You can't lose sight of the importance of doing your best in school. Wherever it is, you're going to go to college."

"And let's not forget that Prince is on trial," Sarah's mother said. "The verdict will come at the end of a month's time. Unless Jack can assure us he will be a safe horse for you to ride, Prince will go back to the racetrack faster than you can snap your fingers. We are not going to change our minds on that."

Mr. Wagner remained somber. "And now we're on to the wolf tooth. Isn't tomorrow the day Prince is scheduled to have it removed?" he asked.

Sarah nodded. "Jack asked me to have him ready to load at nine. I'm going to see if Kayla can come with us." She felt for her cell in her jeans pocket and headed up the stairs. Once in the quiet of her room, she sat on her bed, bent over, and buried her face in her hands. She took a deep breath and closed her eyes, thinking about all that had just taken place. Several minutes passed as she waited for the reality of what had happened to sink in. She knew this day was a turning point in her life.

Sarah got comfortable on her bed with her back resting against the headboard and dialed Kayla's home number. The phone rang several times, and Sarah was about to click off when Kayla, sounding rushed and out of breath, answered. "I just got in from the barn. What's up?" she asked. "How did it go?"

"Ugh, it was crazy!" Sarah said, closing her eyes. "As soon as I got home, I had a terrible argument with my parents. They were afraid turning down Mr. Bolton's offer would be a terrible mistake I'd regret someday. Mom got pretty upset, and Dad tried to convince me I should think about taking the money. No way!"

"So did they say you can keep Prince?"

"There's more. Mr. Bolton came to our house tonight."

"No!" Kayla exclaimed. "He just showed up? You've got to be kidding! What a nerve. What happened?"

Sarah told Kayla about the confrontation. Looking back on it, she was shocked at her own bravado and how she had spoken. Never before had she stood up to an adult like that, especially a powerful man like Hank Bolton.

When Sarah had finished, Kayla admitted she was amazed. "That's so awesome" she said. "You sure have guts!"

"I had to make him know I won't give Prince up. He's the horse I've been waiting for. He's *the one.*"

"I'm proud of you, kid," Kayla said. Sarah couldn't see her face, but she knew her friend was beaming.

"Listen, Kayla, we have an appointment at Dr. Reynolds's vet hospital tomorrow morning. He's going to pull the wolf tooth. Can you come with us?"

Kayla thought for a moment. "I think so. I don't have anything until Jack's lesson in the afternoon."

"Cool. Jack wants me to have him ready to load at nine. Can you bike over?" Sarah asked.

"Sure. See you there. And for your sake, I hope you never hear from Hank Bolton again!"

CHAPTER 14

The Surgery

SARAH ARRIVED AT THE BARN earlier than usual the next morning. She wanted to allow plenty of time to feed the horses before getting Prince ready for the trip to the vet clinic. As she neared his stall, she was surprised to see a note tacked to the door. Coming closer, she read: *Your horse has been fed. Feed the rest.* Gus's name was scrawled on the bottom.

She went into the stall where Prince was eating from a large pile of hay. His feed tub was still moist, so he'd recently eaten his grain. He raised his head and came to her. "You expect a carrot every morning, don't you," she said, as she pulled one out of her pocket and offered it to him.

She stroked her horse gently as he ate the carrot, thinking about Gus's note. He had probably learned from Jack that Prince was having the wolf tooth out this morning, and wanted him to have a chance to eat before they left. This was the first time Gus had done something nice for her. Could it mean he'd noticed she was working hard to do a good job? Probably not—he was just doing what was best for the horse.

She was startled by a voice from outside the stall. "What's up, kid?" It was Kayla, grinning, her short auburn hair especially curly in the summer humidity.

"Hey, I didn't expect you for awhile," Sarah said.

"My dad left for work early, and he dropped me off," Kayla said. She bent closer to read the note. "I guess Prince got a head start on breakfast." She slid through the opening to come into the stall and extended her hand to Prince, who quickly picked up the two sugar cubes she offered.

"Want to help me feed the horses?" Sarah said. She stepped out of the stall and slipped the chain with the grain room key over her head.

"Sure," Kayla said. "I've never been in the grain room or up to the loft."

The girls made the rounds, feeding the morning grain and refilling the pails on the pushcart before heading to the loft. As they worked, they rehashed Mr. Bolton's visit to the Wagner's the night before.

"I can't believe he just showed up at your door," Kayla said. "I bet he thought your parents would make you go along with his deal. You know what they say—money talks."

"I'll never forget how Dad and Mom let me say no to him. They proved they can't be bought," Sarah said as they climbed the steps to the loft. "The DeWitts were on my side too."

"So the battle is over for good?"

Sarah stopped to look at Kayla. "I wish," she said with a sigh. "But in a way it has just begun. I still have to prove that Prince will be safe for me to ride."

After they'd dropped hay to the horses, Sarah grabbed the

push broom and began sweeping the loose hay into the opening over McDuff's stall. When she had finished, she checked the time.

"We've got to hurry," she said. "Prince needs to be groomed before Jack hooks up the trailer, and I need to put on his shipping boots."

They hurried back to Prince's stall, where he had finished his hay and drunk almost all the water in his bucket. Sarah went to get her grooming caddy and shipping boots from the tack room. When she returned, Kayla had put Prince's halter on. "Can he be groomed in the aisle?" she asked.

"I guess so," Sarah answered. "Jack said Prince ties so well in the stall he could be groomed in the aisle on cross-ties, as long as they're connected to the rings on the wall with baling twine."

"Of course," Kayla said. "You wouldn't want this nice halter with his nameplate to be broken if he panicked and pulled back. Fuzzy used to halter-pull. He never ruined a halter, though, thanks to the baling twine. I'm glad Fanny doesn't pull."

Sarah snapped the lead shank onto Prince's halter, but before she could lead him into the aisle, she saw Gus approaching. When he got closer, she said, "Good morning, Gus. Thanks for feeding Prince early." The disagreeable man only shoved his red baseball cap lower over his eyes and grunted as he passed. *He's impossible!* Sarah thought, frustrated. *I don't know why I try to make friends with that man!*

Kayla noticed Gus's rude behavior and raised her eyebrows. "That guy sure doesn't win any personality contests," she whispered. Sarah just rolled her eyes.

Once Prince was in the aisle and appeared relaxed on the cross-ties, the girls began grooming him. Sarah picked out his feet, sending bits of packed bedding and manure to the mat below. "I hope the farrier can pull these racing plates when he comes next week," Sarah said. "Do his feet look long to you?"

Kayla, who was waiting with a broom, checked out Prince's hooves. "They're longer than we ever let Fanny's get," she said, as she swept everything into his stall. "We don't want to give Gus another excuse to be grouchy," she said in a hushed voice. She started to comb out Prince's mane and tail while Sarah got busy with a curry comb and brush. When they had finished, they stepped back to admire the horse's gleaming coat.

Kayla frowned. "His mane is thick and pretty long," she said. "Are you going to pull it one of these days?"

"I got a pulling comb at the tack shop, but you'll have to show me how to use it. I've never pulled a mane before. Do you think he'll mind?"

"Mane-pulling doesn't bother Fanny." She raised an eyebrow. "And if ever there was a horse who'd have a problem with it, she'd be the one," Kayla said. "I only pull a few hairs at a time. But you'd better have a tall stool to stand on. Prince's mane is a long way up!"

As Sarah bent over to put Prince's shipping boots on him, she tried to remember everything Jack had told her when she'd done it at the racetrack. Not too tight, but taut so they wouldn't slip down. When she had finished, Kayla gave a nod of approval.

"It's almost nine. I wonder if Jack is here." Sarah said.

Kayla walked down the aisle to look out the window. "He's backing the truck up to the trailer right now. I guess we're ready just in time."

Sarah took a deep breath and ran her hand down Prince's

neck. Having the tooth out was a big deal. It might make all the difference for this horse with his bad racetrack reputation. She attached the shank to his halter, and with Kayla following, led Prince down the aisle toward the main entrance. The horse trailer was waiting with the ramp down. When they walked out into the morning sunshine, Prince's head shot up, and he stopped, looking warily at the trailer.

"Just walk him on," Jack said. "He's done this before."

Sarah stroked Prince's neck to reassure him. She clucked softly, and they moved toward the trailer. She felt her horse hesitate slightly as they approached the ramp, but she put more pressure on the shank and walked forward onto the ramp. Following her lead, he stepped up after her and walked into the trailer. *He's already learned to trust me,* she thought happily as she rewarded him with a carrot.

"Good job," Kayla said. "Be thankful he's not like Fanny used to be."

Jack lifted the ramp, latched it shut, and Sarah exited the side door. Soon they were on their way, the trailer riding easily on the now smooth farm road. Kayla sat in the passenger seat, with Sarah in the back, as usual, keeping her eyes on her horse in transit. After a few minutes she turned in the seat to speak to Jack.

"I just hope that tooth comes out okay. Do you think the roots could be curled around another tooth? Or maybe around his jawbone? The tooth is so big!"

"There you go, worrying now," Jack said. "The X-rays will tell Dr. Reynolds everything he needs to know before he goes in there. He'll not be chancing it." He looked over at Kayla and changed the subject. "You've got a show coming up this weekend. Will you be bringing Fanny for the lesson this afternoon?"

"You betcha," Kayla said. "This week is not the time to miss a lesson." She paused. "I don't know what to expect at the show. Fanny has never done any jumping except at Brookmeade."

"I guess 'tis more than one worrywart we have with us today," Jack said. "The important thing is to ride Fanny the same, no matter where you are. Use the same aids, remember all the things we've drilled on, and take a few deep breaths to clear your head before you go into the ring. Your mare is ready to compete, and you must believe in her." Sarah glanced at her friend to see how she was taking Jack's pep talk. If Jack said they could do it, then they could do it.

The truck slowed as they approached Yardley village, Jack driving cautiously by parked cars in front of the small shops and restaurants. Now that the summer people were here, the otherwise quaint small town bustled with traffic and shoppers doing errands before they headed for the beach. The Ocean Breeze Bed & Breakfast Inn had posted a "No Vacancy" sign, a sure indication that the summer tourist season was in full swing.

The day was warming up rapidly, and there were already several cars in the beach parking area, but Sarah saw no sign of her father or Abby at The Seaside Creamery as they went by. The truck made a turn by the Yardley House of Pizza onto the road leading to the vet clinic in Winchester, a horsey town that provided many clients for the large animal veterinarians in Dr. Reynolds's practice.

After they had driven a few miles, Jack asked, "I think Rita lives somewhere around here, doesn't she?"

"We just went by the driveway that leads to their place,"

Kayla said. "Her father bought the Mansfield estate and named it Pyramid Farm. It's on a hill, so there's a great view of the ocean, and you should see the barn! It's got a chandelier in the entryway."

"Rita invited some of us from the barn to a pool party she had last summer," Sarah said, "so we got to see the place. The house is a mansion. It has pillars in front like a Southern plantation. I couldn't believe all the turnout paddocks they have for Rita's horses. I'm surprised they don't have an indoor."

"That will be next." Kayla said. "Rita told me there's one in the works. There are trails that lead down the hill to the far end of the beach, but she's not allowed to go down there. She said the trails are rough and rocky in places, and her father is afraid she'll get hurt."

"He might be worrying about that valuable horse as well," Jack said.

"There's no shortage of horses for Rita to ride," Sarah said. "She still has Ajax, her Appaloosa. He was her first horse. There's also a horse her father bought for himself, but Rita says only she rides him—I think his name is Bittersweet. And she still has Sunday Best, the pony she showed as a kid, and who knows how many other horses. She will never have to worry about a horse to ride. And there is plenty of space for all of them in that humungous barn."

"Does she go to your high school?" Jack asked.

"No," Kayla replied. "She goes to the private school in Winchester. She told me her father bought her that Mustang for her 'commute.'"

"I think 'twould be best if you girls remember that lots of

horses and a convertible don't always equal happiness," Jack said firmly. Sarah and Kayla looked at each other.

The countryside became slightly rolling as they continued to the vet clinic, passing a number of fields with horses turned out. Sarah noticed that Prince was looking out his side window. Jack slowed for a sharp curve before putting on his blinker for the turn into the clinic. He followed the sign to the parking area for horse trailers in the back. When the truck rolled to a stop, Sarah and Kayla immediately hopped out and went to the trailer. From the hay strewn on the trailer floor, Sarah knew Prince had been relaxed enough on the ride to eat some from the net, an improvement over his trip to Brookmeade from the racetrack.

Jack disappeared into the office to announce their arrival. He returned a few minutes later. "'Tis lucky we're their first appointment of the day. We won't have long to wait, and you can take him right in."

Once Prince was off the trailer, Kayla held him so Sarah could remove his shipping boots. She tossed them into the back of the trailer. He seemed a little nervous, taking in this new place. He arched his neck and tugged against the shank as Sarah led him toward the entrance to the long building, with Jack and Kayla following. When an overhead door clattered open, he snorted and pulled back. Sarah was able to halt him as a woman with short blonde hair stepped outside to greet them.

"Hi, I'm Dr. Jenson, the new veterinarian here, and I'll be assisting Dr. Reynolds this morning." She smiled at Sarah and pointed to another doorway. "You can bring him right into the examining room. Dr. Reynolds should be right along."

Prince hesitated before stepping onto the rubber mats in the large room, surveying the veterinary stocks in the center of the space. A pungent medicinal smell pervaded the area that was made bright and warm by overhead lighting. No wonder Prince was tense! Sarah clucked to him, and this time he followed her inside.

Dr. Jenson came closer to look at the plate on his halter. "Oh my, he's by Emperor's Gold! That horse is a legend in his time, both as a racehorse and a stallion. I remember when he won the Triple Crown."

Sarah felt a surge of pride in her horse. "Crown Prince never raced," she said.

"Lucky horse," the veterinarian said. "Avoiding the racetrack is a great advantage for a Thoroughbred pointed to another career. Training and racing at the track is stressful on young Thoroughbreds, and those lucky enough to never race have far fewer soundness problems later on."

Jack introduced himself and extended his hand to Dr. Jenson. "We suspect the action of the bit on his large wolf tooth was painful, because he was unruly under tack, to be sure. But as we've seen since Sarah got the horse a few days ago, so far he's been well-behaved at the farm."

"You could be right on the money about the wolf tooth," the veterinarian said. "A bit hitting that tooth would be extremely painful."

Prince tossed his head and pawed the floor. He seemed too nervous to stand quietly, so Sarah circled him in one end of the large room. When she stroked his neck, he felt warm and damp.

"I'm going to give him a sedative to help him relax," Dr. Jenson said, as she approached carrying a syringe. "We need him to stand quietly for the radiograph. Please hold his head steady and cup his left eye, so he can't see what I'm doing back here."

Sarah reached up to put her hand behind Prince's eye. "Like this?" she asked, and Dr. Jenson nodded. The vet swabbed an area with alcohol. She quickly inserted the needle and depressed the syringe with an action so smooth Prince seemed not to notice.

Next she went to a side cabinet and came back with a lead-plated apron that she handed to Sarah. "You'll probably be close to your horse when the X-ray films are taken, so we want you to wear this."

Moments later Dr. Reynolds entered pushing a mobile X-ray machine. "Hi, Jack, Sarah," he said. The veterinarian had been to the Romano barn many times to take care of their horses and administer routine shots, and he immediately recognized Kayla. "How's my favorite Quarter Horse doing these days?" he asked.

"Fanny's great," Kayla said, grinning. "We're going to a show this weekend."

"Good for you," Dr. Reynolds said, as he walked over to look closely at Crown Prince. The sedative had already begun to take effect, and the horse stood quietly with his head lowered slightly. Dr. Reynolds turned and pointed to the stocks with metal railings just wide enough for a horse to walk between. "Let's put our guest of honor in there so we can take a few pictures of that wolf tooth to check out the roots. It will be a close fit for a horse his size, but he should manage okay. Actually, we had a Clydesdale in there last week. Just lead him in from the back, and once he's inside, we'll close the bars, front and back."

Prince awkwardly followed Sarah between the rails, his steps slow and shuffling. With the bars in place, he wouldn't be able to move in any direction while they worked on him. Sarah stood in front of her horse, holding the shank and stroking him as she talked in a low soothing voice. Dr. Reynolds slowly pushed the X-ray machine close to the horse's head.

"We really need him to be immobile for this, Sarah. Hold his head steady and don't let him move." The sedative had relaxed Prince so that now his eyes were partly closed and his lower lip drooped. Dr. Reynolds maneuvered the machine to take plates from various angles. Finally he wheeled the X-ray machine to the back wall where there was a special screen for viewing the pictures once they were developed.

Sarah breathed a sigh of relief. "Part One" was over. While the others gathered to watch Dr. Reynolds develop the films, she stayed with her horse. He was motionless, with his head resting on her shoulder. Sarah stroked the white star on his forehead and ran her fingers through his forelock while she watched Dr. Reynolds from a distance. One by one the vet removed the moist plates from the machine and clipped them to the illuminated screen. There before their eyes were the images of the horse's jaw, showing his teeth and their roots below the gum line.

Kayla gasped when she saw the immense weirdly shaped tooth that grew at a different angle from the other teeth on the screen. Of course this was the wolf tooth. She quickly went to Sarah. "I'll hold Prince. Go and see the X-ray films!"

"It looks like we're in luck," Dr. Reynolds said. "For such a large tooth, it appears the roots are of normal size. They can vary a lot from horse to horse. Sometimes wolf teeth have small crowns with long roots. In this case the crown is extremely large, but the roots are average." He pointed to one of the radiographs.

"From this angle, we can see the root clearly. I don't anticipate any problem pulling that tooth out of there." Sarah took a deep breath and let it out slowly. This was good news indeed. She looked back at Kayla and gave her a thumbs-up.

Dr. Reynolds showed another picture. "And we can see here, there is no sign of a wolf tooth on the other side of his mouth. Sometimes they're 'blind,' lying under the gum, but the X-ray film shows that in this case there's nothing there. Good news. So let's get on with it."

Both veterinarians used the side sink to scrub their hands and put on surgical gloves. When Dr. Jenson was ready, she went to Prince's head and put an equine speculum in place to hold his mouth open. In his sleepy state, Prince did not object, and he gave no resistance when she injected a numbing agent into his jaw in several places around the tooth.

"He won't feel a thing," Dr. Jenson reassured them. "We'll wait a few minutes to make sure the lidocaine anesthetic has taken effect." She reached inside his mouth and ran two fingers between his cheek and gum line. "Once the area of the wolf tooth has healed, you should have his teeth floated with a rasp so he'll be able to chew his food properly. He has some sharp edges on his molars."

All Sarah knew about horse tooth-care was the little she could remember from an article she'd read a long time ago. "How often will he need his teeth floated?" Sarah asked.

"Once a year, if he chews normally," Dr. Jenson said. "It's a good idea to have your vet or horse dentist check his mouth every six months or so."

Sarah stood stroking her horse. Prince seemed like a gentle

giant, so vulnerable and helpless, with his head hung low and his eyes nearly closed.

Dr. Reynolds approached with a tool he used to dig around the tooth's gums to loosen the tooth and separate it from the gum line. Jack came closer to watch the procedure carefully. Then Dr. Reynolds picked up a second tool that reminded Sarah of her father's pliers, but bigger. As Dr. Jenson held Crown Prince's head firmly, Dr. Reynolds carefully placed the tool around the tooth, and when he had a good purchase, pulled hard. The tooth didn't budge from the horse's jawbone.

Sarah wanted to close her eyes and not have to deal with what was happening, but she knew Prince needed her. He continued to stand quietly, not reacting to the procedure taking place.

"This is going to take a bit of muscle power," Dr. Reynolds said. "Hold him tight—here we go again." This time he pulled with all his strength, and the large grotesque tooth finally slid out of the horse's jaw. Dr. Jenson was ready with sterilized gauze pads that she pressed into the gaping hole inside Prince's mouth for a few minutes to minimize the initial bleeding.

"Incredible!" Dr. Reynolds exclaimed. "Unless this tooth has some sentimental value to you, Sarah, I'd like to keep it. I've never seen a wolf tooth anywhere near this size, and I'd like to show it to some of my colleagues. I know they'll find it pretty remarkable."

"Sure," Sarah said. "I'm just glad it's out. I really never need to see it again."

Dr. Reynolds placed the tooth on a nearby cabinet. "Let's get him out of the stocks and into a stall," he said. "The sedative should wear off before long, and you'll be able to trailer him home." He removed the front bar so Sarah could lead Prince out of the stocks. "Dr. Jenson will show you a stall."

Sarah smiled at the veterinarian. "Thanks so much," she said.

"I'm happy we could do something to turn this fellow around. He's too nice a horse to fall by the wayside. You'll have to go easy with his feed for awhile, though. I expect his gum line will fill in quickly, since the roots on that tooth weren't excessively deep, but he's to have no hay for a few days. Dr. Jenson will talk to you more about this, and how to rinse his mouth. I'm coming to Brookmeade on Saturday and will take a look at him then."

Sarah clucked to her sleepy horse and tugged gently with the lead shank. Jack tapped his hindquarters, and Prince walked slowly out of the stocks. They followed Dr. Jenson from the examining room to an area of box stalls in the back of the hospital. She opened the door of the first one, an airy stall lightly bedded with clean shavings, and Sarah led her horse inside. Prince showed no interest in his new surroundings, but stood quietly with his feet wide apart and his head hanging low.

"Let's leave him alone for a bit," Dr. Jenson said. "It will give us a chance to talk about aftercare."

Sarah removed Prince's lead shank and reluctantly joined the others near the stall. When she looked back, Prince hadn't moved.

"Because the root area wasn't deep or wide, this should heal pretty quickly," Dr. Jenson said. "Usually horses can keep right on eating hay and wear a bridle after wolf teeth are pulled, but because that tooth was so enormous, we want to be careful. What you can do to speed up the healing process is squirt a saline solution into that area a few times a day. I'll give you a syringe to use, and we'll practice it once before you go. To make it, just mix two tablespoons of salt with a quart of water."

"What should we feed him?" Sarah asked.

"Like Dr. Reynolds said, don't feed him hay for a day or so. It's stemmy and might cause some bleeding in the area. He'll miss his hay, but roughage will only irritate the opening. Instead of his regular grain, you need to soak complete feed pellets in water, along with some beet pulp, to make a mash that won't require much chewing. Without hay, he can have a few quarts of that mash several times a day. He's a big horse, and needs his groceries. If there are any problems, call Dr. Reynolds or me."

"We always have beet pulp on hand at the farm, and we use a complete feed pelleted grain," Jack said. "Between our barn manager, Gus, and Sarah, Crown Prince will get the care he needs."

"Can he go out in his paddock?" Sarah asked, looking very serious. "And what about the carrots I usually feed him?"

Dr. Jenson smiled. "For a few days, let's swap the carrots for apple slices, which are softer to chew. It won't hurt him to be turned out in his paddock for as long as he usually is, since grass isn't stemmy like hay. Let's hold off on other exercise—in a few days he will hopefully give the green light to go back to his regular diet and schedule."

Dr. Jenson looked back at Prince and saw he remained subdued and resting quietly. "Would you folks like to take a look around at some of our other patients while you wait?" she asked. "I have a little time." The girls nodded enthusiastically.

"Well, let's start over here," Dr. Jensen said, pointing to a handsome chestnut horse with a narrow blaze in the stall next to Prince. "This horse was brought to us with extreme colic in the middle of the night over the weekend. He's a valuable show hunter. His colic required surgery, and we were afraid he wasn't going to make it," the veterinarian said. "But he's doing well now. We expect him to go home tomorrow." The chestnut looked up from his hay as they passed.

"Next to him is a mare that had a difficult foaling," Dr. Jenson went on. They stopped to look in on a leopard Appaloosa who ignored the visitors. Her eyes were dull, and she stood with her head hung low, shifting her weight from one leg to another. A flake of hay in the corner was untouched. "Her foal had the umbilical cord wrapped around its neck, and we couldn't save it," the vet continued. "We almost lost the mare, too. She's not eating well, and is obviously despondent and depressed."

"She looks so sad," Kayla said softly.

"If she's had a foal in the past, she's probably missing the new babe," Jack said. "Horses know when they lose a friend or foal, just like humans grieve when they lose someone they care about."

They walked on through the facility, with Dr. Jenson telling them interesting things about the horses they passed. They saw a light bay with a heavily bandaged right foreleg. "His owner was riding him through a stream and the horse cut his leg severely on a broken bottle someone had carelessly tossed in. He lost a lot of blood and required many stitches."

Just then a young woman hurried up to Dr. Jenson. "The SPCA van is here with the horse they rescued this morning. Shall I have them bring him in now?"

"Yes," the veterinarian said. "He'll go in stall number three."

She opened the sliding side door, and they watched as a young man slowly led in an extremely thin gray horse. For June, when other horses had shed their winter coats, this horse's coat was still long, rough, and disgustingly dirty. He was bony and emaciated, and his hips and spine stood out conspicuously. Sarah's eyes ran down his legs to his grossly overgrown hooves. Sarah and Kayla were sickened by what they saw.

"He looks awful!" Kayla said. "You can count all his ribs, even through his thick winter coat."

"He hasn't gotten enough to eat," Dr. Jenson said. "When a horse isn't fed a diet sufficient in calories, he'll hang onto his winter coat long past the time other horses have shed out. Sometimes older horses do that even on a quality diet." She turned to the young man as he came out of the stall. "What's the story with this one, Jim?" she asked.

"He was found in a small enclosed area by an old barn where someone had apparently abandoned him. Luckily he had access to a brook, so he could get water. That's probably why he's still with us. He's also got a bad scrape just below his left hock. We need you to check him out, treat the hock, and make an evaluation."

"I'll call you when we have the scoop," Dr. Jenson said. Jim thanked her and hung the horse's halter on the stall door before exiting the clinic.

"What will happen to this poor horse?" Sarah asked. She found it hard to believe that people actually *abandoned* horses, when she had always wanted one so badly.

"Hopefully we'll bring him back to good health. The SPCA shelter will try to get the weight back on him, and when he's in better shape, they'll look for a good home for him, one where he'll get proper care," Dr. Jenson said. She entered the stall and approached the horse, who was too dull and starved to move. She opened his mouth to look at his teeth. "This horse doesn't appear to be that old. Someone must have been pretty callous to just walk away and leave him."

Jack shook his head. "There's no excuse in the world for doing this to any animal. I hope they catch up with whoever left this horse to starve and throw him in jail!"

"The authorities are looking into it," Dr. Jenson said, patting the gray before leaving him to join them again in the aisle.

They turned down a corridor leading to the hospital's operating room, and once inside, Dr. Jenson showed them the operating table with its hydraulic lift. "Horses that need to be on their sides during surgery are strapped to this table when it's in a vertical position, and once they're anesthetized, the table is turned. That way a horse can be easily placed back in a standing position once the surgery is complete. We used this table for the colic surgery on Saturday. Larger hospitals often have special swimming pools, which provide a safer place for horses with leg surgeries to come out of anesthesia. Using the pool, a horse won't injure himself further if he thrashes around as the anesthesia is wearing off."

Sarah found the tour interesting and Dr. Jenson very kind, but she couldn't help worrying how Crown Prince was doing. She excused herself and went to check on him. He was walking around the stall when she arrived, more alert and appearing glad to see her.

In a few minutes the others returned, and Dr. Jenson joined

her in the stall. "The sedative I gave him wears off quickly, Sarah," she said. "Would you please put Prince's halter with his shank back on him? I'll be right back."

Dr. Jenson left the stall, returning a few minutes later with a bottle of what appeared to be water in a jar and a plastic syringe. "It's pretty easy to rinse a horse's mouth with this salt-and-water mixture," she said. Sarah and Kayla watched as she filled the syringe from the liquid in the jar, held the horse's head up, and squirted the water into his mouth from the side near where the wolf tooth had been extracted. "Do you think you can handle this?" she asked.

Sarah grinned. "Not a problem."

"As I mentioned, just mix a couple tablespoons of regular table salt to a quart of water to make the solution," Dr. Jenson said. She looked at her watch. "I think that by the time you get Prince's boots back on, he'll be ready to travel."

"I'll get them," Kayla volunteered, and headed to the truck.

"Don't forget to take down the hay net," Sarah called after her.

"Good," Dr. Jenson said. "You remembered about not feeding him hay. It looks like he's in good hands."

With Crown Prince once again on the trailer, Sarah, Kayla, and Jack headed back to Brookmeade Farm. In the back seat Sarah was deep in thought. *Getting rid of that tooth will be a whole new beginning for Prince, a turning point,* she thought. *It's got to be.*

Kayla looked back at her. "Just think, now that the wolf tooth is out, you'll be riding Prince pretty soon." Sarah smiled. She liked the sound of that. "I sure hope so."

But Jack was quick to add a word of caution. "Best not to

get ahead of ourselves here," he said. "You girls are optimistic, to be sure. But we don't know how he'll react until he's actually bridled with a saddle and a rider on his back. Old habits don't always fade quickly, and 'tis possible he'll connect being ridden with the pain he once had, even if 'tis all in his head. We need to be sure his jaw has fully healed before we put a bit in his mouth. Dr. Reynolds has predicted he'll be fine in only a short time, but he'll know more when he sees him on Saturday. I promised your father I'd oversee this thing, and we'll not be in a big hurry to put you on his back."

Sarah's heart sank. She'd allowed herself to believe the tooth's removal would immediately make all the difference. She sat quietly, looking back at her horse, and thought about Jack's warning. She and Prince weren't out of the woods yet.

CHAPTER 15

The Troublemaker

IN LESS THAN THIRTY MINUTES they were back in Yardley and turning into the Brookmeade Farm road. As soon as the truck rolled to a stop near the barn, Sarah and Kayla went to check on Crown Prince. Unlike his first arrival at the farm, when he was extremely nervous, today he seemed quiet and laid-back. Sarah put her hand on his neck. "He's dry. I guess he's getting used to traveling in a two-horse trailer."

Gus was cleaning a stall near the barn's doorway. When he saw the truck pull up, he put down his manure fork and came out of the barn. Jack was getting out of the truck as Gus approached.

"The horse's new stall is ready," Gus said unemotionally. "He can go in it now." With that he turned and went back into the barn, passing Spin and Taco as they came trotting by. Mrs. DeWitt was right behind them, and she hurried over.

"Tell me how the surgery went," she said. "I've been thinking about it all morning."

"Super," Sarah said, reaching down to pet Spin. She straightened, smiling. "The roots were normal, and the tooth pretty much popped right out." She picked up a small stick and threw it for the dogs to chase.

Mrs. DeWitt glanced at Jack, who gave a thumbs-up sign. "So far so good," he said. "There were no complications."

"And the best part is that Dr. Reynolds thinks it will heal fast," Sarah added.

Mrs. DeWitt threw her head back and clapped her hands. "I couldn't be more pleased! And I speak for Chandler as well."

"We got to see the other horses at the clinic," Kayla said, her face becoming serious. "Dr. Reynolds' new vet, Dr. Jenson, gave us a tour." She went on to tell Mrs. DeWitt about the horse rescued by the SPCA. "You wouldn't believe how thin he was. He was starved."

"The vets there see many sad cases," Mrs. DeWitt said. "They try to help every horse, and do a wonderful job in so many ways."

"Yes," Jack said, "'tis too bad some folks get a horse or a pony with no idea what's involved in its care. A man in the next town over bought a pony for his three children, thinking that tethering the pony on their front lawn would provide all the food he needed. They gave him a drink of water once a day. I suspect it was really a lawn mower or a babysitter he was wanting. The kids rode the pony hard, and nobody noticed he was getting thin as a blade. He could hardly stand when a neighbor finally called the authorities."

"It's a good thing there are organizations like the Pony Club and 4-H," Mrs. DeWitt said. "They teach youngsters the right way to care for their animals."

Sarah saw that Crown Prince was standing quietly in the

trailer, not seeming anxious to be unloaded. She turned to Mrs. DeWitt. "Did you know the new stalls are ready? I suppose Medina will be coming back to the barn soon."

"We're one step ahead of you." Mrs. DeWitt smiled. "While you were gone, Gus stripped the stall and put in new bedding, making it ready for Medina. I walked her over here just a short time ago. She was content in the carriage shed, but she seems pretty happy to be back in her old stall with her favorite neighbors. Actually, I think she'd have no complaints wherever she was, as long as her hay and grain kept coming in a timely manner."

"There's a window in Prince's new stall," Sarah said, frowning. "I hope he won't break the glass and cut himself."

"Not to worry," Mrs. DeWitt said. "Gus covered the inside of the window with a screen this morning. Prince will probably like watching the horses in the turnout paddocks. Gus did a wonderful job getting the new stall ready. He scrubbed his water bucket and filled it with fresh water. Then he put lots of bedding on top of the thick mats. But there's no hay in sight. Gus thought the vet wouldn't want him to have any until his mouth has healed."

"He was right about that," Kayla said. "And once Prince's mouth has healed…." She grinned at Sarah, who knew what she was thinking. Riding him would be next.

"Thanks for reminding me, Kayla." Jack said. His gaze turned to Sarah. "It's time for you to go back to Atlantic Saddlery to be fitted to an all-purpose saddle. Of course you'll also have to get the things that go with it. Stirrup irons and leathers, a saddle pad, and a girth are purchased separately. Be sure to get a big enough girth for a large horse." For a bridle, I recommend one with a flash noseband—and pick out a five-inch, fat snaffle bit.

He paused a moment, looking thoughtful. "We'll soon be finding out how he'll react to it."

"Well, this is a coincidence!" Mrs. DeWitt said, delighted with the news. "I'm planning to make a run to the tack shop right after lunch, and I'd love to have both of you girls come with me."

"Awesome!" Sarah said, feeling excited that the moment was getting closer when she would actually ride her horse.

Kayla frowned. "I have a lesson with Fanny this afternoon, so I've got to get home. In fact, I'd better call my mom right now to see when she's picking me up." She pulled out her phone and walked away to make the call.

Sarah thought a moment before speaking to Mrs. DeWitt. "We'll be going by my house on the way. Would you mind stopping so I can get the gift card?"

"Of course not," Mrs. DeWitt said. "I'll be at the barn at one o'clock to pick you up," she said over her shoulder as she turned to walk back to the farmhouse. She whistled for her Jack Russells, and the three of them disappeared around the side of the barn just as Kayla returned.

"Mom should be here in a few minutes," Kayla said. "She's in a hurry and wants me to be in the parking lot."

Sarah smiled at Kayla. "Thanks for coming. You helped a lot."

"Let's get your horse unloaded and into his new stall," Jack said to Sarah.

Sarah was beginning to feel more comfortable getting Prince on and off a horse trailer. She stepped inside and disconnected the trailer tie after attaching the lead shank to his halter. Once Jack lowered the ramp and unhooked the butt bar, she asked Prince to move backward. He was quieter than usual, and calmly backed down the ramp. This time there was no hesitation as they approached the barn's entryway, and Prince willingly walked inside.

"Your horse seems a little on the lackluster side," Jack said, walking behind them. "Perhaps he'd still be affected by the sedative." Prince's racing plates rang on the cement floor of the aisle, and Jack raised his voice to call out to Sarah, "He needs to have his shoes pulled and his feet trimmed when the farrier is here next week."

As they neared Medina's stall, where up until now Crown Prince had lived, Sarah saw the lovely mare standing close to the bars, watching them with her ears pricked. There was no doubt as to her breeding—everything about her screamed Arab. Her large dark eyes, which contrasted sharply with her almost white coat, were set far apart, and her head tapered to a dainty muzzle. Viewed from the side, she had the concave dished profile typical of Arabians. The mare had beautiful movement when Mrs. DeWitt was riding her—with her tail held high, she seemed to skim over the ground.

Moving with his head lower than usual, Prince didn't notice Medina until she nickered softly in greeting. He came to a sudden stop and turned to look closely at the mare before answering with a throaty neigh. Sarah tried to get him moving past the stall, but he strained against the lead shank, pulling toward Medina, until the two horses touched noses between the bars. Both sniffed the other curiously, their nostrils quivering.

Sarah laughed. "I guess Prince has found a girlfriend." The horses continued to sniff noses until Jack slapped Prince's rump to urge him forward. He reluctantly turned away from Medina and followed Sarah along the aisle and into his new stall. It looked beautiful! The sun's rays coming in the window brightened the new wood on the walls and turned the deep bed of pine shavings golden.

After she removed the shipping boots and left him free in the stall, Prince went immediately to the casement window to look at the horses turned out in the paddocks. Finally turning to the new red feed tub Gus had hung in the corner, Prince found a mash waiting. *Gus is on top of everything,* Sarah thought. *He knew just what the vet would want Prince to be fed.*

Jack must have been thinking the same thing. "Gus usually gets a blue ribbon in the horse care department," he said.

Sarah was removing Prince's halter when she heard Tim Dixon's voice behind her.

"Are we playing musical stalls at Brookmeade Farm?" he asked.

"Hey, Tim," Sarah said, as she slipped out of the stall and slid the door shut. "What do you think of the new stalls?"

"I'd say this one is larger than Medina's. Your big guy should have plenty of room. Do you know if anyone is taking the other new stall across the aisle? It's huge, too."

Jack nodded. "I believe Richard Snyder has reserved the stall for Rita's horse for the next few weeks. With the show season about to heat up, he wants Rita to have a number of private lessons without having to truck the horse over here each time."

"Cool," Tim replied. He looked at Sarah, who wasn't thrilled to hear the news. Having a steady diet of Rita wasn't something she looked forward to.

"Jack, now that I'm going to get a saddle, should I put it on

Prince when I longe him?" Sarah asked.

"The more you can provide experiences much like being ridden but without any pain the better. But I think for the first time he's saddled, 'twill be best if I'm the one who longes him. Your new saddle will be far different and heavier than the postage stamp saddles they use at the track, and we need to be sure it fits him. But we should allow him a little more time, at least 24 hours following the surgery. I'll have some free time late tomorrow morning when we can school him, but make sure you turn him out for a half hour or so before hand."

"I'm glad it's okay for Prince to graze in a paddock," Sarah said.

"Once you get your tack, you should oil the bridle, if you'll be wanting it to last a long time. Hold off on doing anything to the saddle until we try it on your horse. If 'tis not a good fit, you can exchange it for another. I don't see anything out-of-the-ordinary about Crown Prince's conformation that will be problematic in fitting a saddle, so pick out an all-purpose that fits *you*, and then we'll try it on him," Jack instructed.

After Jack left, Sarah and Tim turned to look at Prince in his new stall. He'd finished the mash and was pawing the shavings. As expected, he lowered himself to roll in the bedding, nimbly twisting back and forth on his back. Finally he sprang to his feet and shook like a retriever after a swim.

"How did the tooth pulling go?" Tim asked.

"Great! That huge tooth had normal sized roots, so Dr. Reynolds was able to yank it out. Now I can hardly wait for the hole in his mouth to heal so I can ride him. I just hope he'll be okay with a bit."

"Which reminds me," Tim said, "Rita offered to let me borrow her Dr. Bristol snaffle bit, and she told me she left it with you. That's what I came to pick up."

Sarah's cheeks warmed with embarrassment. "Oh, I'm so sorry! When Rita asked me to give it to you, I put it in my sweatshirt pocket. So it went home with me. I was hurrying this morning and forgot to bring it."

Tim looked disappointed. "I really wanted Jack to see how Rhodes will go with that bit in the lesson this afternoon."

Sarah searched for a solution. "I'm not riding with you guys today, and Mrs. DeWitt is dropping me off at my house on the way back from the tack shop. Can you stop by and pick the bit up before your lesson? Will that work?"

"Yeah, sure," Tim said, agreeably. "Then I guess I'll head out. Can you call me when you're leaving the tack shop?"

"Not a problem," Sarah said, wishing she had thought of the bit earlier.

When she was sure Prince was relaxed in his new stall, Sarah got her lunch from her backpack in the tack room and went outside to the bench in a shady spot. She had just finished eating her turkey sandwich when Mrs. DeWitt pulled into the parking area. Sarah jumped up from the bench and hurried to Mrs. DeWitt's Mercedes. She was disappointed the terriers weren't there, but it was just as well. It was too warm on this summer day to leave them in a vehicle while they were shopping.

Mrs. DeWitt smiled at Sarah when she climbed in beside her. "Are you excited to be getting your own saddle?"

Sarah flashed a broad smile back. "I sure am, because the next step will be riding my horse, just as soon as his mouth has healed."

Mrs. DeWitt put the car into gear, and soon they were moving along the farm road, heading to the beach and Atlantic Saddlery. From regularly riding this way on her bike, Sarah was getting to know every rise, fall, and bump on the road. She waved to Kathleen O'Brien, who was coming out of the bungalow as they passed.

When they turned onto Ridge Road, Mrs. DeWitt became serious. "Sarah, you've had quite a week, bringing Crown Prince back to the farm and then dealing with all the problems that have come up. But I think you've turned the corner. I feel strongly that having the wolf tooth out will make all the difference for Prince. I won't be surprised if he's left all his bad behavior at the racetrack."

Sarah was reassured to hear her say that. "I knew when I first saw Prince that he was a special horse."

"Did you know that Hank Bolton stopped to see Chandler and me before he left Yardley last night? He told us about the surprise visit he paid to your family. We had no idea he was planning to do that. I hope his call wasn't upsetting to you."

"He caught all of us by surprise," Sarah said, "but I knew right away why he was there. Sometime yesterday he put a copy of the letter he'd given me in our mailbox, so my parents had read it before I got home."

"Hank said you were adamant you wouldn't give up Crown Prince for anything in the world. He said you never wavered. I must say, that was one sweet deal you turned down, and it must have taken a lot of courage to do that!"

Sarah was quiet, as the memory of the meeting with Mr. Bolton played back through her mind. It seemed like an eternity ago. She remembered her words and the way she had spoken to him. "I'm afraid I was totally rude. I don't know what came over me," Sarah admitted.

"Hank said he observed something that impressed him a great deal. He told us that your parents backed you up one-hundred percent. Even with the large amount of money involved, they were willing to let you make the final decision. Do you know how fortunate you are to have parents who will stand behind you like that?"

"Oh, I do," Sarah said. "I tried to tell them last night. There have been times when I've felt sorry for myself, thinking that I'd never have a horse of my own. Now I think I'm the luckiest girl in the world."

"There's more than luck involved. You've always worked hard in your lessons here, and you've developed into a talented rider."

The car turned into the Wagners' driveway, and Sarah ran into her house, quiet with the other family members all working. She quickly grabbed her wallet and returned to the car. In a few minutes they were in the Atlantic Saddlery parking lot, which wasn't crowded as it had been on Sarah's last visit. "Now let's find you a saddle," Mrs. DeWitt said, patting Sarah on the knee.

With only a handful of customers in the shop, a salesperson greeted them as soon as they came through the door. In no time Sarah was trying out saddles perched on the back of the wooden horse, with both the salesperson and Mrs. DeWitt checking the saddles for fit. It helped that Sarah knew the size of the saddle she used for her lessons at Brookmeade. She finally decided on a Crosby saddle that could be used for both dressage and jumping. It appeared to be a very good fit, but Sarah gulped when she saw the price tag. She had no idea if there was enough money on her gift card for a bridle and the other things she'd need to go with the saddle. The salesperson volunteered to keep the saddle at the checkout until they finished shopping.

After finding the things she would need to go with the saddle, they looked at bridles. Both Sarah and Mrs. DeWitt loved a beautiful German-made bridle with a flash noseband and laced reins. Prince would look so handsome in it! After looking at the many bits on the rack, she chose a fat eggbutt snaffle to go with the bridle. It was gleaming stainless steel and the size Jack had suggested. Mrs. DeWitt applauded her choice. "Classy!" she said. Sarah next found some longeing equipment. *I'm glad I won't have to borrow Jack's anymore*, she thought.

She turned to Mrs. DeWitt. "Don't you have some things to pick up?"

"I just need hoof dressing and fly spray," Mrs. DeWitt replied, "and it won't take long to find them. But what about something for oiling your new tack?" Sarah followed her down another aisle to look at the leather care products. She scooped up a container of neatsfoot oil and some saddle soap.

This shopping trip was far different from the visit on the tack shop's opening day. There was no line at the checkout, and soon they were paying for their purchases. Sarah was relieved when there was enough money left on her card to cover everything. When it was time to put their purchases in Mrs. DeWitt's car, everything fit in the back except the longe whip, which extended all the way forward between the seats to the dashboard.

As they were leaving, Sarah remembered her promise to Tim. "Mrs. DeWitt, would you mind dropping me off at my house? I want to oil my new bridle, and I have a bit at home that Rita is going to loan Tim. He needs it for the lesson this afternoon."

Mrs. DeWitt nodded. "Certainly, dear. I'd offer to deliver it to Tim myself, but I have another appointment after I drop you off." Sarah pulled her phone from her pocket to call Tim.

Once back home, she prepared to oil her new bridle and saddle accessories. Having to clean her tack after her lessons at Brookmeade had been good practice. She covered the kitchen table with layers of old newspapers and found a soft cloth in a bag of rags in the basement for applying the neatsfoot oil. She had just started taking the stiff new bridle apart when she saw Tim's black Jeep pull into the driveway. She picked up Rita's bit and went to the back door.

"I'm sorry you had to make this special trip," she said, as Tim stepped into the mudroom.

In addition to the Dr. Bristol bit, he saw the reins in her other hand. "Did you get everything you need at Atlantic Saddlery?"

"Come take a look." Sarah beckoned him into the kitchen, where her saddle sat on the back of a kitchen chair. "I'm not going to oil it until we're sure it's a good fit for Prince."

Tim walked over to get a closer look. He picked up the saddle, squeezed the cantle, and ran his hand over the seat. "It's not as heavy as some all-purpose saddles, and the leather is really nice." He grinned. "You're getting closer to sitting on that horse."

"Not soon enough for me. If Prince was really a wild bucking bronco once, those days are over now!"

Tim turned to leave. "I'd better get back to the barn to get Rhodes ready for the lesson," Tim said, heading for the back door. "See ya!"

"I hope Rhodes likes the bit," Sarah said, as Tim walked down the porch steps.

Later that afternoon, after she had finished oiling all the pieces of her new bridle and the saddle accessories, Sarah stepped back to look at the leather pieces that covered the kitchen table. Each piece was shiny and much softer. Along with her stirrup irons, stirrup leathers, and girth, the gleaming stainless steel bit lay on the table, waiting to be attached to the new bridle. She was going over the leather pieces with a clean cloth to remove any excess oil when her cell phone rang. She wiped her hands quickly before answering the phone. It was Kayla.

"Hey, what's up," Kayla said. "I thought you might be around after the lesson. I was bummed you weren't there. I'm dying to hear about your new saddle."

"A Crosby all-purpose. I just hope it fits Prince. It can be so tricky to fit a horse correctly. I oiled my new bridle, girth, and leathers. You should see the pieces of the bridle spread all over our kitchen table. I'm glad Mom is at work!"

Sarah pulled over a chair and got comfortable. Her phone conversations with Kayla were rarely short.

"Tell me about the lesson. How did Fanny go?"

"She was super, especially over fences. Jack says I need to work on keeping my hands steady to have better contact with her mouth. But I'm feeling good about the show on Sunday." After Kayla commented on how the other horses and riders had performed that day, she changed the subject. "Did you know Rita was moving Chancellor to Brookmeade this afternoon?"

"Jack told me."

"She didn't waste any time," Kayla said. "Chancellor came in practically the minute the new stalls were finished."

"He's right across the aisle from Prince, right?"

"Yeah," Kayla said. "Rita brought all her things over in her van's dressing room, and Judson unloaded them in the boarders' tack room while she was riding. After the lesson, Mom walked Fanny a few minutes so I could check out the new stalls. I peeked into the tack room. You should see how much stuff Rita brought with her! She has tack trunks and boxes stacked up all over the place, along with three saddles and four bridles."

Why does she need all that?" Sarah asked. "I heard she's going to be at Brookmeade for just a couple weeks until her show season starts. Give me a break!"

"Well, knowing Rita, she'll have a different saddle for jumping, dressage, and hacking. She probably has a bridle for every bit in her arsenal, so she doesn't have to bother to change them. And she has Judson to take care of her tack. I'll bet she doesn't know how to clean and oil a bridle. I don't know what's in her tack boxes, but believe me, there's not much space left in that tack room for you!"

Sarah pondered this a moment. "So she's going to have regular private lessons with Jack. You can imagine what that will cost. It must be nice," she said in a lilting tone.

"Rita did something totally weird," Kayla said. "When Tim was a little late coming to the indoor with Rhodes, Rita commented that she'd seen Tim's car at your house, so maybe he'd miss the lesson. She pretended to say it just to me, but her voice was loud enough for Paige to hear. I think Rita is trying to make trouble between Paige and Tim."

"Are you sure Paige heard her?" Sarah asked.

"I saw Paige's head jerk our way after Rita said it."

"Great," Sarah said sarcastically. "I just hope Paige didn't take the bait. Tim stopped here to pick up the bit that Rita is loaning him. That's all. I brought it home by mistake. Tim only stayed long enough to check out my new saddle and get the bit, but Rita must have driven by our house on the way to Brookmeade and seen his car in our driveway."

"Exactly," Kayla said. "I think she's hoping she can make Paige jealous, worried that Tim is interested in you."

"This is so like Rita, and so ridiculous." Sarah said. Just then she heard a car coming into the driveway, and turning, saw her mother's SUV pass the window. "Gotta go," she said to Kayla. "I wanted to clean up the mess before Mom gets home. She's not going to be thrilled when she sees tack strewn all over the kitchen!"

Sarah quickly began collecting the various parts of the bridle, although she knew she'd never have it put together in time! Already she could hear her mother entering the mudroom through the back door. Mrs. Wagner noticed the strong smell of new leather and neatsfoot oil when she came into the house. "Sarah, honey," she called out, as she used her cane to make her way through the mudroom. "You must be home."

Sarah gulped. "I'm here, Mom. I've just finished oiling my new tack."

Her mother's gaze hit upon the table when she entered the kitchen, and her eyes widened. Sarah knew the look. "I'll have everything out of here in a few minutes. I promise, Mom."

Sarah was relieved when her mother said nothing before leaving the kitchen to go directly upstairs. Sarah hurriedly began putting the pieces of the bridle together, making sure the bit was attached correctly. When the bridle was assembled, she hung it on the chair with the saddle. She quickly gathered all the newspaper to put into the trash, and after a final hand washing, wiped down the kitchen table.

Now she could hardly wait for her father and Abby to arrive home! When the Seaside Creamery contingent walked through the door fifteen minutes later, the family gathered to admire her new tack. "This must have cost a good piece of change," her father remarked. "Did it finish off your gift card?"

"Almost," Sarah replied. "But now I could use some help getting the saddle to Brookmeade. I also need to pick up my bike. Mrs. DeWitt dropped me off here this afternoon, so my bike is still at the farm."

"Sure," her father said. "I think that could be arranged. But after dinner."

Mr. Wagner started toward the den, but stopped and turned back to Sarah. "Now that you have a saddle, I expect it won't be long before you'll want to ride that horse, providing his mouth has healed. I know that Jack plans to get on him first, and your mother and I would like to be there when he does. Remember, we're concerned for your safety. Crown Prince has got to prove himself."

Sarah shook her head. Here it was again, the question of whether or not Prince was hers for good. She was reminded that he would be on trial for at least three more weeks.

Her father wore a serious, I-mean-business look. "Ask Jack to schedule his first ride on Prince so we can be there. I'm sure he'll understand."

What if Prince acts up when Jack rides him? she thought. *What then?*

CHAPTER 16

The Conflict

THE STRING OF SUNNY DAYS continued, and it was already quite warm when Sarah arrived at the barn the next morning. She parked her bike near the side door and hurried down the aisle. From his new stall at the back of the barn, Prince was, as usual, watching for her through the bars, but across the aisle Chancellor was restlessly moving around in his stall. *It looks like he hasn't settled in*, Sarah thought.

As she neared Prince's stall, Sarah noticed a cardboard box in front of the door. Rita must have been true to her word and donated some of her castaways. Sarah couldn't resist checking out the contents. There was quite an assortment of partly or nearly used up bottles and cans of everything from hoof dressing to liniment. She liked the hoof pick with a brush attached and the black crop, but wasn't thrilled with the other things in the box. A plastic mane comb with two teeth missing, a worn cribbing strap, and a pair of tired-looking polo wraps rounded out the collection. Sarah didn't know whether to be grateful or insulted. *What makes her think Prince needs a cribbing strap?* she thought.... She nudged the box to the side and turned her attention to her horse.

Prince immediately shoved his muzzle against her when she entered his stall, asking for the carrot he'd come to expect. Instead she offered him a few peeled sections of Macintosh apple she'd brought in a plastic baggie—they would be softer to chew. As he chomped on pieces of apple, the juice running from his lips, Sarah watched Chancellor pacing in his stall. She noticed how different the Dutch Warmblood and her Thoroughbred were. They were both large horses, but there the similarity ended. Prince was more streamlined, built for speed, with a more refined head and longer back. Chancellor was heavier, more muscular. He had far more bone, larger feet, and massive hindquarters that could push him over tall fences.

Chancellor continued to move nervously about his stall, frequently pausing to change direction. Sarah left her horse and approached the black Warmblood. She could offer him some of the pieces of apple, and perhaps a little treat from a human friend would help him relax. Slowly she pulled his stall door open wide enough to squeeze through. Chancellor whirled and looked at her with his ears pinned, the white ring surrounding his left eye showing prominently. Sarah stood still, speaking softly. She held out a few apple sections to him, but the horse showed no interest.

Suddenly Gus appeared outside the stall, glaring in at her. "Get out of there," he growled. "You've got no business going into another boarder's stall without an invite. And we've got hungry horses waiting to be fed!" With that he turned and strode off.

224

Sarah hung her head. For wanting to help a nervous horse, she'd gotten into trouble with Gus. But he was right. She wouldn't want anyone going into Prince's stall without her permission. She immediately left Chancellor, being careful to securely fasten the stall latch, and headed for the grain room. There were nickers and soft neighs from the horses along the way who anticipated what was coming next.

She went about the morning feed drill, loving the smells of the barn and the horsey greetings. The air from the loft was still fragrant with the aroma of new hay. After tossing two flakes of the seasoned hay down to every horse except Prince, Sarah started down the stairway from the loft on her way to prepare his bran mash. Paige Vargas was walking up the aisle and spotted her.

"Oh, there you are," Paige said. "Jack wants to see you in the office, if you have a minute."

Sarah hesitated before answering, wondering again how Paige had interpreted Rita's remark of the day before, one obviously designed to raise doubts in her mind about Tim. The comment was straight from Rita's imagination, but did Paige realize that? Paige was a total knockout! No way could Tim have a wandering eye and want to dump her. But commenting on Tim's whereabouts was Rita's attempt to start trouble. Sarah decided to try to put out the fire, if there was one.

She waited for Paige at the foot of the stairs. "Thanks, Paige. I'll head down there now. And by the way, how did Rhodes go yesterday with the bit Rita lent Tim? He came to pick it up at my house yesterday." There. She'd offered her explanation, and hopefully it would seem innocent enough. She met Paige's gaze squarely.

Paige eyed her back for a moment, and then smiled. She'd read Sarah's between-the-lines message. "Rhodes actually went pretty well," she said. "All the horses did. Yesterday's lesson was a good school for show jumping, and Jack said we may do some cross-country obstacles next week."

"Awesome," Sarah said, giving Paige a thumbs-up. "I hope I'll be here to watch."

"By the way, Sarah, I'm going to ride Quarry early if you want to turn Prince out in the small paddock for a while."

"That will be perfect. Thanks." Walking away, Sarah breathed a sigh of relief. She was pretty sure Paige wasn't upset with her. Sarah imagined how nice it must be to have good looks and a sense of humor—and be a thoughtful and considerate person to boot. No wonder Rita was jealous of Paige.

In the office, Jack, Kathleen, and Lindsay were going over a lesson scheduling sheet. Jack looked up when Sarah walked in. "Mrs. DeWitt tells me you've got yourself a saddle and bridle," he said. "But before you go riding to the hounds, we need Dr. Reynolds's blessing, and he comes on Saturday." Sarah nodded, feeling excited, just thinking about riding Crown Prince.

"In the meantime, we need to be sure the saddle you got fits your horse," Jack continued. "If all's well, you can begin to longe him under saddle, starting today. But we should try it on him for size. You need to be sure there's enough clearance for his withers and that it's broad enough for his back and shoulders."

"My dad and I brought it over last night. Paige is getting ready to ride Quarry, so I thought I'd turn Prince out before I longe him. I also need to rinse his mouth out like Dr. Jenson showed me."

Jack nodded approval. "I'm going to school French Twist in a few minutes, and at ten I'm giving Rita a lesson. We should have time to try the saddle on Prince in between."

Sarah was glad she and her father had brought the saddle to the barn the night before. They had found the tack room an unbelievable mess. The amount of stuff Rita had crammed in there was unbelievable! Her many boxes and tack trunks were strewn around the room, and her three saddles had been placed on any available saddle rack. The other boarders used the racks over their trunks for their own saddles, and Sarah had planned to do the same. But when Rita came to town, she'd put one of her saddles on the rack directly over Sarah's trunk! When her father stepped into the room, Sarah could just imagine what he was thinking.

"Rita Snyder moved her horse in here this afternoon, and this is all her stuff," Sarah had said. She placed her saddle on top of her tack trunk, a tight squeeze. All the bridle brackets on the wall were also taken, so Sarah nested hers with her saddle.

When Sarah returned to Prince's stall, she attached him to his stall tie and squirted some of the saline solution into the side of his mouth where the wolf tooth had been. He wasn't crazy about the salty water and tossed his head, trying to rid his mouth of it. "That will help you heal, Prince," she said. She put on his shank and led him to the small paddock. He was happy to be outside, and cantered once around the paddock before stopping to lower himself to the ground. He rolled over on his back, his legs flailing as he twisted against the soft earth. Jumping to his feet, he ran for a few more minutes before burying his nose in the green grass.

This gave her a chance to clean his stall. Back in the barn, Sarah grabbed a manure fork and backed a wheelbarrow up to the stall. While she was working, she heard Rita's Mustang pull up by the side door. A few minutes later Rita burst into the barn, carrying still another plastic box of horse equipment and a longe whip.

"I forgot my longeing equipment yesterday," she explained to Sarah, who stared in disbelief. "You know, they need to build a bigger tack room here. I couldn't find space for all my things. I'm going to talk to Jack about it. And Chancellor is used to straw bedding, not these cheap shavings." Sarah decided not to comment. With Rita's horse right across the aisle, the last thing she wanted was an argument with her.

"Thanks for the horse stuff," Sarah said. "I can use the hoof pick."

"Cool," Rita said as she headed to the tack room. A few minutes later she returned with an overflowing grooming caddy. *How many different brushes does she need to groom one horse?* Sarah thought. Rita clipped a lead shank on Chancellor's halter and put him on cross-ties in the aisle.

Just then they heard Jack's Irish brogue. "Sarah, have you got your saddle?" he called, as he strode up the aisle toward them.

"Yes, I'll get it," she answered. She pushed the wheelbarrow to a corner where it would be out of the way and hurried to the tack room. When she stepped inside, she noticed that Rita's things were scattered around the room even worse than before. It wasn't easy for Sarah to pick her way through the clutter to get her saddle, but she retrieved it and brought it to the collapsible saddle rack in front of Prince's stall.

"I'm going to bring Prince in from the paddock," she called to Jack.

As she was walking away, Sarah heard Rita say to Jack, "I'm having a tough time finding space for my things in the tack room. Is there any chance Gus could put up some extra saddle racks? I could also use some shelves on the side wall near my trunk." Sarah couldn't resist turning to watch what was coming next. She wasn't surprised to see Jack walking toward the tack room, no doubt to assess the situation, with Rita following behind.

Sarah sprinted to the paddock. She didn't want to keep Jack waiting. When she returned with Prince and put him on crossties further up the aisle from Chancellor, Jack and Rita were just emerging from the tack room. Rita was scowling and Jack looked grim. His words were clipped and had an authoritative ring when he spoke to Rita.

"And now that you've organized your equipment properly, you'll be moving your car to the parking lot, now won't you?"

Rita's scowl became even more embedded and her thin lips were pursed as she walked out of the barn. "Watch my horse!" she demanded over her shoulder. A few minutes later they heard the convertible's motor start up and then grow fainter as Rita it drove away. When she returned a few minutes later, she went back to grooming Chancellor, but not before looking daggers at Sarah.

Jack came over to see Sarah's new saddle. "'Tis a beauty," he said, "and should be just what you need. Mrs. DeWitt steered you in the right direction. Now let's see if it fits Crown Prince."

While Sarah stood at his head, Jack removed the pad and girth from the saddle. "We need to see how it really fits, without the pad hiding any problem areas." He gently lifted the saddle onto Prince's back, looking to see if there was adequate clearance over the withers and if the saddle was wide enough for the horse's shoulders. He ran his hand between the saddle and the horse's back to check for any bumps, lumps, or tightness that could cause problems for Crown Prince over time. Prince stiffened and looked around nervously when he felt the saddle's weight on his back. Sarah stroked his head to reassure him.

Jack stepped back to look at the handsome horse with his new saddle. "You're in luck, Sarah," Jack said. "'Tis a good fit, and I notice that the lowest point of the seat is right in the center. You'll be in good balance with this saddle."

"Mrs. DeWitt and the sales woman at the tack shop talked about that," Sarah said.

"I'll show you how to secure the stirrup irons when you're longeing, so they don't come down and start clanging against his sides when he's moving. Do you want to longe him now?"

"Sure," Sarah said, and together they resaddled the horse, adding the saddle pad, girth, and stirrups. Prince moved sideways and tossed his head when Sarah tightened the girth. "Go easy with that," Jack said. "Better to tighten it just enough to keep it in place now, and then again later on. Just before you start longeing, you should check the girth once more to be sure the saddle hasn't loosened. Some horses blow themselves up when being girthed, but the walk to the ring should bring him down. Then longe him as you've been doing."

"Got it," Sarah said. "I bought a longeing cavesson, longe line, and whip, too, so I don't need to borrow yours."

Jack nodded his approval and turned to go, walking past Rita while she groomed Chancellor. Again his words were terse. "I'll meet you in the indoor on schedule. You'll have a few minutes to warm up." Jack noticed the mats where Rita had picked out her horse's feet. "You'll not be forgetting that boarders are supposed to sweep up after their horses," he said. Rita didn't reply, but her eyes narrowed and her mouth twisted into a grimace as she continued brushing her horse.

Sarah left Crown Prince on cross-ties and went back to the tack room to get her lunging equipment. She noticed that Rita's things had all been placed neatly in the far end. The two saddles she wasn't using were stacked on one saddle rack, and there were two bridles squeezed onto the bridle bracket below it. All of Rita's plastic and cardboard boxes had been neatly placed near her large green tack trunk with the Pyramid Farm logo. Sarah saw that the saddle rack and bridle bracket over her own trunk were now vacant.

Ouch! she thought. *This probably didn't go down well. No wonder Rita is steaming.* As she walked back to Prince's stall with her cavesson, longe line, and whip, Sarah saw that Rita had finished tacking up Chancellor and was standing with him near Prince's stall, obviously waiting for her. When Sarah was just a few feet away, Rita let her have it. Rita's face was twisted in anger.

"Who do you think you are?" she hissed. "You act like you own this place! Just because you got a new saddle, you have to go complaining to Jack about where I put my things in the tack room. My father is paying a ton of money for my board and lessons here, and you don't pay anything!"

Sarah stared at Rita, completely taken off guard by her sudden outburst. "I don't know what you're talking...." she began, but Rita cut her off.

"That horse of yours is nothing but a racetrack reject. I don't know what you saw in him, and I don't care. He can't begin to compare to Chancellor! My dad bought him for ten times what yours will ever be worth. You think you're Jack's pet. Well, just stay out of my way!" With that Rita jerked Chancellor's reins and spun him around to follow her as she stomped down the aisle toward the indoor.

Sarah watched her go, a slow burn mounting. *What a spoiled brat! No one can tell her anything. She always has to have her own way.* Sarah set down the longeing equipment in front of Prince's door and grabbed her cell phone from her pocket, quickly punching in Kayla's number. Kayla didn't immediately pick up. *With the show only two days away, she might be riding Fanny,* Sarah thought. But on the third ring, Kayla answered.

"You'll never guess what happened!" Sarah said. "Jack made Rita pick up the tack room, and after he left, she flipped out, accusing me of complaining to Jack about her." Sarah stopped to catch her breath. "You know what the problem is, Kayla? Rita gets as many horses as she wants, but she can't stand for me to have just one."

"Slow down," Kayla said. "Did this just happen? Tell me everything!"

Sarah filled her in on the rest of Rita's hissy fit. "And I bet the final straw was when Jack told her she had to sweep the aisle after she finished grooming Chancellor."

"Sarah, listen," Kayla said. "We both know Rita is used to having her own way. She doesn't hesitate to order people around, but she can't take it when it's reversed. She hates to hear any compliments about anyone else's horse. She knows you've got an awesome horse and is just plain jealous. What did you say to her?"

"She didn't let me get a word in edgewise before she took off with Chancellor for her lesson with Jack. You know, Kayla, I can't deal with this right now. Making sure I can keep Prince gives me enough to think about. I wish Rita and her wonder horse would just go away!"

"Look, Sarah, I wouldn't let her off that easy. I'd give her a piece of my mind! But I need to get back to Fanny, so I gotta go. I'll call you later."

Sarah slowly put her phone away. So many things were whirling around in her head. She went up to Crown Prince and hugged his neck until she felt calm return. *I'm not going to let Rita spoil my day! I've got to think about Prince right now. This will be the first time he's been longed under saddle.*

A few minutes later she put the longeing cavesson on Prince and walked him to the outside ring. She watched for signs of nervousness, but Prince walked calmly, more interested in what was going on around the farm than the saddle on his back. Once in the ring, she checked the girth and tightened it a hole.

Sarah eased herself away from her horse, the whip pointed at his hip. When asked, Prince began walking around her, his ears flicking back and forth in her direction, listening for her voice. He tossed his head occasionally in annoyance at some black flies buzzing around him, but when asked to trot, he broke into the gait smartly. He had already learned what was expected and seemed to enjoy his work. She loved the picture he made! With the saddle on his back, Sarah had an urge to run to her horse, leap onto his back, and ride off with the wind! She longed to feel his powerful muscles carrying her forward, and to become one with this majestic horse. Together, they would leave all their problems behind.

CHAPTER 17
The Tragedy

SARAH LOOKED AT HER WATCH. Dr. Reynolds was late—forty minutes late. She had done most of her chores early to be ready for the nine o'clock vet appointment, and now she was waiting on the bench outside the barn where she'd have a good view of the entry road. Earlier she'd turned Prince out while she cleaned his stall and got started on her regular chores. Then she cleaned his mouth with the saline solution and gave him a thorough grooming. It wasn't necessary, but she wanted him to look his best for the vet.

Sarah turned as Paige stepped out the side door. "Hi, Paige. How was your ride this morning?"

"Okay. Tim and I did a little dressage school and then went for a hack. Our horses are getting pretty fit, and Quarry was a handful. He was trying to take off with me in the lower meadow. I had to use the pulley rein—like you!" She sat down on the bench with Sarah. "Are you waiting for Dr. Reynolds?"

"Yeah, he's late, but I guess that's not unusual for a vet. He'll be here sooner or later." Sarah put her arm to her forehead, shielding the sun, as Tim came out of the barn to join Paige. "Your Fair Pines event is pretty soon," Sarah said. "You guys must be psyched."

"I just hope Rhodes and I do a better test than we did last time," Tim said. "You can't expect to be in the ribbons if you don't start out with a good dressage score. You should have seen Quarry this morning. He's probably fit enough to do three cross-country runs the same day!" His eyes were drawn to the farm road by the white-capped pickup that was approaching. "I think this might be your vet," he said.

Sarah turned to look. As the truck got closer, she saw that Dr. Jenson was with Dr. Reynolds. She knew the plan at Brookmeade was for them to take a look at Crown Prince first, since it wouldn't take long to check his mouth. Afterward they were going to see Nicole's horse, Jubilee, who was lame in the right foreleg. The leg had remained swollen even after Nicole followed Jack's advice—for the last few days she'd been letting cold water from a hose run down her mare's leg several times a day, but the swelling had diminished only a little, and Jubilee's leg was still warm to the touch.

Sarah went back to Prince's stall to put on his halter and lead shank. A short time later the two veterinarians and Jack arrived at the stall. Prince must have associated them with the vet hospital, because he eyed them warily when they came into the stall. She had to hold him tightly when he tried to move away.

"How's our guy been doing without hay?" Dr. Jensen asked Sarah. "I hope he didn't call his lawyer."

Sarah smiled. "He wasn't exactly happy, but he's been getting yummy mashes and eating grass in the paddock."

Dr. Jensen sized up the handsome, well-filled-out horse. "He certainly doesn't look underfed," she quipped.

"We don't need the speculum on him to check his gum," Dr. Reynolds said, removing a flashlight from his pocket. After Dr. Jenson forced Prince's mouth open, Dr. Reynolds adjusted his glasses and focused the flashlight inside where the wolf tooth had been. He peered into the dark cavity and then gingerly ran a gloved finger over the horse's gum. Sarah was relieved when Prince didn't flinch at his touch, and she was even happier with what Dr. Reynolds had to say.

"The area has completely closed in where the wolf tooth's roots were, not surprising, when you consider they were of normal size to begin with," Dr. Reynolds said. He stepped back from the horse as he put the flashlight back into his pocket. "I'm going to give him a clean bill of health," he paused to wink at Sarah, "and a license to eat all the hay you want to feed him."

"What about bridling?" Jack asked.

The veterinarian didn't hesitate. "There's no reason why he can't have a bit in his mouth, as long as it isn't severe."

"You hear that, Prince?" Dr. Jenson said, giving the horse a pat. "You're back in the hay business and ready to run in the Derby!"

Sarah was relieved, but at the same time a worry gnawed at her. Prince's tryout under saddle and bridle would take place sooner rather than later, and her parents would be right there watching every move he made!

When the veterinarians and Jack left, Sarah stayed behind with her horse. The skin around his eyes wrinkled as she talked softly to him. "You're not a bad horse, and together we'll show them you're a great horse, even if you never set foot on a race-track again."

Stepping back, she took her cell out of her pocket and dialed Kayla, who picked up on the second ring. "Hey, what's happening?" Sarah asked.

"I'm getting Fanny ready for the show. I just gave her a bath, and her white stockings look like Mr. Clean was here. Now if they'll stay that way until tomorrow," Kayla said. "Clipping her whiskers and bridle path is next. What about you? Has Dr. Reynolds been to your barn yet?"

"That's why I'm calling," Sarah said. "He said Prince can be ridden anytime! Did I tell you that my parents are insisting they be here when Jack gets on him the first time?"

"Are you serious? It sounds like they're expecting the worst."

"They want to be sure he's not crazy. The stories his trainer told my father made Prince seem like a lunatic. I don't believe he'll act that way with me, and I'll be so glad when he's no longer on probation. I'm going to see what time is convenient for Jack. I want to get this over with."

"Chill out! And let me know when Jack's going to ride him. I don't want to miss it."

Sarah immediately went to the loft and tossed down some hay for her horse. Standing over the opening, she saw him dive into it as if he hadn't eaten in a week.

Now to find Jack. He might still be with the veterinarians checking out Jubilee. On her way to Jubilee's stall, Sarah saw that Dr. Reynolds's truck was gone from the parking lot. She wanted to ask Nicole what the vets had said about Jubilee. As she got closer, she saw Nicole come out of her horse's stall, but Nicole didn't look particularly pleased to see her, so Sarah changed her mind and turned toward the office. She was curious about Jubilee's leg, but she'd have to find out about that later. *I wish those girls would knock off giving me a hard time,* she thought.

Lindsay was talking to a noisy group of young riders in the office about the horses they would ride that day, but there was no sign of Jack. Sarah stepped outside just as Mrs. DeWitt and Grace came up the steps. They were both dressed in jodhpurs and paddock boots, obviously planning to ride, and Taco and Spin were right at their heels.

"Hi, Sarah. Has Dr. Reynolds seen your horse yet?" Mrs. DeWitt asked.

"He sure has." She gave both dogs a quick pat. "He said Prince's gum has healed so he can have hay again." She paused. "And he can have a bit in his mouth now."

"That's great news! This is what you've been waiting for. So when's the big day? When will Jack ride him?" Just hearing Mrs. DeWitt say those words sent a shiver up her spine. It wouldn't be long now.

"Actually I'm looking for Jack to ask him that question. Have you seen him?"

"Call him. Unless he's on a horse, you should be able to reach him on his cell."

Sarah smiled at Grace, who held up her riding helmet for Sarah to see. "Grandma's taking me on a trail ride."

"I'll bet Pretty Penny will love that!" Sarah said. She waved as they started off to groom and tack up.

Sarah dialed Jack's cell, and he answered right away. "I'm

at the carriage shed working with the foals," he said. "And how may I be helping you?"

"My parents want to be here to watch when you ride Prince for the first time. Do you have any idea when that might be?"

"Hmmm, let me think," he said. "'Tis soon we want to get started." He paused to consider his schedule for the day. "I'm tied up this afternoon. How about in an hour?"

Sarah clutched her cell tighter. "So soon! Actually I think that might work, since it's my dad's day off. I'll let you know if they can't make it," she said.

"I'll meet you at Prince's stall," Jack said. "I want to check the bridle, in case it needs adjusting. The side pieces need to be short enough to keep the bit stabilized in his mouth, and the flash noseband needs to be tight enough. Please have it ready, but don't try putting it on before I get there."

Her next call was home. "In an hour?" her mother said. "You're lucky we're both here now. Your father is mowing the grass, but I'm pretty sure we can be there in time. I'll let you know if there's a problem."

Sarah stood still, clutching her phone. It was all coming together! In an hour, her future with—or without—Crown Prince would be decided. She had to let Kayla know. And in the meantime, she still had sweeping to do.

When she'd finished her chores, Sarah saw it was almost time for Jack to arrive. They were ready for him. From his earlier grooming, Prince's dark coat shone like a mirror, and her tack was neatly arranged in front of the stall. Prince seemed to know that something was up, and he moved about uneasily. She combed his mane, trying to make it lie neatly on his off side, but a few minutes later he shook his head, sending it flying in different directions. *He can probably pick up nervous vibes from me,* she thought. *I've got to chill out.*

Chancellor was eating hay in his stall across from them, finally relaxed in his new place. Sarah and the other boarders were relieved that Rita had taken several boxes of her things and one saddle home. Kelly Hoffman was one of the few who seemed to enjoy Rita's company, and they'd been spending a lot of time together. Kelly rode her horse, Midnight Jet, on the trails with Rita after Rita's private lessons.

Most of the boarders had ridden that morning, and the barn was quiet enough for Sarah to hear Jack's boots on the cement as he approached. "'Tis the day we've been waiting for," he said in his most cheerful voice. "Your horse is going to pass this test with flying colors."

Sarah suspected he was trying to calm her fears. She swallowed hard. "So much depends on this," she said. "I'm glad you're the one getting on him."

"Let's get him tacked up," Jack said. "You hold his head while I put the saddle on. The bridle will come last."

With the saddle in place, Jack picked up the bridle and looked at it carefully. "I think your bit is stout enough not to irritate his gum, but these side pieces on the bridle might need to come up a notch. It's important they're short enough to stabilize the bit, so it moves around in his mouth as little as possible. We'll be able to tell once 'tis on." Jack put the reins over Prince's head and removed his halter. It only took him a few seconds to deftly insert the bit in the horse's mouth and pull the bridle over his ears.

Prince reacted by throwing his head up and violently

pulling backward. He began to nervously chomp on the bit and toss his head. Jack held onto the reins loosely, not trying to bring the horse's head down. "I'm giving him a chance to find out for himself that things are different now. He's got to learn that a bit won't cause him pain anymore."

Jack and Sarah watched the horse, who continued to nervously toss his head. "Once he's settled down, I'll adjust the side pieces if need be," Jack said, "and tighten the noseband just enough to keep his mouth closed. We don't want him opening his mouth to evade the action of the bit."

They stood in the stall for several more minutes, letting Prince chomp on the bit and occasionally shake his head. The bridle appeared to be a good fit, and after Jack buckled the noseband, he took the reins, preparing to leave the stall. "I saw your folks waiting on the hillside above the ring with Mr. DeWitt. Don't worry. I think they're going to like what they see."

With Jack leading Prince, they made their way out of the barn and along the roadway to the outdoor ring. Sarah gulped when she glanced at the slope in back of the ring. She hadn't expected this much of an audience! Kayla was sitting on the grass with her mother, Abby, Paige, and Tim. Sarah's parents and Mr. DeWitt were in lawn chairs near them. A number of boarders Sarah didn't know sat with Kathleen and Lindsay, and Kelly and Nicole were under the large oak tree. She noticed that even Gus was leaning against a tree on the other side of the road, waiting to see what would happen. There was no sign of Mrs. DeWitt or Grace, which meant they were still on their trail ride, and as usual, the Jack Russells had gone with them.

Prince continued to sporadically chomp on the bit, but not as often, as his attention was drawn to the spectators. *They're probably wondering if this will be a rodeo,* Sarah thought. *I can think of a couple who are probably hoping it will.*

When they reached the ring, Jack led Prince inside, and Sarah closed the gate behind them. Jack seemed calm and composed, entirely focused on the horse beside him, and after his regular longeing sessions in that ring, Prince also seemed relaxed. Sarah didn't notice Kayla walking casually down the hill to join her next to the rail.

Hey, kid," Kayla said, appearing beside her, "what do you think?"

"I'm freaking out, Kayla. If he does one bad thing, it will be all over."

"Jack will do a good job. You must know that. Be glad that Rita isn't here. Paige said she went out to pick up some lunch. It didn't take long for the word to get out, though. It looks like everybody in the barn knew Jack was going to ride Prince, so maybe Rita purposely skipped out. She doesn't like to see Chancellor sharing the spotlight with any other horse."

"You've got that one right," Sarah said.

Jack led Prince around the ring once in each direction and then approached the mounting block, something he reserved for very large horses. Sarah leaned against the rail and found herself gripping it tightly. The time had come. Soon they'd know if Prince's bad behavior of the past was behind him.

Before stepping up on the block, Jack halted Prince and lifted the saddle flap to tighten the girth. He pulled the stirrup irons down, checked their adjustment, and prepared to mount. When Jack gracefully swung his leg over the horse and sat lightly in the saddle, Prince immediately walked forward. He was still somewhat preoccupied with the audience above the ring, but he chewed the bit occasionally as Jack gradually took up more contact with the reins.

Sarah felt like clapping her hands! There hadn't been the explosion she'd feared, but she knew the test was far from over. Jack's legs were firmly against the horse's sides, asking him to move forward into a slightly resisting rein that controlled where he went and how fast he traveled. When they reached one end of the rectangular ring, Jack asked Prince to circle before continuing along the rail. Later he changed direction across the diagonal, and Prince continued to march forward, sometimes chewing nervously on the bit, but for the most part seeming to accept it.

When they reached the other end of the ring, Jack sat deep on his seat bones, closed his legs, and with a gentle but firm hand asked the horse to halt. Sarah held her breath. She knew this would apply more pressure on Prince's mouth. His head came up, as if he anticipated pain, but he halted when asked. Jack stroked his neck and praised him. They walked forward and repeated the exercise several more times, until finally Prince not only refrained from throwing his head up, but even brought his nose down slightly.

Sarah knew the real test would come at a faster gait. When Prince was moving willingly forward at walk, Jack closed his legs and used the voice command "Trot." *He's building on what we've been doing on the longe line,* she realized. *Prince knows the word.* Sure enough, Prince broke into a trot, and although he continued to chew the bit and toss his head occasionally, he showed no discomfort or real inclination to be unruly. Those watching could tell he was nervous, but his movement was still beautiful to watch.

"He doesn't act like he's on the verge of blowing up," Kayla whispered to Sarah.

Jack circled Prince before sitting the trot and asking him to spring forward into canter. Not sure of the aid, the horse at first trotted faster, but then broke into the three-beat gait and continued to canter around the ring. This was the horse who had supposedly acted like a nutcase at the racetrack? It was hard to believe!

After circling the ring once more, Jack asked Prince to come back to trot. While sitting deeply and continuing to apply his legs, he closed his fingers, putting pressure on the bit to ask the horse to slow down. The audience on the hillside watched closely, hoping the transition would go smoothly, while at the same time worrying it might not. But like a seasoned trouper, Prince came back from canter to trot and then to walk. Those spectators witnessing this demonstration who knew Crown Prince's actual background realized what an amazing performance it was!

Jack, usually serious, was smiling broadly. He praised the horse loudly, stroked his neck, and felt relaxed enough to give him a free rein so he could stretch his head and neck down.

"He couldn't have gone better!" Jack called to Sarah. "Come into the ring, please."

After Jack dismounted in the center of the ring, he checked Sarah's footwear. "Good. You're wearing paddock boots with a heel, I see, not sneakers. I want you to ride your horse." Jack unbuckled his riding helmet and gave it to her. "But first put this on."

Sarah stared at him in disbelief. It hadn't occurred to her this would be part of the plan! "You want me to ride him *today*?" she asked.

Without responding, Jack led Prince to the mounting block and motioned for her to follow. "Just do everything the same as you would if you were riding Lady Tate," he said, as he shortened the stirrups. "Breathe deeply and relax. It won't help him if he senses you're nervous."

Sarah's heart was pounding as she stepped up on the block and prepared to mount her horse. This was truly the final test, and she knew her parents were watching with worried and critical eyes. Thank goodness Jack was right there, holding Prince by the bridle. She picked up the reins, put her foot in the stirrup, and slowly swung her leg over her horse's back. When she had settled herself in the saddle, she looked at the ground. It was a long way down!

Prince's ears flicked back in her direction as she reached forward to stroke his neck. "It's me Prince. It's just me, boy." After Sarah had shortened the reins to establish a soft contact with his mouth, Jack released the bridle. The horse moved forward into an energetic walk, his head up, again looking at the spectators. Prince didn't object when, with her legs on his sides, she guided him to the rail and began walking him around the ring.

Sarah felt so many things at once. She was ecstatic to finally be mounted on her horse, to feel the powerful muscles working beneath her. They were as one being, this large powerful animal who trusted her completely and responded to the wishes she communicated through her aids. As he carried her forward with his amazing long strides, Sarah felt such pride that Crown Prince was *her* horse, hers alone. He was *the one*, the horse she would give anything in the world to keep as long as he lived.

For a brief moment, Sarah closed her eyes and imagined Crown Prince as a Pegasus-like creature, a glorious winged horse, soaring to unimaginable heights before coming back to earth. Carrying her on his back, he'd gallop through green fields and leap towering barriers in their path. Nothing could stop them when they were together!

When Sarah opened her eyes, the sight of the spectators spread out across the hillside brought her back to reality. With a jolt she remembered what this moment signified and the consequences if Prince didn't perform well. Some of those people watching her would determine their destiny: Jack, Mr. DeWitt, and most importantly, her parents.

"Try circling him at one end of the ring," Jack called from the rail. "Don't be afraid to move him forward with your legs while you contain him with your hands. You must use all your aids to have a conversation with him. He'll be okay—and his training starts *now*."

As they came out of the circle, with Prince energetically striding forward, Sarah began to feel more confident. His attitude seemed no different than when he was on the longe line, happy to be in work and willing to do as she asked. Sarah wanted to go faster! Without waiting for Jack's suggestion, she pressed her legs against her horse's sides and distinctly said, "Trot." There was no hesitation in her horse. As Prince broke into his ground-covering trot, Sarah was immediately taken with the length of his stride. She'd never ridden a horse that moved like this, his strong hindquarters powering them forward. She remembered what Jack had taught her: sit tall, and let the horse's motion move you into posting—forward and backward, not up and down.

When Sarah turned her horse across the diagonal of the ring to change directions, she became even more aware that she wasn't just a passenger on Crown Prince. He was listening to her! She was in control, and he was accepting of that control. And he was so smooth. No jerky strides, no up-and-down motion. She sensed a wonderful moment of suspension in her horse's stride, as if they were airborne for a brief moment. Crown Prince was like no other horse she'd ever ridden!

Sarah was trotting her horse down the long side of the ring when she became aware of a humming noise in the distance, that of a car approaching on the farm road. From the direction she was facing, she saw the car top the rise and start down the long hill toward the barn. On its way to the parking area, the car would pass close to the ring.

Suddenly the approaching car picked up speed, a lot of speed, and as it drew closer, Sarah saw that it was Rita driving her Mustang convertible. A ripple of fear ran through her, unsure of how Prince would react to the noisy car. Why was Rita coming so fast? At that rate she would have a hard time stopping when she reached the parking area. The road was posted at fifteen miles an hour, but Rita was breaking the speed limit just like she seemed to ignore any other rule if it pleased her. Would Prince spook, rear, or maybe bolt like Gray Fox when the speeding car got to them? Sarah felt panic rising.

The speed of the Mustang didn't slacken as it bore down on the riding ring. Sarah suddenly understood what Rita was planning. *Rita wants to frighten my horse,* she thought. *She knows the ring is very close to the road. She wants Prince to spook at the car and blow up, maybe even throw me off!* She immediately turned her horse toward the far end of the ring, distancing them as much as she could from the road and the fast approaching car.

As the vehicle bearing down on the ring continued to pick up speed, it drew the attention of the spectators. Mr. DeWitt also noticed subtle movement through the trees and under-brush where the woods trail connected to the farm road, and he jumped up from his chair. Yes, the gray Medina and the smaller chestnut pony were approaching the road, as Mrs. DeWitt and Grace returned from their trail ride. Pretty Penny, always anxious to get back to the barn, was in the lead, and at the rate Rita's car was going, the pony might step out in the roadway right in front of the speeding car!

The others could also see the imminent danger, and a wave of terror swept over the group. A collective cry rose from the people near the ring as Gus Kelso came from nowhere, running toward the trailhead at a breakneck pace no one would have believed possible from the barn manager. At that moment everyone was aware of a tragic accident about to happen, one they all felt help-less to prevent, even when every voice on the hillside screamed "Stop! Stop!" at the speeding driver.

Now all eyes were on Gus, the speeding car, and glimpses of the pony approaching the road. Even with Gus in plain sight, the Mustang didn't slacken its pace, but rather seemed to come even faster. It looked like the three of them would reach the same spot at the same time!

The moment Gus reached the trailhead, he lunged for Pretty Penny's bridle just as the pony was about to step out into the road. Only then did Rita hit the brakes hard, but going that fast, the car only fishtailed and slewed forward for a long distance in the gravel roadway, leaving deep tire tracks behind.

At the far end of the ring Sarah did a flying dismount from Crown Prince and pulled the reins over his head. When she turned, she could see Gus holding Medina and Pretty Penny while Mrs. DeWitt bent over something in the road. Jack and Mr. DeWitt raced to the sobbing woman as she stood up holding her little Taco, who lay motionless in her arms.

CHAPTER 18

The Confrontation

SARAH RAN FORWARD, Prince trotting beside her. She had to get to Mrs. DeWitt! Prince was startled by the commotion and pulled to the side, his head high, but Sarah managed to hang onto the reins. She looked for her father.

"Dad!" she yelled. "Dad, please come hold Prince!" Mr. Wagner sprang into action and slipped through the fence boards. When he got close, Sarah quickly thrust the reins into her father's hands. "Just walk him around," she called, as she sprinted away. Before her father could say anything, she was running the length of the ring, out the gate, and down the road. She made a beeline for Mrs. DeWitt, ignoring Rita's Mustang, which she passed on the way.

Sarah reached the small group gathered around Mrs. DeWitt and pushed her way to the front. Grace was still astride Pretty Penny, tears streaming down her face. Mr. DeWitt hurried to his granddaughter and lifted her from the pony. He held her tightly as she cried. Jack was speaking into his cell next to Mrs. DeWitt, whose face was ghostlike as she sobbed, still holding Taco. His eyes were shut and a trickle of blood flowed from the little dog's nose onto her yellow polo shirt. There were snatches of muffled conversation. "There's nothing a vet can do…. He's gone…."

Spin ran in a tight circle around them, looking up at his fallen comrade, sensing that something was terribly wrong. Sarah felt hot tears as she got down on her knees and called to Spin. When he came to her, she wrapped her arms around the distraught dog and hugged him as she wept. How could this have happened? Rita's stupidity and recklessness had taken Taco from them!

The spectators parted to make way for Kathleen's car as it pulled up near them. Kathleen flung the door open and rushed to where Mr. DeWitt stood holding Grace. A few minutes later they walked to the car, the little girl still in tears. *Kathleen must be taking Grace back to the bungalow,* Sarah thought. She picked up Spin and hurried to Kathleen's car as Mr. DeWitt carefully eased Grace into the front seat, giving her a kiss before heading back to his wife.

"Can you take Spin with you?" Sarah asked Kathleen.

"Of course," Kathleen said. "Good idea." Spin did not resist when Sarah placed him in Grace's lap, and the little girl held him close. After Kathleen had driven away, Jack turned to the shaken onlookers.

"I think 'tis best if we all take leave," he told them in a quiet voice. "There's nothing to be done here. Let's give the DeWitts a few minutes alone." They all turned almost in unison and began to trudge back toward the barn or the parking area, talking in quiet groups. The ride on Crown Prince was all but forgotten. Kayla's mother beckoned to her daughter as she headed to her car. Before hurrying to catch up with her mom, Kayla ran to Sarah and gave her a hug.

Sarah started back to the ring, her mind racing, a cutting sorrow overwhelming her. She was trying to deal with what had happened—she'd never lost a pet before, and she felt like Taco was almost her own dog and a part of her family. She would never see him again, never hear his paws skittering on the barn aisle as he raced to see her, and never again pet his beautiful face. And poor Mrs. DeWitt! How awful for someone so kind-hearted to lose her beloved dog in this way!

Ahead of Sarah, Gus was slowly walking Medina and Pretty Penny back to the barn, his head down, shoulders slumped. Sarah saw her father still dutifully leading Prince in a circle in the ring. Prince was animated, occasionally dancing beside him. He wasn't being unruly, but he tugged against the reins, excited and unsure what all the commotion was about. For someone not accustomed to handling horses, her father was doing a good job. Sarah hurried to her horse.

Sarah took the reins. "Thanks, Dad," she said, her voice breaking. Sarah's mother was watching from a nearby vantage point on the rail. "Was it one of the dogs that Rita's car hit?" her mother asked with concern. When Sarah nodded, Mrs. Wagner shook her head. "Mrs. DeWitt must be devastated, and you, too. I'm so sorry, Sarah. I know you had a special relationship with those dogs." They turned to watch Jack drive by in the farm pickup and stop when he got to the DeWitts. When Sarah saw him lift Taco from Mrs. DeWitt's arms, she turned away. She couldn't bear to watch.

"I'm going to take Prince back to the barn now," Sarah said to her parents, unable to meet their gazes. "I'll be home later." She led her horse to the gate and onto the roadway, holding the reins tightly as he pulled her toward the barn. "Easy, boy, easy," she said, holding him back.

She was relieved when they got back to the barn. Inside, an unusual silence prevailed, surprising since a few people were still going about the business of caring for their horses. Most had witnessed the accident and bore their sadness privately. Usually there was a radio playing in the background, but not now. Sarah gave a half-hearted wave to Paige, who was grooming Quarry, but the girls didn't exchange words.

As she passed by Medina's stall, Sarah saw Gus inside with the mare, leaning against the wall with his hand on his forehead. His eyes were closed, and she could see the wet tracks of tears on the man's craggy face. Sarah was astonished to see such emotion from the usually stone-faced man. She'd never seen him pay any attention to Mrs. DeWitt's dogs. *But he must have thought a lot of Taco,* she thought. *He just never showed it. I guess that's just the way Gus is. He must care a lot about the DeWitt family, to run like he did to save Grace.*

Sarah led Prince to the back of the barn, glad that the area was deserted. She decided to untack him in his stall, instead of the aisle. After removing the bridle, she looked down at the beautiful eggbutt snaffle bit balanced in her hand. Today her horse had discovered that it wasn't painful to have a bit in his mouth, and free of pain, he'd been extremely well-behaved under saddle. This should be a day to celebrate another major turning point in her life, but she felt only sadness. They'd all lost a friend. Thinking of Mrs. DeWitt and how much she had loved her little Taco,

Sarah's eyes welled up. How lonely Spin would be without his brother! She brushed the tears away and pressed her face against her horse's neck. Prince stood quietly, as if he understood.

A few minutes later Sarah took a deep breath and went back to the business at hand. She removed the saddle and put her tack outside the stall. After running a brush over her horse, she started for the tack room with her bridle and saddle, leaving Prince drinking from his water bucket.

Going by Chancellor's stall, she paused to look at the grand horse, relaxed with one hind leg drawn under himself. He was beautiful, his black coat gleaming. *How could someone with a horse as lovely as Chancellor begrudge another person having a horse? And then to act so stupidly that she'd killed one of Mrs. DeWitt's Jack Russells!* She felt anger boiling inside her.

Shaking her head, Sarah continued on her way to the tack room where she used her new saddle soap to clean her tack. As she worked, vivid images of the events of the afternoon flashed before her. *Perhaps Rita would no longer be welcome there. Maybe the DeWitts would ask her to leave Brookmeade Farm.* It was a thought she relished.

When she had finished, Sarah put her tack away before turning off the lights and walking back to Prince's stall. As she was passing Chancellor, she stopped in her tracks. Rita was in the stall with her horse! She stood on his off side, so Sarah couldn't see her clearly, but there was no doubt it was Rita. Her long dark hair fell over part of her face, and one arm was draped over Chancellor's neck. Sarah stood still, watching. In her mind's eye she could again picture Rita's green Mustang convertible barreling down the hill, speeding dangerously toward them, going faster and faster.

Sarah's voice was low and measured when she spoke. "Rita, I want to talk to you."

Rita's head snapped up in surprise. She glared out through the bars before stepping away from her horse and into the aisle, sliding the stall door shut behind her. She approached Sarah with deliberate steps, her face twisted in a sneer.

"I have a thing or two to say to you, too, little Miss Perfect, Miss Goody-Goody," Rita began. Her voice was cold as ice, and her words came in short, clipped bursts. "Everything was fine until your horse came on the scene. You think Jack and everyone else should be catering to you every minute."

But Sarah cut her off, her hands clenched into fists. "Shut up, Rita!" she snapped. "I think it's time you did some listening for a change. You were an idiot today, driving way too fast on the farm road, and because of you, Taco is dead!" Rita looked surprised in the face of Sarah's outburst. But Sarah hadn't finished. For too long she had listened to this spoiled brat without speaking up. But no more. She strode toward Rita, pointing a finger in her face.

"You act as if you own the world, and you think everything should revolve around you! You can't stand it when anyone pays attention to my horse. You can't stand it that I even *have* a horse!"

Rita had backed up against the bars of Chancellor's stall, and for perhaps the first time since Sarah had met her, she looked intimidated. Rita struck back. "You've got some nerve, freaking out and talking to me like this," she hissed. "You still ride a bicycle. What do you know about driving a car? It was an accident. It's not my fault that a dumb dog didn't know enough to stay out of the road when a car was coming!" she said, glaring.

Sarah hadn't thought she could get any angrier, but now she

was so mad her hands were shaking. "You can't even take responsibility for what you've done! You're out of control. I know what you were planning today. You drove toward the riding ring with your pedal to the floor because you wanted my horse to explode in front of my parents, so I would lose him. Nothing would make you happier." Sarah stopped and breathed in audibly. She was close enough to see the green of Rita's eyes flashing at her from beneath her thick dark brows.

Sarah's words came again in clipped bursts. "Your father gives you everything you want. You could have a dozen horses if you wanted them. But you hate that I have just one. And now you've killed Taco! I don't know how you'll be able to look at yourself in the mirror."

This time Rita had no reply. It was as if Sarah's words had finally penetrated her stony expression, and the façade she had always managed to throw up was crumbling. Rita attempted to snap back at Sarah, but her voice broke. She turned to face the stall, and Sarah saw small tremors through the girl's shoulders as she wept quietly. Rita had broken. Sarah stepped back, her arms limp at her sides. Her wrath was spent, and she suddenly felt incredibly tired, like she imagined a marathon runner must feel at the end of a race. Rita slowly turned to face her, as she brought her tears under control.

"You say I can have anything I want," she said, her voice quavering, "but there's one thing no one can give me. I'll never have my mother back." She bit her lip as she reached up to wipe her eyes. "*You* have your mother, but *my* mother died. I never knew her. *Your mother* survived her car accident. *My mother* didn't make it. The only thing I have is her name. There are no memories." She slumped as if all the air had gone out of her, leaning back heavily on Chancellor's stall door. "It isn't fair," she choked out.

Rita's words hit Sarah like a rushing wind. She was stunned. She had never even considered this vast difference between them. The girl who always seemed so confident was actually covering up a huge vulnerability, and all the material possessions she flaunted were an effort to fill a void. She'd never known her own mother. Sarah didn't know what to say.

Rita flung her hair out of her face with a toss of her head and continued. "My dad tries to make it up to me, and you're right—he gives me everything I ask for. He never says no." She struggled as she began to break down again. "But sometimes I wish he would. He lets me do anything I want. And today...." Rita's body shook, the tears coming anew. "I didn't mean to hit Taco. I don't know what came over me. When I saw you on your horse so close to the road, I just gunned it. I was going to lay on the horn when I got close to you." She reached to again wipe the tears from her face. "You are right. I *am* a horrible person."

For what seemed an eternity, the two girls stood in silence, staring at each other. Sarah's voice was low when finally she spoke. "You need to talk to Mrs. DeWitt. You need to tell her you're sorry."

Rita shook her head. "She probably never wants to see me again."

"It's something you've got to do," Sarah said. "It's important. Wouldn't your father want you to apologize?" As Rita looked unconvinced, Sarah stepped closer. "Rita—your mother would want you to."

Rita hesitated. "I won't know what to say to Mrs. DeWitt."

"Tell her what you've told me. The DeWitts must be home by now. Come on. Do it now. I'll go with you."

Sarah took a few steps toward the side door, tugging on Rita's arm until she reluctantly followed. Together they stepped outside and started up the gravel driveway toward the DeWitt's farmhouse. A few minutes later, they turned the corner and the house came into full view. Only Mr. DeWitt's Blazer was parked outside, and the place was quiet. There were no barking Jack Russells to rush toward them. When they reached the terrace and Mrs. DeWitt's flower garden, Rita stopped. She looked ahead to the front door.

"I don't know if I can do this."

Sarah stepped closer to look into Rita's eyes. "You have to. Come on."

The house appeared deserted as they moved past the geranium-filled urns and started up the broad porch steps. When they got to the top, Sarah pointed to some wicker rocking chairs and a bench. "Wait here," she said.

An eerie quiet hung over the place as Sarah approached the doorway, the stillness broken only by a lone nuthatch in the nearby woods. She pressed the bell on the door decorated with a large hydrangea wreath. A few moments later, Mr. DeWitt appeared. His face mirrored the sorrow they all felt, as he looked beyond Sarah to Rita sitting on the bench. His gaze came back to Sarah.

"Mr. DeWitt," Sarah began. "I hope you don't mind our coming here now." She found herself fishing for the right words. "I mean, you and Mrs. DeWitt must feel so bad about what happened to Taco. But I wonder if Rita and I could speak with her for a minute. That is, if she feels like she can see us."

"I really don't know if she's able to talk to anyone right now," Mr. DeWitt said. He hesitated a moment. "But I'll see." He walked back down the hall and into a side room. Several minutes elapsed, and Sarah was about to retreat when Mrs. DeWitt came to the door. She had changed into a pink robe, and her eyes were red and puffy. Her face was uncharacteristically somber, with no trace of her usual warmth and smile.

"Hello, Sarah. It's kind of you to come here in person to let Chandler and me know you share our sadness. I know you loved Taco, too."

"He was such a special little dog. I'm going to miss him a lot, but of course not as much as you will."

Mrs. DeWitt brought a handkerchief to her nose and blew loudly. "You're very sweet, dear, to be so considerate." She looked beyond Sarah and noticed Rita sitting on the bench. "Rita, is that you?" she asked, her voice registering surprise.

Rita hung her head, not able to meet the woman's gaze. Mrs. DeWitt paused a moment before pushing the screen door open and stepping onto the porch. She walked slowly to one of the wicker rockers and sat down, motioning for Sarah to sit as well. There was an awkward silence until Rita raised her head to look directly at Mrs. DeWitt.

"I know I acted like a total jerk today, Mrs. DeWitt. There's no excuse for my driving so fast on the farm road. It's my fault that Taco got hit, and I want you to know that I'm really, really sorry." Rita lowered her head and covered her face with her hands.

"What was going on, Rita?" Mrs. DeWitt asked in a low even

voice. "Why were you driving so recklessly? If Gus hadn't gotten there in time, this accident could have been far worse, with consequences that would have changed our lives forever. I can only be thankful my granddaughter is okay. But you put her—us—in very real danger."

Rita looked directly at Mrs. DeWitt and slowly, her own sadness stumbled out. When she had finished, she again lowered her head. Mrs. DeWitt turned away to gaze over the sweeping lawn into the woodlands. Finally she rose from her chair and went to sit beside Rita. She looked at her pointedly. "If it hadn't been for Gus's fast and calculated action, we might be mourning Grace and Pretty Penny right now as well as Taco. Gus is the hero who saved them both. I realize you have your own pain to overcome, but causing others pain is not the answer."

Rita looked into Mrs. DeWitt's sad blue eyes. In a broken voice, she said, "I don't know if you can understand. My father lets me off the hook all the time. With him, anything goes. I boss Judson and our housekeeper around, and I even got into trouble at school for arguing with the teachers. My dad's the greatest, but sometimes I wish he'd draw the line. I sometimes feel so out of control."

Mrs. DeWitt shook her head. "Rita, you can't blame your behavior on your father. *You* were driving that car today, no one else." She paused for a moment before continuing. "Have you learned anything from what happened today?"

Rita took a deep breath as she looked up at the porch ceiling and then back at Mrs. DeWitt. "I guess when you do something stupid like I did, bad stuff can go down."

"Ah, yes," Mrs. DeWitt said. "Those unintended consequences

when you break the rules. There's a reason why Chandler put up those speed limit signs on the road."

Sarah sat quietly, her eyes glued to the porch floor. She felt uncomfortable being there, listening to such a private conversation. But she was rooted to her chair.

Mrs. DeWitt continued. "It's obvious you're carrying a lot of anger, Rita, and that anger makes you act irresponsibly. Losing your mother when you were just a baby was a terrible thing. Life can be so unfair. But now you need to find a way to deal with your anger. Lashing out at others never solves anything." Rita didn't answer, but sat looking off into the distance.

"This needs to be addressed, Rita," Mrs. DeWitt continued. "I feel you would benefit greatly from sessions with a trained counselor. But first your father needs to know that your unsafe driving caused a dreadful accident, and he needs to know why."

Mrs. DeWitt rose from the bench. "I'm going back in the house now," she said. "But before I do, I need to be open with you, Rita. Up until a few minutes ago, I was considering asking you to sever your ties with Brookmeade Farm. The way you drove your car today makes you a menace. But I'm glad you made this visit and offered an apology and an explanation. Will you promise me you'll be open and honest with your father?"

Rita looked serious. "Yes, I promise," she said, "even though this may be one time when he lays down the law. He'll probably take my keys away, and I'll be totally grounded. But I'll tell him everything."

"Good. And there's something else that needs to change— your attitude. We need to see a different Rita at Brookmeade

Farm, one who doesn't need to be better than her friends, and a Rita who is considerate of others."

Both girls stood up, preparing to leave. Mrs. DeWitt walked over to Sarah and gave her a hug. "I suspect you had a role in this meeting," she said quietly in her ear, "and I appreciate it." Then she returned to Rita and hugged her as well before going back into the house. Rita looked surprised.

The girls started down the porch steps and onto the gravel driveway. They walked without speaking until Sarah said, "Don't you feel better, Rita? Aren't you glad you did it?"

Rita kicked a stone out of her path. "I didn't have a choice."

CHAPTER 19

The Test

SARAH PAUSED A MOMENT before leading Crown Prince into the indoor arena. For weeks she had longed for this day, when Prince's trial period would be over and he would be pronounced hers for good. Now that the thirty days were up, she was going to demonstrate to her parents that Prince was sane, well mannered, and most of all *safe*. She was eager to show them how well he was going under saddle, but with so much at stake, she couldn't help feeling anxious.

As they entered the arena, she was taken aback by the number of people seated on the bleachers. So many people had taken an interest in Crown Prince! She wasn't aware that Mrs. DeWitt had spent some time on the phone calling the Brookmeade boarders and staff. It was expected that her parents, Abby, and the DeWitts would be here, and she wasn't surprised to see Kayla and her mom sitting in the top row. She wasn't totally surprised to see Paige and Tim, since they'd ridden earlier in the afternoon, but Tim's parents and Paige's grandmother were also with them. Kathleen and Lindsay were sitting with Gus, and even Kelly and

Nicole were on the bottom row with a few other boarders. Standing by the side of the bleachers, of course, was Jack.

But no Rita. With the rest of the class in attendance, she was almost conspicuous by her absence. But then, true to her prediction, Rita's father had grounded her and taken her car away when he'd learned of her behavior and the events at the farm. Judson had come the day after Taco's death to take Chancellor back home, and for the last few weeks, Rita's only visits to Brookmeade were with her horse for her weekly lessons with Jack's Young Riders.

Mrs. DeWitt had gone to bat for Rita. She said everyone makes mistakes, and Rita had owned up to hers. Mrs. DeWitt made it clear to everyone who rode at Brookmeade that she felt no bitterness toward Rita for her behavior on that tragic afternoon, and she said she would be disappointed if anyone else held it against her. Others noticed that Rita's hard edges seemed to have softened slightly, and while she never mentioned Crown Prince, a few times Rita even said nice things about Quarry, Rhodes, and Fanny.

Sarah pushed thoughts of Rita out of her mind. She needed to focus on her horse right now. Prince had stopped in his tracks to eye all the people on the bleachers. Sarah had ridden him many times inside the indoor the last few weeks, but having an audience was something new. She clucked softly and led him toward the mounting block. When she swung easily into the saddle, Prince didn't immediately move off, but rather was frozen, his eyes never leaving the bleachers. Sarah could feel the tension in his body as she gathered her reins and pressed her legs firmly on his sides. Only then did he walk forward.

Sarah sat tall, feeling proud. As many times as she'd ridden Crown Prince, she'd never gotten over the thrill of being on the back of this incredible horse. Now the time had come to show everyone, once and for all, that he wasn't a racetrack lunatic. He was *her* good boy. He was *her* dream!

She looked at her parents. What were they thinking? They'd been hearing her excited reports on how well Prince was doing since the wolf tooth was removed, but there was always the chance something could go wrong today, especially when the people in the arena made him edgy. She didn't want to blow it!

In the last few weeks, Sarah had found that Prince could indeed be spooky of new things, but thankfully he quickly got over his fear once she allowed him to check them out. With this in mind, she took him to the bleachers so he could see the visitors up close. As they walked by, Jack spoke to her. "Why don't you walk, trot, and canter your horse in both directions, doing the schooling figures we've practiced. Exactly how you do it is up to you." Then he went to sit with Kathleen.

With her legs firmly against her horse's sides, they walked halfway around the arena before she felt the tension leave his body. She then shortened her reins and asked him to trot. He eagerly made the transition, trotting along the long wall where she could see his beautiful reflection in the mirror. He was so easy to post to, his long legs moving in a delightful one-two cadence as he trotted. After going around the arena a few times, she took up more contact with his mouth and started some schooling figures. She changed direction across the diagonal and then made a circle at the other end of the arena, asking him to bend in the direction of the circle. While still on the circle, she sat the trot and reached back with her outside leg to ask for a canter departure. She was relieved when Prince sprang into the faster gait on the correct lead, and Sarah practiced what Jack had taught her: sit tall, look ahead through her horse's ears, and lightly polish the saddle from back to front with her seat.

After they had cantered in both directions, Sarah brought her horse back to walk and asked him to halt. But Prince had other ideas. He was primed to move forward and resisted at first, pulling against her hands. At these times she always worried that he would react like he had before the painful wolf tooth was removed. She sat deeper into the saddle, and again asked Prince to halt. This time he halted agreeably. As a reward, she asked him to walk forward while offering a long rein so he could stretch his head and neck down.

If she hadn't feared it would upset her horse, Sarah would have whooped and hollered. Prince had performed beautifully! But she became apprehensive when she noticed Jack walking toward the part of the ring where some jump standards and rails were set up. *Oh, no,* she thought. She hadn't expected any work over fences today, because Prince was still too green to do much jumping. But Jack was making some adjustments on a gymnastic line of three fences with one stride between each one, setting them to a low height typically used for inexperienced horses just learning to jump.

She tightened her grip on the reins as Jack walked up to her. "He'll have no problem with this, Sarah. Pick up trot, circle at the far end, and then come straight to the first fence. Just keep your eyes up and maintain a steady pace to the fence. You are *both* ready to include a little gymnastic work in our training sessions."

In their last lesson Jack had introduced Prince to a simple cross-rail, but it had been an easy single jump preceded by cavalletti poles on the ground to help him approach with the right striding. Without the poles, the horse would have to pick his own spot for the takeoff and continue through the line of three fences. What they'd be doing today was something new and much more difficult! Why was Jack making them do this now, when so much was at stake?

She felt her heart beating faster as she asked Prince to trot. They circled at the end the arena until she could point him straight to the first jump in the gymnastic line. Jack had made it into a cross-rail, followed by two low verticals with one stride in between each jump. This series of fences could be a challenge for a horse just off the track. And if he jumped through the line, would he stay quiet and relaxed? Jumping was an exciting activity for many horses, and that excitement often translated into speed—or worse. Maybe he'd try to bolt! He'd never tried to buck her off, but there was always a first time. Wouldn't it be awful if that first time was today?

Prince raised his head when he saw the jumps ahead, and Sarah felt his body hesitate. She remembered Jack's story about Donegal Lad needing to sense his rider's confidence to clear big fences, and she closed her legs on Prince's sides. *You can do it,* her heart sang to her horse, and when they reached the first jump, he pushed off with just enough lift to clear it cleanly. He continued cantering through the line, jumping the two verticals as if he'd done this exercise a thousand times. Sarah was ecstatic! *How could I have questioned Jack? If he asked us to do it, then I should have known we could!*

The onlookers all were aware how inexperienced Crown Prince was, and they erupted into cheers and clapping. They had just seen proof that the horse deserved to stay with Sarah. No one could argue that he was not a good match for her! Startled by the noise, Prince jumped sideways, but Sarah nimbly moved with him, keeping her seat. Recognizing the talent this young rider possessed, the audience cheered even louder, causing Prince to prance with his head and tail high.

Mrs. DeWitt stood up and faced the group. "This is a special day, and we hope you can all come to the lounge for a little celebration with cake and ice cream," she announced. After a month's trial, Crown Prince is here to stay! And we have a surprise to show all of you!" There was more clapping as Sarah, laughing, guided her prancing horse out the gate Jack held open for her.

She had halted in the courtyard and dismounted when Abby came flying toward them. She was a little out of breath as she came up to Prince. "You and Prince were awesome," she said, stroking the horse's neck, "and I heard Mom say that 'Prince has proven himself today.' Dad thought so too."

Sarah wasn't surprised, but it was great to hear. "Want to help me untack him?" she asked. Abby's coast-to-coast grin was her answer, and together they walked Prince back to his stall.

"Can I brush him too?" Abby asked.

"Sure, after we take his saddle and bridle off," Sarah said. "But just a quick job this time. We don't want to miss the party."

Sarah decided to leave her saddle and bridle outside the stall for now—she could stretch the rule just this once. She'd clean them and put them away later. She wanted to get to the party to thank everyone for coming. And hadn't Mrs. DeWitt mentioned something about a surprise? After giving Prince a hug and a peppermint, she started for the lounge, with Abby trotting to keep up with her.

The lounge was a little crowded, but that didn't seem to dampen the spirits of Sarah's friends as they chitchatted, laughed, and drank the punch Lindsay was serving from a glass punchbowl. Mrs. DeWitt beckoned for Sarah to stand beside a beautiful cake that was decorated with the words *Congratulations Sarah and Crown Prince!* Mr. DeWitt was poised with a camera and he took several shots before Kathleen began cutting the cake.

Sarah took charge of the first slice of cake and ice cream, and she carried it to Gus, who seemed somewhat uncomfortable in such a social setting. He was dressed in khaki pants and a plaid short-sleeved shirt, and his hair was neatly combed to the side. It was the first time Sarah (or anyone else) could ever remember seeing Gus when he wasn't wearing jeans and his red baseball cap. Sarah smiled at the usually grumpy man, as she offered him the cake.

"Thank you for all your help, Gus," Sarah said. Gus didn't reply, but he didn't scowl, and Sarah thought she saw the trace of a smile on his face, as he accepted the cake and ice cream and promptly applied his spoon to the side with the most frosting.

Paige held her glass over her head and announced, "Here's to Sarah for never giving up on the horse who was 'The One,' and to Crown Prince for being 'The One.'" There was laughter as everyone touched glasses and drank more punch.

Sarah held up her glass and added to the toast. "If anyone here deserves credit, it's Jack, who convinced my dad to let me take Prince on trial, and then advised me every step of the way. Prince and I owe him so much. And to the DeWitts, who made it possible for me to follow my dream."

The clapping continued as Sarah went to her parents, sitting on the couch. "Can I ever thank you two enough?" she said, leaning to give them both a hug. She knew they were both genuinely pleased with the events of the day, and any lingering reservations they had harbored about Crown Prince were gone.

"Seeing you ride that big horse so well today makes us proud," her father said. "We can look forward to the two of you getting better and better in the months ahead." Her mother said nothing, but her eyes were moist as she gave Sarah a big squeeze.

Jack spoke from his spot near the hearth. "We Brookmeade folks actually have a lot to celebrate today, beginning with another of my Young Riders, Kayla Romano, who brought back some impressive ribbons from the Quarter Horse show she took Fanfare to a few weeks ago. Those two have come a long way and have a bright future." Jack paused to look around the room. "I'm also very proud of our two young eventers, Paige Vargas and Tim Dixon, who competed in their first three-phase event at the Fair Pines Horse Trial just last weekend. Tim and Rhodes Scholar came in third out of a big division, and Paige also did well in another novice division. She has a bright green ribbon hanging by Quarry's stall to show for it." Jack looked around the room once more. "And although she isn't here this afternoon, I'll mention how proud we are of Rita Snyder and Chancellor. They won a championship at the Rally Round Farm show last Sunday."

Mrs. DeWitt had quietly slipped out of the lounge a few minutes before, and just then she returned. With Spin dancing beside her, she carried a small brown and white Jack Russell Terrier puppy that squirmed and twisted in her arms, her small stub of a tail wagging furiously. "I want you all to meet the newest member of our Brookmeade family," Mrs. DeWitt said. "This is Cameo, and she's eight weeks old." There was more clapping as everyone tried to get a closer look.

Sarah stepped back to watch her friends crowding around Mrs. DeWitt and the puppy that was trying to lick every hand that came her way. Abby pressed close enough to place a pat on the small dog's head. Spin wanted his share of the limelight, and he bounced from one person to another.

Even with all the hubbub going on around her, Sarah's thoughts returned to her horse. Rudy Dominic and Sam would probably have a hard time believing Crown Prince could perform like he did today! Now that the trial was over and he was hers for good, she could think about what might lie ahead— riding him on the trails with her friends, learning to do dressage movements, jumping him on the hunt course, and taking him over cross-country obstacles. She even dared to think of the time when they could one day compete in shows and events like her friends.

She remembered Jack's words when he first saw Crown Prince: "*Who knows the heights Sarah and this horse might reach if we can turn him around?*" Now they had a real chance. With the wolf tooth gone and Hank Bolton out of the picture, it would be smooth sailing. Her horse would be super—she just knew it. And the change in Rita's attitude meant that things would be different around here. The kids in her class would pull together to make a name for Brookmeade Farm and their favorite instructor.

As Sarah imagined what it would be like without Rita as a rival, an unsettled feeling invaded her happy thoughts. Why had Rita ignored Mrs. DeWitt's invitation to come to this party? Rita had been contrite and full of apologies when she'd spoken to Mrs. DeWitt that terrible day that Taco was killed. Was she being sincere, or just expedient? Only time would tell.

Mr. DeWitt seemed pleased as he walked over to Sarah and her parents. "You're on your way, young lady," he said to Sarah. "I notified Rudy Dominic that Crown Prince is doing well at Brookmeade Farm and won't be coming back to the racetrack. Rudy is going to mail you his Jockey Club registration papers. Now Crown Prince is yours, all yours."

Sarah smiled. Another turning point in her life—she couldn't wait for what came next.

Glossary

This glossary is designed to help readers better understand various terms that appear in this book. The definitions are short and general in nature, and in some cases readers may wish to consult other sources for a more complete explanation.

Aids Used by riders to give horses directives. The natural aids: hands, legs, seat or weight, and voice. The artificial aids: whips and spurs.

Anglo/Arab A horse with one Thoroughbred parent and one Arabian parent.

Appaloosa A versatile breed developed by the Nez Perce Native Americans, which is commonly known for its distinct spotted coat.

Baker blanket A brand of horse clothing with a distinctive plaid pattern.

Bars The area without teeth in the horse's lower jaw where the bit rests.

Bascule The natural round arc of a horse's body when it jumps a fence athletically, putting its withers at the highest point.

Bat A short crop (whip) with a wide head.

Blaze A white marking on a horse's face that extends from its forehead to its muzzle.

Blemish A mark left from a former condition or injury that may be unattractive but does not indicate unsoundness.

Bone The measure of the circumference of the foreleg below the knee, which is considered to reflect a horse's proclivity toward soundness.

Bran mash A nourishing and easy-to-digest feed for a horse made by mixing bran with warm water, and letting it soak until it expands.

Bridle path A trail intended for recreational use by horses and riders, or the area behind the horse's ears where the mane is clipped short to accommodate a bridle or halter.

Buck When the horse attempts to unseat a rider by leaping in the air with its back arched and its head lowered while kicking out with its hind legs.

Canter The fastest of the horse's three main gaits, which include the walk, trot, and canter. The canter has three beats.

Capped hock A swelling at the point of the hock, which may or may not contribute to unsoundness in the horse.

Cast When a horse rolls against a stall wall in such a way that its legs are pinned and it becomes trapped. This can lead to potentially fatal injuries if the horse isn't assisted to its feet.

Cavalletti Rails placed on or just above the ground in various patterns, which the horse is walked, trotted, and/or cantered over. They are used in the training of the horse in a number of disciplines.

Cavesson The noseband of a bridle, or the headstall with a sturdy noseband commonly used when longeing the horse.

Chaps An article of clothing riders wear over pants when riding to prevent chafing of their legs.

Cleveland Bay A breed of horse originally developed in England for carriage driving.

Cluck The sound a person makes with the tongue commonly used to encourage a horse to move forward.

Cob A small, stout horse of strong build—refers to a body type rather than a specific breed.

Colic Abdominal pain in the horse, ranging from mild to severe and indicating a digestive disorder, which due to the horse's unique intestinal system, can be fatal.

Combination Two or more jumps placed in close proximity with a specific number of strides between each jump.

Conformation A horse's physical form and shape.

Cooler An item of horse clothing used to prevent a hot, sweaty, or wet horse from being chilled.

Coop A type of jump modeled after a chicken coop, which was originally placed over wire fencing to make it safe for jumping on foxhunts.

Counter-canter To canter on the opposite lead from the direction the horse is traveling.

Crest The upper portion of a horse's neck.

Cribbing A vice when a horse pulls against a solid object with its teeth, often while swallowing air.

Crop A small riding whip used by the rider to reinforce the leg aids.

Cross-ties A method of tying a horse, usually in a barn aisle, using ties attached to opposite walls and to each side of the horse's halter.

Curry comb A grooming tool with rows of small teeth used to loosen dirt prior to brushing.

Dam A horse's mother (mare).

Dandy brush A grooming brush made of a stiff material used to remove dirt from the horse's coat.

Diagonal (correct) A way of posting (rising) to the trot so the rider rises in unison with the horse's inside hind leg and outside front leg.

Dispersal sale When an owner puts all his horses up for sale.

Dressage test When a horse and rider are judged on how they perform a series of specific movements and patterns, which demonstrate the horse's level of training.

Dropped noseband A type of bridle noseband that encircles the muzzle to prevent a horse from opening its mouth to evade the action of the bit and is often used on horses that require more control.

Dutch Warmblood A European breed selectively bred as to excel in equestrian sports such as dressage and show jumping.

Eggbutt A type of snaffle bit with egg-shaped (slightly oval) rings to which the cheek pieces and reins of the bridle are attached.

Equitation A type of horse show class in which the rider's form and riding ability are judged.

Equus Scientific term for the species known as horse.

Eventing A three-phase type of equestrian competition in which horses are tested in dressage, cross-country jumping (natural obstacles across varied terrain), and show jumping.

Farrier A person who trims the feet of and "shoes" horses.

Flake (of hay) One measured section from a bale of hay.

Flash noseband A type of bridle noseband used to help keep the bit steady in the horse's mouth and hold the horse's mouth closed, preventing evasion of the rein aids.

Flea-bitten gray A horse coat color that features small splotches of brown and black hairs among predominantly white hairs.

Flexion tests A diagnostic tool often used to test for joint pain (and related unsoundness) by holding the horse's joint (commonly in the legs) in a tightly flexed position for one to two minutes and then having the horse trot off.

Float To remove sharp edges from a horse's teeth by filing them with a rasp, enabling the horse to chew its food more efficiently.

Fly sheet An article of horse clothing designed to protect the horse from insects.

Flying change When a cantering horse changes his lead to the opposite canter lead without slowing to walk or trot.

Forward A term used to describe energetic movement or impulsion in the ridden horse.

Founder A term commonly used to describe the equine vascular disease of laminitis, which impacts the sensitive structures of a horse's hooves. In advanced stages of laminitis, a bone within the horse's hoof can actually detach, rotate, and/or sink, hence the term "founder."

Frame (in a) When a horse is moving forward with energy in response to the rider's leg and seat aids into a restraining hand, often assuming a desirable "profile" or appearance with a rounded topline and the nose positioned just in front of the vertical.

Frog The firm, resilient V-shaped "cushion" that sits in the center of sole of the horse's foot and helps absorb the shock of concussion.

Galloping boots Horse clothing used during exercise to protect a horse's lower legs from injury.

Gelding A neutered (castrated) male horse.

Girth The piece of tack that attaches to either side of the saddle and wraps under the horse's belly, holding the saddle in place on the horse's back.

Going large When a horse is ridden on the outer track of the riding arena around the entire riding space.

Gooseneck trailer A trailer that attaches to the bed of the hauling vehicle, rather than to the bumper.

Green Used to describe a horse in the early stages of training, when it is inexperienced and often lacking confidence.

Half chaps A type of chaps used by riders that begin below the knee and help keep the rider's leg steady as well as offer some protection from chafing.

Half-halt A sequence of aids that ask a horse to adjust its balance in preparation for the rider's request for a particular movement or transition.

Halter A headstall generally made of leather, nylon, or rope used to lead or otherwise control a horse.

Hand The four-inch unit of measure used to determine a horse's height from the ground to its withers.

Hand gallop A controlled gallop, with a speed between canter and full gallop.

Heartgirth The distance around a horse's body when measured just behind the withers.

Homebred A horse whose owner owned its dam at the time it was foaled.

Hot walkers Racetrack workers who walk horses to cool them out following exercise, or the mechanical machines used to serve the same purpose.

Hunter A horse used in the sport of foxhunting (field hunter) or one competed in horse shows (show hunter), where the horse is judged on its way of traveling on the flat and its form over fences.

Impulsion The energy in a horse's forward movement.

In-and-out Two jumps placed in close proximity and jumped consecutively, with a specific number of strides between them.

Interfere When a horse hits one leg against another due to a faulty way of moving its legs.

Irons A common term for the rider's stirrups, which are often made of metal.

Jigging A term that describes the up-and-down movement of a horse between a walk and trot, usually occuring when a horse is excited or nervous.

Jumper A horse competed in classes where the horse's ability to jump fences cleanly in the shortest period of time determines the winner, while its form over fences isn't considered.

Kimberwicke bit A shanked bit with minimal to mild curb action that is more severe ("stronger") in a horse's mouth than a snaffle bit.

Lead To walk a horse with the aid of a rope or lead shank, or the word used to describe the leg extending furthest in front when a horse is cantering. The lead leg is the last hoof to make contact with the ground during each canter stride. The rider is said to be on the "correct lead" when the lead leg matches the direction of travel (for example, the right leg when traveling on a circle to the right).

Leg-yielding When a horse moves laterally, traveling both forward and sideways when cued by the rider's leg, seat, and rein aids.

Liver chestnut A deep shade of chestnut horse coat color.

Liverpool A jump with a ditch or tray of water under it.

Long and low The phrase used to describe the way a horse moves on a long rein with his head and neck stretched out before him; a movement often used to stretch the horse during warm-up.

Long in the tooth An expression meaning "getting along in years," since horses' teeth get longer as they age.

Longeing (lungeing) The exercising and / or training of a horse on a circle using a long lash (longe whip) and a long webbed line (longe line) that is attached to a sturdy headstall (see cavesson).

Martingale, standing A leather strap running from the bridle's noseband between the horse's front legs to the girth, used to prevent the horse from carrying its head too high and evading the rider's rein aids.

Near side The horse's left side.

Never started A phrase often used to describe a horse that was never in a race.

Off A term used to describe a horse whose way of traveling indicates lameness.

Off side The horse's right side.

On the bit When a horse moves forward energetically from the rider's leg into a supporting rein with a rounded topline and the nose positioned just in front of the vertical.

On the flat A phrase describing a horse's ridden performance when it is not jumping.

OTTB An off-the-track Thoroughbred.

Oxer A spread jump featuring the challenge of both height and width.

Paddock boots A low, heeled boot worn by horseback riders.

Palomino A horse coat color that comes in varying shades of gold with a white mane and tail.

Pastern The portion of the horse's lower leg that connects the ankle joint and the hoof.

Pinto A horse coat color featuring mainly white hairs with black or brown patches.

Polo wraps A type of bandage used to protect a horse's legs during exercise.

Pony The term to describe a horse under 14.2 hands high, or a way of exercising a horse by leading it while riding astride a second horse.

Prince of Wales spurs A mild type of spur with a short neck (shank).

Pulled (mane) The term used to describe a horse's mane that has been thinned and shortened by selectively removing the longer hairs.

Quarter Horse A popular breed of horse developed in the United States and commonly used for ranch work, racing, and both English and Western pleasure riding.

Rasp A metal file used to reduce the points on a horse's teeth; also the name for the tool used to file down a horse's hooves.

Revet A way of stabilizing a bank often used in the construction of cross-country obstacles.

Roll-top jump A solid jump with a rounded top.

Run up (stirrups or irons) When the stirrup iron is slid to the top of the stirrup leather as a way of stabilizing the stirrup on the saddle. Usually done when the rider is walking beside the horse, as it prevents a low-hanging stirrup from catching on doors and fences, for example.

Running out When a horse runs to the side of a jump at the last moment to avoid jumping it.

Saddlebred An American breed of horse known for its flashy, animated gaits.

Schooling figures Movements horses are asked to perform on the flat when being trained.

Scribe A person who assists a dressage judge during a dressage test by writing scores and comments on a test sheet as the judge dictates.

Shank The chain on the end of a shank lead, which can be attached over the horse's nose for greater control, or the side pieces of a curb-type bit, or the neck of a spur.

Sheet An item of horse clothing lighter than a horse blanket, usually used in milder conditions or to protect the horse from rain.

Shipping boots An item of horse clothing used to protect the horse's legs when it is being transported.

Simple change When a cantering horse changes his lead after first slowing to a trot or a walk (see flying change).

Sire A horse's father (stallion).

Snaffle The simplest and mildest type of horse bit, which is usually jointed in the middle.

Snip A small grouping of white hairs on the front of the horse's muzzle.

Sound Term used to describe a horse free of lameness or other conditions that would compromise its ability to perform.

Sport horse A horse used for equestrian competitions or recreational purposes.

Spurs An artificial aid attached to the rider's boots to accentuate the leg aids.

Stall walking A vice demonstrated by a horse excessively moving around in its stall.

Stallion A male horse used for breeding purposes.

Standards (jump) The structures on the sides of a manmade jump that support the horizontal rails.

Star A grouping of white hairs on a horse's forehead.

Stocks An enclosure used to constrain a horse, usually used to assist a farrier or vet.

Stride A single coordinated movement of the four legs of a horse, completed when the legs return to their initial relative position.

Sweet feed A palatable horse feed containing various grains plus molasses.

Tack up To saddle and bridle a horse in preparation for riding.

Thoroughbred A breed of horse used for racing at a gallop.

Transition A change from one gait to another.

Triple bar A type of spread fence that includes three sets of standards and rails.

Trot The second gait of the horse's three main gaits, which include the walk, trot, and canter. The trot has two beats, and is faster than the walk but slower than the canter.

Tucked up The phrase commonly used to describe when a horse's flank area is tight and contracted following hard exercise or dehydration.

Twitch A device placed on a horse's sensitive upper lip to restrain it.

Two-point position When a rider lifts his or her seat slightly out of the saddle, leaving his legs and hands in communication with the horse.

Tying-up A muscular disorder occurring in horses usually following stressful exercise or dietary changes, which can cause painful muscle and kidney damage.

USEA The United States Eventing Association.

Vertical jump A jump with height but not width.

Vice An undesirable horse behavior, such as cribbing, weaving, and stall walking.

Walk The slowest of the horse's three main gaits, which include the walk, trot, and canter. The walk has four beats.

Weaving A vice demonstrated by a horse swinging its head and neck from side to side while shifting its weight from one front leg to the other.

Withers The highest part of a horse's back located at the base of its neck.

Wolf tooth A tooth sometimes appearing in the horse's mouth in the area directly above the bars; generally removed to prevent problematic contact with the bit.

Points of the Horse

ABOUT THE AUTHOR

Linda Snow McLoon was *that girl* who always wanted a horse of her own but had to wait until she was an adult for her dream to come true. She and her horse Bayberry competed in horse shows, dressage competitions, and horse trials. Linda taught young riders as a U.S. Pony Club Affiliate Coordinator of Instruction, and along the way bred and raced Thoroughbred racehorses. She lives in Portland, Maine. You can get in touch with Linda and find out more about the Brookmeade Young Riders Series by visiting www.lindasnowmcloon.com.

ABOUT THE ARTIST

Jennifer Brandon is the painter, illustrator, and graphic designer behind Jaché Studio. Her passion is to share with you a piece of a beautiful moment through the medium of paint. Jen offers original and custom oil paintings, where the personality of each horse, person, or pet is expressively depicted and the energy of the moment is relived through the medium of paint. Visit Jaché Studio on Facebook and view more of Jen's work at www.jachestudio.com.